FOURTH CRISIS

THE BATTLE

FOR

TAIWAN

By Peter von Bleichert

Books by Peter von Bleichert

Fiction

Crown Jewel: The Battle for the Falklands

Dragon Fire: The Battle for the Falklands

Non-Fiction

Bleichert's Wire Ropeways

Blitz! Storming the Maginot Line

TABLE OF CONTENTS

CHARACTERS

PEOPLE'S REPUBLIC OF CHINA (CHINA):

Ambassador Fan Wei

Captain Kun Guan

Senior Lieutenant Peng Jingwei

General Zhen Zhu

...and, Vice President Ai Bao Li; President Xu Wai Li; General Piao Bai; & Chief Executive Yao Ou Pei.

REPUBLIC OF CHINA (TAIWAN):

Major Han Ken

Senior Master Sergeant Li Rong Kai

Major General Tek Foo Chek

...and, President Bing Rong.

UNITED STATES OF AMERICA:

Captain Anthony Ferlatto

Richard Ling

Lieutenant Cynthia Pelletier

Secretary of State Georgiana Pierce

Captain Shane Whidby

Commander Max Wolff

Jade Zhang

...and, Vice President Elias Campos; Special Agent Hunter Jackson; Rear Admiral Norman Kaylo; President William Keeley; Secretary of Defense Shawn Tillison; & National Security Advisor Nathaniel Westermark, Ph.D.

NOTES

Taiwan sits 75 miles due east of mainland China's Fujian Province. The island is 245 miles long from north to south and 89 miles wide. The East China Sea is north of it, the Philippine Sea east, south is the Luzon Strait, and the South China Sea is located to the southwest. Taiwan is mountainous with a chain of jagged peaks running vertically down its middle that slope away to coastal plains. The island spans the Tropic of Cancer and has both tropical and subtropical vegetation.

In 1979, the American Congress ratified the Taiwan Relations Act. The Act stipulated that the United States of America "...will consider any effort to determine the future of Taiwan by other than peaceful means a threat to the peace and security of the Western Pacific area, and of grave concern to the United States." The Act was later supplemented with recognition by the United States of a One China policy. This policy recognized a single China, of which Taiwan was a part, though it did not express the form of government that should control One China.

In 2005, the Politburo of the Communist Party of China announced the Anti-Secession Law. This Law authorized the use of force against Taiwan in the event of a declaration of independence or a threat to regional security.

BRIEFING

By the end of the Second World War, the Chinese Civil War had stalemated with the Communists on the mainland and the Nationalists on the island of Taiwan. Since this time, there have been three crises that have threatened total war between the People's Republic of China (China) and the Republic of China (Taiwan):

The First Crisis began when Taiwanese preparations to invade the mainland were discovered. The Chinese pre-empted the attack by assaulting and seizing several of Taiwan's small island territories. With war raging on the Korean Peninsula, and convinced Communism must be contained, President Truman sent the US Navy into the Taiwan Strait, effectively separating the combatants and ending the crisis.

A continuation of the First Crisis, the Second Crisis opened with Chinese shelling of Taiwanese territory. Taiwan returned fire. The bombardment claimed thousands of lives on both sides as the two air forces met over the Taiwan Strait. One hundred Chinese MiG 15s faced off against 32 Taiwanese F-86 Sabers in aerial combat. There was no clear winner and the Second Crisis subsided.

The Third Crisis began when the president of Taiwan accepted an invitation to deliver a graduation speech at his alma mater, Cornell University. The United States granted him a visa. Massive Chinese airborne and amphibious military exercises commenced, and ballistic missiles began to splash-in and near Taiwan's ports. As a show of American determination to defend Taiwan, President Clinton sent the USS *Nimitz* carrier battle group into the Taiwan Strait. This temporarily cooled things off. Then, in the run-up to Taiwan's presidential election and as a warning to voters not to put the pro-independence party in power, hundreds of Chinese missiles were fired and impacted within Taiwanese waters. Despite these attempts at intimidation, the Taiwanese people called China's bluff. With more American firepower arriving on scene, the Third Crisis ended, and a long and uneasy peace began.

At the beginning of the 21st Century, China had become Earth's most populous nation. It also became the planet's second largest economic and military power.

The near future…

1: MACHINATIONS

"All warfare is based on deception. Hence, when able to attack, we must seem unable; When using our forces, we must seem inactive; When we are near, we must make the enemy believe we are far away; When far away, we must make him believe we are near."— Sun Tzu

Cranes and smokestacks pierced the blanket of noxious gases hanging over Beijing. The unnatural stew tinted the low-hanging full moon a rusty orange. Beyond the Forbidden City's Meridian Gate lay the vast flatness of Tiananmen Square. Only the Monument to the People's Heroes and the Mausoleum of Mao Zedong interrupted a historical meeting place, the great plaza. Flanked by the massive Qianmen and Tiananmen gates, the west side of the square was hemmed-in by the Great Hall of the People, and, on its east side, the National Museum of China. The vibrant, modern Chinese capital that surrounded the old city center throbbed with midsummer activity.

Bicycles and cars sped in all directions. An elderly vendor hawked barbecued scorpions outside a high-fashion boutique. A rickshaw runner yelled at a passing luxury sedan. Beneath the neon glow of video screens and billboards, a sleek, modern tram glided along its street track. It passed the Ministry of National Defense's compound where the 'August 1st' building stood. Named for the founding of the People's Liberation Army, it loomed over the neighborhood.

Wearing a peaked, stylized roof adorned with antennae and satellite dishes, the building constituted a modern-day fortress. From its summit hung the red and gold flag of the People's Republic, and, in a basement bunker far from the reach of foreign spies and twitchy locals, Party officials attended a late-night meeting.

The bunker's reinforced concrete and exposed steel columns and girders were made more welcoming by elegant antique Gansu carpets, cloisonné vases, and intricately carved mahogany-paneled screens. A large golden Seal of the People's Republic of China hung on the bunker's long wall, opposite a painting of Mao Zedong, the Chairman surrounded by happy workers. Marble busts of Lenin and Marx stared at the aged men seated around a large oval table. Most wore uniforms of the Chinese armed forces, and a few more were dressed in suits. Most of those gathered were spotted and bloated from excess, mere reflections of their former glorious selves. A tiny woman entered the chamber and fanned her hand at the thick-hanging tobacco smoke, moving it from her disapproving, crinkled face. She coughed and drew a colorful tapestry draped across the wall. Behind it were exposed two large video screens. The screens flickered on. Maps of the Pacific Ocean and the Taiwan Strait Theater exploded into view.

"The Military Commission of the Politburo Standing Committee of the Communist Party of China is hereby called to order," intoned Xu Wai Li, president of the republic and chairman of the gathered military commission. President Xu reiterated the purpose of the late night meeting: How to react to the announcement that the United States would furnish the renegade Chinese province of Taiwan with advanced weapons. People's Liberation Army General Zhen Zhu sat among the members of the commission.

A squat square of a man, General Zhen had a grey crew cut and one blinded eye, the consequence of a parasite during his youth. A golden aiguillette, collar insignias, star-covered epaulets, and a chest full of medals and ribbons adorned his olive-drab uniform. Perched forward, a peaked cap shaded Zhen's dark brown gaze. Its black visor, outlined in yellow braid, served as a billboard for the red star insignia of the People's Liberation Army.

General Zhen contemplatively ran his finger over scar tissue. During the chaos of the 'June 4th Incident'—the name chosen by the Party for the massacre of citizens at Tiananmen Square—a chunk of glass had been embedded in his cheek. A medic's sloppy stitching left him with the Frankenstein-like blemish, though Zhen wore the mutilation with honor. Having personally shot nine of the pro-democracy demonstrators that summer night, his only regret was he had carried a pistol instead of a machinegun. Besides this Tiananmen blemish, combat in Vietnam, at the Indian border, and Tibet all had exacted their toll upon his aging body, leaving the old warrior with a shambling gait and sleepless, aching nights.

General Zhen sighed with impatience as he surveyed the men of the supreme martial committee. Most of them were half-drunk from dinner, and the rest, on the verge of sleep. All waited for People's Liberation Army Air Force General Piao Bai to finish his droning statement.

"In conclusion," General Piao half-mumbled, "I would advise against the army's plan to invade Taiwan, continuing instead on a path of rapprochement, softly integrating Taiwan into our economy with agreements; essentially a de facto non-violent unification." One man yawned. "As for the Americans," Piao continued, "we all know they will defend the island, so why fight those we can instead starve? Our 20-year plan to dismantle the economy of the United States and pilfer its technological jewels is on track. Soon, the Americans will no longer be able to afford aircraft carriers. Yes," he exclaimed, nodding with self-agreement, "We must ignore this latest transfer of weaponry by the Americans and stay the course." General Piao smiled to the president—his old schoolmate—and the rest of the committee attendees. Feeling his position unassailable, he creaked back down into his seat.

The president took back the floor. He reminded the committee that they had all read the air force's proposal, and trusted all were in agreement: the plan would be adopted, energies focused on pressing issues at the Indian frontier, and with the restive Muslim population in the northwestern province of Xinjiang. General Zhen cleared his throat for attention and raised his hand. The interruption, a veiled challenge to paramount authority, and, therefore, the president's nod of approval met wholly unenthusiastic acceptance.

"Thank you President Xu. With all due respect to the chairman and this body, General Piao is *wrong*." Zhen stood, buttressing himself on the table with straightened arms. "Perhaps my distinguished colleague in the air force would be more comfortable wearing the uniform of the girl scouts?" Zhen taunted Piao. Piao's blotches turned several different shades, and he looked to the president for intervention. None came, and Zhen proceeded. "Taiwan..." the poisonous contempt he held for the island came through clearly, "is no longer about an unfinished civil war, or the disrespectful meddling of a foreign superpower. Taiwan is about the ascendance of China to a place of glory befitting her new global power. My comrades…" the general paused, scanning the membership. "Let me take Taiwan and deliver China to this rightful place of glory." Zhen raised a fist and began to pace behind the now wide-awake men. "We are blocked from the Pacific by the first island chain, of which Taiwan is the keystone," the general tantalized. "Once the island is back in the fold, I will use its air and sea bases to drive the Americans all the way back to Hawaii. After that, gentlemen," he smiled wolfishly, "it will be *our* bombers and warships conducting exercises off San Diego and King's Bay, *our* aircraft carriers that steam on the horizon."

"Insanity," an admiral of the People's Liberation Army Navy scoffed, Zhen's rant. "You presume much general." The admiral looked around for eye contact and support. However, most of the commission stayed neutral by looking to Mao's portrait. The admiral hung in the wind. General Zhen continued:

"Must the commission be reminded of the massive firepower at our disposal? Of the new weapons deployed along the coast? While some…" Zhen looked to the fuming General Piao, "cling to faint-hearted policies; it is we who possess the advantage and the initiative. Gentlemen, it is time. If I may?" Zhen asked, though he was already in motion, reaching an arm under the table. President Xu extended an arm in invitation. Zhen produced a small remote control from a drawer. He strode to the map, and, like an ireful magician, waved his arms. Computer-generated icons populated the screen: little red airplanes, infantrymen, parachutes, rockets, ships, and tanks.

"In Fujian..." Zhen said as he pointed to the Chinese province adjacent to the sweet potato-shaped Taiwanese island, "I have under my personal command over 1,500 East Wind ballistic missiles, and over 400 highly-accurate East Sea and Long Sword cruise missiles." He paused to allow his declaration to sink in. Then, with the push of a button, the computer simulated a massive single coordinated missile launch against the island; a 'wargasm,' as it were. "Then," Zhen continued, "I command an entire airborne corps, four amphibious divisions, and countless armored, infantry, and mechanized divisions ready to be air- and sea-lifted across this...miserable little Strait." Zhen sneered, and his tobacco-stained teeth glistened. "Our enemies cannot match our cyber-warfare capabilities, and the limitations of the Taiwanese armed forces are well known to this body." The general activated a laser pointer on the remote control. With the red dot it projected, he circled the measly number of blue icons that represented Taiwan's defenses. "Taiwan can at most field a few trifling divisions, and their air force and navy cannot endure our overwhelming onslaught. My staff has programmed several attack simulations into the new 'Blue Lantern' supercomputer, with each employing a multi-phase attack. First, our surface-to-surface missiles will rain down upon Taiwan's military and air defense bases and critical infrastructure. Then, our long-range surface-to-air missiles will blast scrambling Taiwanese aircraft as they take to the air. Next, our air force will fly in, cudgeling any surviving enemy aircraft and ground targets; and, the final blow will be delivered by our amphibious and

14

airborne forces as they land at Taiwan's air and seaports, fanning out across the island. Blue Lantern has predicted that, against all possible defenses, we will have total victory in six days." On the wall display, computer-generated arrows swept east from the Chinese coast, and turned the simulated island of Taiwan blood red.

"That is enough," People's Liberation Army Air Force General Piao shouted, standing again, his legs cracking and popping as he rose. Finally, on his feet, he growled, "We all know where this will lead: nuclear war with the Americans."

"And risk our atomic reprisal? Never," General Zhen roared at his counterpart. "The United States is bankrupt, distracted, and divided. The Americans have no stomach for a nuclear exchange. They would not risk Los Angeles for Taipei. Your conclusions are flawed and clearly exhibit diffidence. Perhaps retirement would better suit you general?" Zhen stabbed.

"How dare you?" General Piao rumbled, shaking with anger. "You ask us to risk everything; all our hard-won progress, just to satiate your craving for battle and conquest."

"Gentlemen," President Xu interjected, with the lilt of a man entertained. "I suggest we proceed with General Piao's plan. We will boycott the American companies that provided the weaponry, but otherwise, do nothing. Time is on our side. We will use it. This is my executive recommendation. Is there any more discussion?" The president looked right at Zhen, and his glare willed the general to sit again. With that, a vote was called.

Zhen dissented in disgust. He scanned the old men. He despised their obediently raised hands and pudgy faces that looked to the president like submissive pets awaiting their master's praise. In that moment, deep beneath the 'August 1st' building, General Zhen decided China could no longer wait for those lapdogs to become men.

◊◊◊◊

Having retired for the evening to his government apartment, Zhen settled into an over-stuffed couch. He lit an unfiltered cigarette, spit a bit of tobacco from the tip of his tongue, and then gulped the last of his glass of Scotch. He looked out at one of the Sea Palace's two lakes, and, beyond, the Imperial Palace and the Hall of Harmony. With wisps of blue smoke still curled about him in the still air, he stared far, as though in a trance. The general swirled the golden alcohol about the crystal glass before he took another sip. With a deep breath and sigh, he reached for a cellular telephone and dialed a memorized number.

Zhen reached one of his 'Four Fiends'—a loyal cadre comprising three men and one woman. All were equally devoted to China becoming the planet's supreme power, and each possessed a unique authority or skill. In a loose hierarchy beneath the 'Four Fiends' also awaited 'Nine Dragons'—a rogue's gallery with the power and will to change the world. Zhen took a deep, wheezy breath and uttered a single code word: "*Qiongqi*," the Chinese word for deceit. With preordained plans set in motion, the general hung up and refilled his crystal tumbler with single malt.

◊◊◊◊

Northeast of Beijing, in Hohhot, was a cramped and dingy apartment. Within, a thin, greasy-haired man sat before a jury-rigged collection of hard drives, multiple flatscreens, racked boards, and humming processors. A skilled hacker, he was one of the Nine Dragons. Having received his go code, the hacker put down the telephone and typed frantically at the computer's keyboard. He held a finger over the keyboard's [Enter] button, and the dragon tattoo that adorned his forearm stared; egging him on. Lowering the finger with a click that resonated, the computer screens flashed as lines of code streamed across them. His program had been irretrievably launched, and began to worm its way into cyber-space.

Dongyin Island lay northwest of Taiwan proper and just a veritable stone's throw from the Chinese mainland. Atop its rocky cliffs sat the Dongyong lighthouse that broadcast a cone of light that pierced the sea fog and the black night. Near it lay 'Sea Dragon Cave,' across from Reclining Alligator Islet, a flat-topped rock that Taiwan's engineers had chosen, to drill 50 evenly spaced silos into its solid schist. Within these silos, the air force had placed Sky Spear short-range ballistic missiles. Overlooking the missile field, two Taiwanese airmen sat in a bunker.

They worked a panel of lights and switches, and monitored 'Strongnet,' Taiwan's command and control computer network. One airman looked to the bunker's small armored window and the dark sky beyond. It was 0400: time for the delivery of a breakfast of hot soup. A buzzer sounded to indicate someone at the other side of the blast door. Authenticating their identity on a video screen, the supervising airman unlocked the door and swung it open.

An attendant entered and placed a covered tray on a table. He poured glasses of cold water, and then exited the bunker. The heavy door swung closed and locked with an echoing click. The airmen uncovered the bowls of soup and began to slurp it down greedily. But then, an alarm shrilled and interrupted their feast. A red ceiling light began to strobe. One airman spilled soup into his lap, and cursed and grimaced in pain as his superior rolled his chair to the Strongnet terminal and read the order. Blood drained from his face as he noted the words. He scurried to a wall safe and spun the tumbler. He threw the unlocked safe door open, grabbed a binder from inside, returned to his still-spinning chair, and matched the Strongnet code with that listed within the binder.

"I have a valid launch code," he yelled, and handed the order to his colleague. "Verify." The subordinate complied and double-checked the numbers.

"Sir, this is a valid launch code. We are in launch mode," his voice trembled.

The superior ordered the control room into lockdown, isolating the room from outside air. In a cave deep beneath their feet, a generator kicked on, and took over from the island's grid. Both men removed revolvers from a second safe, holstered them, and returned to their control panels. As in a hundred previous exercises, the Taiwanese activated missiles one through 50. Unlike in training, however, the telephone began to ring, and there was an urgent clanking rap at the thick steel door. Although one man was seemingly disturbed by this, the other ignored the noise and proceeded by the numbers.

"Green lights. All missiles are ready to fly," the supervisor said. The rapping at the door became ever more insistent. "Shoot anybody who comes through that door," he pointed. The unanswered telephone continued its plea for attention. Floodlights came on and washed over the missile field where silo covers slid open and exposed the red tips of the ballistic missiles within. A soldier approached the control room window. He screamed, but the men inside could not hear his pleas. Frustrated, the soldier frantically waved his arms, gesturing that they should discontinue the launch. The airmen ignored him and proceeded with their duty. The soldier then pointed his assault rifle and sprayed the window with bullets. Although it remained intact, the window became an opaque web of unitized shards.

"Sir, they're shooting at us," the subordinate stated the obvious.

"They are traitors," the superior said, with a glare at his colleague. "We expected saboteurs. Stay focused, lieutenant. We will fire our missiles as ordered. Now, report all missiles or *I* will shoot you." The supervisor drew and cocked his revolver.

"Yes, sir," the man stuttered, and regained his focus. "Missiles one through 50: silos open and clear."

"Acknowledged. Prepare to launch." Both men inserted keys into their panels. With a cracking voice that momentarily revealed the human behind the cold professional, the supervisor counted down: "Three, two, one, launch." With both keys turned, that which could not be stopped, began. Mere spectators now, they sat back. The control room began to shake as the missiles started their launch sequence.

A large explosive detonated outside the control room's door, and a rocket-propelled grenade blasted through the window, killing ·

both men inside instantly. The door jumped off its bent hinges and slammed to the ground with a clank. A flash-bang grenade was chucked into the room. An assault team stormed the room, and the beams of gun-mounted flashlights swept the smoke-filled space. A Taiwanese officer followed the team and strode to the missile control panel. He evaluated the read-outs, and, understanding any efforts to stop the launch would be futile, pounded his fist in frustration. A hiss and suction emitted from the nearest Sky Spear silo.

A column of sparks and flame erupted; a manmade volcano. A Sky Spear burst from its protective hole and began to climb into the sky. The missile in the next silo ignited, and within minutes, all 50 climbed from Taiwan's Dongyin Island. The missiles pierced low-level clouds, illuminating them from within as they arced west toward the Chinese coast.

Minutes later, the Sky Spears dove over the shipyards, skyscrapers, and temples of Fuzhou, China. Chinese surface-to-air missiles climbed to meet them, and claimed three of the 200-pound high-explosive warheads. Forty-seven Taiwanese missiles slipped through the defenses and impacted. Several blocks of downtown Fuzhou were carpeted with destruction and death. The supersonic bombs shattered and collapsed one commercial high rise, and with occupants tucked between sheets, immolated several residential ones.

A heavy summer rain had drenched the American capital. Richard Ling and Zhang 'Jade' Jiao dined at their favorite Cantonese restaurant in the neighborhood of Adams Morgan. They sipped steaming Jasmine tea as they awaited a break in the weather. When the downpour subsided, they agreed this was their chance to head out. Richard paid and helped Jade with her raincoat.

Hand-in-hand, they walked out into the drizzle and headed for the Metro station at DuPont Circle. The couple pushed through the throng of college students, pickpockets, and tourists that spilled from bars and out into the potholed streets. Richard towered lankily over the crowd. He drew the bloodshot, blue-eyed stare of an entitled college student. As the couple sauntered, Richard contemplated rumors of promotion at work.

Born in Illinois, Richard was a proud second generation Chinese-American. He worked for the State Department's Bureau of Intelligence & Research, serving as an analyst of Chinese economic, military, and political issues, and their role in Sino-American relations. As he pored over open-source material, covert intelligence, satellite photos, and foreign newspapers Richard had continued to distinguish himself from the ranks of anonymous analysts; even those across the river at CIA. His insights had benefited the secretary of state, as well as other high-level American decision makers. All this meant Richard was in line to become Assistant Secretary of East Asian and Pacific Affairs. A colleague in administration had already confirmed the whispered rumor.

Jade glanced at her man; pensive and inattentive as they nudged through the people. She leaned in to kiss his cheek.

A native of Hong Kong, Jade was in DC to study international relations. She never had expected to fall in love with an American, let alone a Chinese one; an inconvenience that went against her every reason for being in the United States. Together for several months now, Jade and Richard had met beneath the grand rotunda of the Library of Congress's Reading Room. Jade studied at one of the long wood tables. Richard was seated there, too, clacking away on his laptop. Jade had noticed his nerdy good looks, and caught him looking her way and. To, hook him, she pouted her full lips and ran fingers through her long, black hair. Then, to reel him in, she had then flickered almond-shaped green eyes. The lure of her feminine powers did not disappoint. Within minutes, Richard had nervously approached and offered a simple, 'Hello.' The memory of their meeting made her smile. Richard turned to Jade and suggested they stop at their favorite club for a nightcap. Still unnoticed by Richard, a staring, loutish college student crashed into him.

"Hey, watch it," bloodshot eyes slurred. Richard pondered the hate-filled eyes and remembered the countless times he had been surrounded by white kids on the playground and worked over for being different. Richard apologized anyway and pushed on. "I'm not done with you, chonky," bloodshot spat. Richard looked to Jade, who shrugged in ignorance of the epithet. Richard turned back to the college student, who leaned in close to intimidate. "My old man lost his job because of you people," bloodshot stated and stabbed his finger into Richard's sternum. Surprised to find muscle where he expected only bone, the soused student stepped back a little. Richard moved forward and filled the void.

"I'm from Chicago," Richard rebutted, leaning in closer and puffing his chest.

"Ah, you're not worth my time," bloodshot declared, before turning away. His frat brothers saw he had retreated and, to save face, pulled him away for more shots of tequila.

"Let's just go," Jade murmured, tugging at Richard. They took a few contemplative steps. "You'll always be a foreigner here, you know? Just another ABC," she muttered. Richard knew this term well. Like many first and second generation American-Born Chinese, his type often existed in limbo. Despite patriotism that Oscar Wilde would label vicious, Richard struggled with the alienating racism so many Americans showed him. While many called him smart and hardworking, deep down he knew his impetus for success was rooted in this dichotomy. Moments earlier, Jade and Richard had been happy to share a much-needed date. Now, they strolled silently past their favorite club. *Guess there won't be any dirty martinis tonight*, Jade thought. The couple reached the Metro station. They stepped onto its steep escalator.

Jade and Richard bumped along in the subway train and stared out through blackened windows. Richard's inverted triangle of a face was lit intermittently by passing tunnel lamps, and his dark brown eyes reflected in the safety glass.

Walking from Foggy Bottom/GWU station, Jade and Richard strolled along the cobblestones of Olive Street toward their place, the townhouse they had shared for several weeks now. Jade grabbed Richard's ass, making him smile again. They paused in the yellow of a streetlamp and shared a long kiss. Walking again, their step quickened. Jade giggled with anticipation. Once through the apartment door, they began to strip each other. Richard was slow to indulge at first, seemingly preoccupied with his discouraging encounter. However, when Jade guided his hand to her moistness, he soon forgot all.

Panting heavily, Jade slid off Richard and collapsed beside him. Now at the outer edges of sleep from the powerful, shared orgasm, Richard flashed into a dream: The world was on fire.

"I'm hungry," Jade declared, startling Richard awake. "You men," she laughed. "If I were a spider, I'd sting and kill you now." She donned a robe and went to the kitchen. Richard stirred from his cocoon of sheets, and clicked on the bedroom television with the remote. Breaking news from Taiwan came on. Richard squinted against the glare and sat up.

"Hon,' come here. You need to see this," he exclaimed with urgency. Jade ambled back into the bedroom cupping a bowl of chocolate syrup-covered ice cream.

"What is it?" she asked, as she fell into her favorite overstuffed chair. She shoveled some ice cream into her mouth.

"Look…" Richard turned up the volume.

A reporter explained that Taiwan had launched ballistic missiles at Communist China, killing thousands of innocent civilians in a blatant act of war. Taiwan, in turn, claimed the attack was unauthorized—the act of a rogue missile captain—and offered profuse apologies while warning China against escalation. Beijing promised retaliation for the act of terror, and to solve the Taiwan question, 'once and for all.' The United States had called for calm on both sides. As a prudent precaution, the American president ordered the nuclear supercarriers *George Washington*, *John C. Stennis*, and *Ronald*

Reagan to the area. The journalist then concluded her report with, "Ladies and gentleman, the events of the last few hours are undeniable—the Fourth Taiwan Crisis has begun."

Jade swore in Chinese, and Richard dropped the f-bomb in English. They both looked at each other with mouths agape. Richard's cell phone began to ring. He glanced at the flashing, vibrating thing, and then back to the news.

"There goes the weekend," he sighed. Richard stood and walked to the nightstand. Wanting privacy to take the call, he carried the phone into the kitchen.

On the San Diego embarcadero, near the Spanish colonial revival Santa Fe Depot, and past the tall masts of the Maritime Museum's full-rigged sailing ship, *Star of India*, a white pickup truck pulled up outside a tall glass hotel. Wearing US Navy dress white, Lieutenant Cynthia Pelletier hopped out of the pickup and blew a last kiss to its driver, her dad. He smiled widely and told her to be safe, and that he was very proud of her.

The hotel's bellhop took Lieutenant Pelletier's sea-bag from the truck and nearly collapsed under its weight. He shuffled off, groaning, maneuvering the unwieldy canvas sausage to a luggage cart. Out of breath, he directed Pelletier to the front desk. She entered the air-conditioned lobby and tucked her short blond hair behind a smallish ear. Her long bare legs carried her quickly past the gawking concierge who slammed his open jaw shut. Pelletier placed her plain handbag on the cold marble check-in counter, and pulled a reservation confirmation from the bag's side pocket. When her green eyes locked on the manager, he flushed for the first time in years. *She's too pretty to be a sailor*, he thought.

Pelletier had grown up surrounded by Colorado's saw-toothed and snow-peaked mountains. At a young age, she had traded a love of horses for that of airplanes. While others her age swooned for Tom Cruise, she instead was seduced by the movie's other star: the big swing-wing F-14 Tomcat fleet defense fighter. Cindy would sit on her pink bike at the end of her driveway and pretend the asphalt was the steel deck of an aircraft carrier. Cindy's best friend would stand beside her and salute. This signaled Cindy to start pedaling. She would pump the pedals as hard as her skinny legs could manage, and got the bike up to speed. Trailing sparkly streamers from the handlebars, Cindy's bike would hit a makeshift plywood ramp and go airborne. These were her first imaginary carrier take-offs. She cherished those few weightless moments before the bicycle hit the ground again. Often sent tumbling through the brambles, she always had a righteous laugh, and did it all again and again.

Years later, she had found her teenage sweetheart, and fell harder than those bicycle wipeouts. He had proposed on the dance floor at their senior prom. She turned him down and left him in the flicker of the disco ball, with the thump of music and a broken heart filling his chest. Although she was handed true love, Cindy wanted more from life: Cindy wanted wings. With a bit of help from her father, she put herself through college and earned a degree in aeronautics. With diploma in hand, Cindy went right to the navy recruiter. He immediately showed her where to sign.

United States Naval Officer Candidate Cynthia Pelletier had then gone on to Officer Candidate School at Naval Station Newport, Rhode Island. There she had endured the Marine Corps' 'House of Pain,' and earned a healthy fear of drill instructors, and a place at Primary Flight Training. Now a distinguished naval aviator, Lieutenant Pelletier accepted her hotel card key. She headed upstairs for room service and a few hours of sleep.

Early the next morning, Lieutenant Pelletier trailed another bellhop. He lugged her sea-bag, as she strolled through the hotel's lobby doors and out into the cool pre-dawn dark. Pelletier breathed in the moist salty air and looked at the seagulls that were already awake and complaining as they wheeled above. Attracted more by Cindy's splendor than by the bellhop's wave, a taxi screeched to a stop beside her, and the driver emerged to open the car's door. He was unkempt and reeked of old cologne. Pelletier stated her destination: "North Island Naval Air Station," and took a deep breath before shuffling into the car. She quickly lowered the windows to aerate the interior, and, in the side mirror, watched the driver cram her sea-bag into the taxi's trunk.

They passed the venerable aircraft carrier *Midway* on Harbor Drive, and then the Marina and Gaslamp districts of Old San Diego. The taxi turned onto Highway 75 and crossed the elegant blue ribbon of viaduct that linked Coronado Island to the city. The sun began to rise, tinting the morning sky deep purple. In the distance, Pelletier spotted the white-barreled towers and red witch hat-shaped roofs of the beachside Hotel Del Coronado. The taxi passed Coronado Island's Tidelands Park and turned onto 4th Street. Pelletier thought about her ship: USS *Ronald Reagan*. This would be the first time she was to serve aboard the nuclear supercarrier, and she would be doing it in the navy's newest airplane. With fifth generation aircraft trickling into the fleet, Pelletier was one of the first to learn and fly the new jets. One of the stealthy machines awaited her on North Island's flight line. She would fly it out to meet the carrier.

Nudged by tugs, *Ronald Reagan* had already put to sea beneath the twinkling stars, and departed San Diego Harbor early that morning. With her decks bare and cavernous hangar empty, 'The Gipper,' as *Ronald Reagan* was affectionately called, would meet her air wing and escorts south of San Clemente Island. Once formed-up in southern California waters, the *Ronald Reagan* carrier strike group was to head west toward the continental shelf.

Pelletier's taxi arrived at the outer gate of North Island Naval Air Station. Her identification checked by the sailor on duty, she handed in her sea-bag. The cabbie, who clutched his lower back as he mumbled, fell back into his car. Pelletier strolled a promenade where a gauntlet of palm trees rustled, and headed for one of the naval station's old buildings. She returned salutes from those she passed and smiled all the while.

Squeezing into her flight suit, Pelletier checked her flight plan and strode out to North Island's ramp and the warplane that awaited her. She went about her pre-flight routine and watched two fat carrier cargo aircraft take off from the base's main runway. Propeller-driven and heavy with spare parts, mail, supplies, and Pelletier's sea-bag, the cargo planes required the most time to catch up with *Ronald Reagan*, and were, therefore, first to depart. As she watched them struggle into the air, Pelletier began her own airplane's start up sequence.

◊◊◊◊

The American nuclear supercarrier *George Washington* was engaged in an exercise with the Royal Australian Navy south of Palau. She was the closest to Taiwan, so her strike group got orders to steam northwest at full speed, and entered an area of the Philippine Sea called the 'Dragon's Triangle.' *George Washington* was super in all respects. She towered some 20 stories over the water and reached four more beneath it. The 1,096-foot hull—as long as the Chrysler Building was tall—got pushed at over 30 knots by twin nuclear reactors that powered four giant bronze propellers. With a four-and-a-half acre flight deck and an air wing larger than most national air forces, *George Washington* was twice the weight of *Titanic*, and some 97,000 tons of American diplomacy.

Plying the waves off *George Washington*'s port bow was the guided-missile cruiser *Lake Champlain,* a sleek vessel and, at about half the size of the carrier, the largest of *George Washington*'s escorts. Although five-inch deck guns were her only apparent armament, *Lake Champlain* hid anti-air, anti-ship, and land-attack missiles below her spray-soaked decks. At the ship's prow, snapping in the headwind proudly flew a red-striped flag with a yellow snake that menacingly declared 'Don't Tread on Me.' A single black anchor hung beneath it, and, below the waterline, a bulbous sonar stem protruded. With helicopters and torpedoes, *Lake Champlain* was an enemy submariner's worst nightmare. On the cruiser's superstructure, below the bridge's band of windows, hexagonal radar arrays scanned the sky for threats. Arrayed around the ship were dishes, domes, and antenna masts that talked to satellites. They also linked *Lake Champlain* to the group's other ships, and to command at Pearl Harbor. With sensors and weapons controlled by a sophisticated computerized combat system, *Lake Champlain* projected a protective bubble high into space and deep below the sea. All by her lonesome, *Lake Champlain* constituted an armada.

On *Lake Champlain*'s bridge, US Navy Captain Anthony Ferlatto stood between the quartermaster and lookout, his legs spread wide to brace against the roll of the ship. With squinted beady black eyes, Captain Ferlatto studied digital charts and chewed an unlit cigar. "If I ain't chewing on this, I'll be chewing on you," he told those who questioned the nasty habit. The soaked cheroot occupied his mouth, and his sharp hooked nose whistled as he breathed. Ferlatto scanned the ship's helm console and looked to the officer-of-the-deck, who gave a curt nod. The OOD knew the captain hated minced words— what he called 'noise'—especially when a simple gesture would suffice. Ferlatto walked forward and rested a hand on the ship's steel wall. He determined from its vibration that the cruiser's gas turbines were at the correct power setting, and running good and healthy. He grunted with satisfaction. Ferlatto was always happy at sea. He squinted through the armored, tinted windows and looked to the other ships spread around the supercarrier.

A bit smaller than the cruiser at just over 500 feet, two guided-missile destroyers—*Mahan* and *Paul Hamilton*—steamed with *George Washington* and *Lake Champlain*. Bringing up the rear and rounding out the posse was the smallest ship of the group, the guided-missile frigate *Rodney M. Davis*. Ten miles ahead of this main body of ships, the nuclear attack submarine *California* ran 200 feet beneath the choppy surface leading the charge.

California was a 377-foot high-tensile steel shark. Although she looked like most submarines, with a hemispheric bow, dive planes, a tall sail, and a long black cylindrical hull that tapered at the stern, *California* went beyond common appearances to represent the cutting edge of American submarine technology. Like other boats of the new *Virginia*-class, *California* sported a wide array of advanced sensors and weaponry. She could dominate shallow green and deep blue water against any submerged foe, conduct covert surveillance, deliver special forces, or pummel land and sea surface targets with cruise missiles and torpedoes. With the alignment of complex factors like availability, personal desire, rotation, and shipyard experience, Commander Max Wolff had the good fortune of being *California*'s very first skipper.

Commander Wolff came from a long line of submariners… German ones. His great-great-grandfather was a U-boat captain for von Tirpitz during the Great War, and his grandfather manned one for Dönitz. Max was born in Philadelphia a few years after his father left the rubble of Germany for the 'Land of Opportunity.' He graduated from the US Naval Academy in 1985, attended submarine school in Groton, Connecticut, was assigned to a *Permit*-class boat and, a year later, received the coveted gold dolphins, pinned on his uniform. Several boats and decades later, Wolff distinguished himself with a first command on a *Los Angeles*. Possessing recognized proficiency in nuclear propulsion and an instinct for submarine tactics, the stars came together for Commander Wolff, and he took command of *California*.

With the big white hull number on her sail and her new skipper's ethnicity, *California* was informally referred to as 'Unterseeboot-781', or, simply, 'U-781.' When Wolff was informed of the boat's new nickname, it was the only time his crew had seen him smile. Used to his expressionless face and frosty steel eyes, they knew full well that behind this façade lived a deeply caring man and a consummate submariner who would give anything for those who served with him. As *California* sailed into dangerous waters, Commander Wolff's inherent stoicism became amplified, leaving greetings unanswered as he finished lunch in the submarine's wardroom.

Wolff's tense jaw flexed and churned the soft sandwich. His crew-cut of blonde hair was spiked back to attention with a backward sweep of his hand. Wolff punched the air to look at his watch. *It's time*, he thought, and stood. A pillar of a man, he headed for *California*'s control center. He passed and respectfully brushed with his fingertips, a brass plaque stating *California*'s motto: *Silentium Est Aureum*—'Silence Is Golden.' Although quiet at most speeds, *California* was racing at 32 knots with the rest of the carrier strike group. She was making plenty of noise and her ability to collect sounds from the water was degraded. Wolff entered the submarine's control center. He announced his presence with an order to reduce speed and deploy the towed sonar array.

Chiayi Air Base sat on Taiwan's northwestern coastal plain, one of the many Taiwanese military complexes that lived under the gun. Home to the 455th Tactical Fighter Wing, 4th Group, Chiayi was well within range of Chinese missiles. Like the rest of Taiwan's air bases, Chiayi practiced alerts and scramble take-offs so its aircraft could not be caught on the ground. Since the Fourth Crisis had begun, all Taiwanese air bases had been on ground alert. On Chiayi's flight line, Major Han Ken waited in the seat of his F-16 Fighting Falcon.

The Fighting Falcon's look was classic: dart-tip nose, crisp and sharp edges, distinctive bubble canopy, tricycle landing gear, and an ovoid engine inlet nestled between slender wings. Like tail feathers, the notched empennage had, beneath it, a big, silver nozzle that marked the end of the engine tunnel. Although built in the 1990s, the Americans had kept Taiwan's Fighting Falcons upgraded, making the jets practically new under the skin. Major Han proudly served as flight leader of Chiayi's 21st Squadron; 'The Gamblers.' Freshly painted on the side of the warplanes the squadron's insignia was displayed: two playing cards, the ace-of-hearts crossed by the king-of-spades. Upon the vertical tail was a blue roundel with the white sun of Taiwan with '455-4's painted beneath it. Parked with Han on the tarmac were the squadron's nine other fighter-bombers, all outfitted with external fuel tanks and air-to-air missiles. The sweating pilots suffered, strapped into their reclined seats. Beside those of 'The Gamblers,' the wing had 40 more Fighting Falcons ready to go, with six others getting armed and fueled within Chiayi's shaded shelters. . Even with the canopy wide open, the pilots enjoyed no breeze, and cockpit temperatures climbed.

Han tugged at his flight suit, itching through the thick fabric at the tickle of streaming sweat. A welcome air conditioning cart pulled up, and an airman snaked a flexible yellow duct into his cockpit. Cool, dry air blew over him. Relieved, Han tried to relax. Unlike the other men in his wing, he had no photos of family to stare at longingly, to pass the minutes. However, he did have Erica, Playboy's 'Miss August, her picture taped to his cockpit console. She accelerated time like no other. Han sighed; her ample bosom made the uncomfortable wait pass faster. The cool air seeped into his suit. Han shifted in the ejection seat and tried to stretch.

Like other young Taiwanese men, Han had been conscripted. His academic records in math and other sciences, however, allowed him to apply for a place at the Air Force Academy at Kangshan. He was accepted and, soon enough, it became clear that Han had an innate ability to fly. Shunted to fixed-wing aircraft and then jets, Han smoked anyone who tried to down him. After he had 'shot down' countless hotdogs in mock combat, and showed his absolute control in flight after flight, it was realized Han was an artist who worked in the medium of airspace; his brush: precise proximity flying and aerial combat maneuvers. Han, ever the doubtful prodigy, stood sweating in his flight suit as he was ordered to be the youngest pilot ever to join the air force's 'Thunder Tiger' air demonstration team. After wowing air shows and dignitaries for years, all while training Taiwan's greatest aviators, Han now had a wing of warplanes under his command.

Han checked his watch. It was two hours since the siren had summoned the men to their aircraft. In another four, backup aircrews would relieve them all. In hopes of a nap, Han closed his eyes.

A sharp, jagged, illuminated silhouette, Taipei was a human beehive. 'Taipei 101'—a graceful skyscraper shaped like a bamboo frond—punctuated the city's skyline. Taiwan's capital since being so declared in 1949 by the leader of the Chinese Nationalists, Chang Kai Shek, Taipei was an effervescent city of festivals, towers, shopping districts, and dazzling light. It was also contrasted by shadows, with narrow alleys where smoke and grease, sucked from sizzling woks, discharged around laundry flapping on poles. Arcades jutted from colonial and Chinese style storefronts, and sheltered pedestrians from the hard rain as they strolled along the red tile sidewalks and beside endless rows of parked motorbikes. Taipei, kissed by warm sea breezes and the hot sun, and, with nearly seven million people crammed in, the city comprised the economic, cultural, industrial, and political heart of the Taiwanese nation.

Taipei's metropolitan area sat at the northern tip of the island, blooming on the Danshui River between the Keelung and Xindian river valleys. Land was scarce, so every inch of the cityscape had been utilized, with neighborhoods that sprawled in a jumble of lanes and backstreets. Crisscrossed by high-speed rail and highways, the city was served by an international airport—Taoyuan/Chiang Kai Shek—as well as one that handled domestic and trans-Strait traffic: Taipei Songshan. Southeast of downtown and across the Danshui River sprawled the Jhongjheng District, the capital's civic soul. Surrounding the city, scattered among its fields and on its hilltops, a ring of air defense sites stood guard. A road climbed a hill on the eastern side of Taipei. It switched back and forth through a dense and steep stand of trees, and then emerged at the gate and electrical fencing of Songshan-East Air Defense Site #2.

This air defense site, known as 'Hill 112' for its altitude in meters, guarded Songshan Airport and the eastern part of the capital from aerial attack. Hill 112 comprised a cruciform reinforced concrete platform and a massive bunker built into the hill. Atop the platform stood a rotating radar antenna, three anti-aircraft guns, and a single surface-to-air missile battery. A parking lot doubled as a helicopter landing pad, and camouflage netting draped over an observation tower precariously perched on the hill's slope. Two airmen occupied a machinegun position guarding the main gate. In command of Hill 112 was Republic of China Air Force Senior Master Sergeant Li Rong Kai.

Senior Master Sergeant Li left the command bunker to get some fresh air. He was young, tall, and thin, but with hard, intelligent eyes. He took a deep draw of the wet, warm summer air. It would be a beautiful day if not for the unfolding events, a day when he and his family might have driven to a mountain park for a picnic. Li drew the delicate fragrance of plum blossoms into his nose and tasted its sweetness on his tongue. He brought binoculars up to his face and focused on the cityscape.

The usual buzz of the capital—its heartbeat—was clearly subdued. People had skipped work to hoard supplies and huddle around televisions. Li panned away from the hazy view of skyscrapers and fixed his magnified gaze on the building where he lived with his wife, young daughter, and mother. Li hoped his family had left by now for their farm on the eastern side of the island. Traffic had clogged the highways for hours to days, so the journey was sure to be long. Li prayed it would end with them safe. Although he had left them just yesterday, it felt like days. Buses roamed the city to collect Taiwan's airmen, marines, sailors, and soldiers. They packed into the sweltering coaches that drove them to marshaling areas and waiting trains. Li's bus had met another that then dropped him at a junior high school parking lot where a Humvee and driver waited. During the short drive to Hill 112, they passed one of Li's favorite restaurants, an Italian eatery where he and the wife would steal away for a romantic dinner. Li wondered if he would ever dine there again. He continued his stroll around Hill 112.

◊◊◊◊

A lone Chinese J-15 Flying Shark banked over the golden Bohai Sea. Off the warplane's right wing menaced the massive Chinese mainland, and, to its right was the Korean Peninsula. A menacing twin-engine heavy fighter, the Flying Shark sported dark-blue tiger stripes across its grey skin, and a distinctive drooped nose, large forward canards, and a candy-striped tailhook tucked under its pointed tail, Chinese naval aviator Senior Lieutenant Peng Jingwei at the stick. One of China's best pilots, Senior Lieutenant Peng was counted among the few qualified to land an airplane on the corkscrewing deck of an aircraft carrier. Peng turned the jet over Liaodong Bay and toward the coastal city of Huludao.

In the distance, just outside Huludao's urban expanse, and among neatly rowed crops, a long, single runway stretched. Beside the strip sat a squat, concrete building shaped like an aircraft carrier hull. Topped by a steel flight deck and superstructure, it served as China's carrier flight school, known simply to the rank and file as '91-065 Troop.' The faux ship hull housed student pilots and the Russian and Ukrainian advisors who trained them on flight simulators and in classrooms. On the 'dry ships' flight deck, sailors worked with mock-ups of aircraft and helicopters, practicing arming, fueling, moving, and repairing these aircraft. After Peng had been transferred from the People's Liberation Army Air Force to the Army Navy Air Force, this school was where Peng learned carrier operations, and graduated to lead China's first naval aviation squadron known as 'The Garpikes.' Peng lined up his Flying Shark with the runway, deploying flaps and dropping the landing gear.

◊◊◊◊

People's Liberation Army Navy Captain Kun Guan served the Party from deep beneath the sea. Despite a natural aptitude for nuclear propulsion and subsurface tactics, Captain Kun had never felt comfortable in submarines. 'Unnatural contraptions,' he called them, and he cringed with every creak from the metal constructs. Despite hailing from China's political class, Kun's rapid rise through the ranks of the People's Liberation Army Navy was self-accomplished. When the Party sought to expand Chinese subsurface power, Kun—in command of a destroyer at the time, and a surface warfare man at heart—had been shunted to submarine school at Qingdao Naval Base.

Kun's new career track under the sea began on a *Romeo*-class boat. He was chief officer on the obsolete Soviet diesel-electric that occasionally flared a nasty habit of choking the crew with engine fumes. After several patrols and some high-profile encounters with the American navy, Kun, promoted took command of *Changzheng 6*, one of China's new *Shang*-class nuclear attack submarines. *This one is better*, Kun thought of *Changzheng 6*, although he still did not like being hatched into the steel tube.

Kun leaned against the cold steel of *Changzheng 6*'s attack center bulkhead. Kun's was the sixth hull of the brand-new *Shang*s, all of which were named 'Changzheng' after the year-long 8,000 mile Long March of the Red Army retreat from Chiang Kai Shek's Nationalists. Designed and constructed with Russian assistance, *Shang*-class nuclear attack submarines compared roughly to early flights of 1970s American *Los Angeles*- or Russian *Victor III*-classes. They were generally quiet and heavily armed with tube-launched torpedoes and missiles. Captain Kun stood straight again and tugged the wrinkles from his uniform. Used to old analog dials and gauges, Kun admired the colorful glow of the attack center's new-fangled digital screens. With a well-padded roundish frame, Kun seemed built for the confines of a submarine. It was his brain, however, that revolted

He was perpetually aware that the ocean wanted in. With a muffled pop, the submarine's alloy skin adjusted to changing sea pressure. Kun's heart beat faster. Training and willpower were all that kept him from running to a hatch, and he took deep breaths to collect himself. Even though the air smelled like the submarine's air filters, the extra oxygen helped Kun suppress the sensation that the hull contracted, squeezing him tighter and tighter. *Environmental systems were one area that still needed work*, he thought. His rational mind came back from that dismal place of fear. Kun dried his nose with a pocket kerchief. Although he had remained perfectly still during the anxious episode and projected a well-practiced collected façade all the while, he did not realize his chief officer had become aware of his unease. Captain Kun clasped his hands behind his back and meandered behind the submariners seated at the attack center terminals. *Trained children*, Kun thought as he patted one nervous young man on the back. *Changzheng 6*'s chief officer looked to a screen and cleared his throat.

"Sir," the chief officer yelled, "The submarine is in position: 14.094 degrees north, 143.6572 degrees east."

◊◊◊◊

The statue of President Abraham Lincoln looked pensively to the east, his unblinking gaze locked on the National Mall's hazy distance, staring at the World War II Memorial and the Washington Monument. A gentle breeze danced across the Reflecting Pool, refreshing Jade and Richard, who shared a sandwich on the steps of the Memorial.

Jade's university was close by. Richard worked even closer, so the couple often met for lunch here. They sat on the cool, white marble, and staked out part of the landing to eat the food Jade brought: sandwiches from home, or take-out. The meals had become a ritual of political debates, meddling in friends' affairs, and soaking up the sun. This particular day was tropics-hot and oppressively humid, and with the Taiwan crisis, Jade and Richard had become especially grumpy.

"Taiwan is part of China," Jade again proclaimed. "It's even part of China's extended continental shelf."

"You're right. It is Chinese. Just not authoritarian, totalitarian Chinese," Richard replied. Rarely able to hold his tongue, even when he knew it would be best to do so, he rolled his eyes and took another bite. *Probably why I ended up in the diplomatic corps*, Richard weighed with a private smirk.

Jade huffed, but offered no riposte.

"It's about political systems, not race," Richard added, in hopes of ending this thread of the conversation. Knowing the effort had failed, he quickly took another bite of his sandwich.

"I hope we liberate the island," Jade muttered passive-aggressively, drawing a sharp glare from her lover.

"Don't you mean invade?" Richard retorted. He turned away, signaling he really did not want an answer, and looked to a group of schoolchildren that climbed toward the looming former president. Their children's teacher began to read the Memorial's bronze plaque aloud. He annunciated each word in his 'best Lincoln:' "Four score and seven years ago…"

"You cannot invade what is rightfully yours?" Jade pushed-back his hanging question. "And, as usual, you Americans will stick your nose where it doesn't belong."

"Oh, now I'm American? I thought I was just a lost Chinese. Anyway, the US belongs in the Pacific. We've earned the right," Richard forced.

"The *right*?" she hissed.

"Stand on any Pacific beach, my darling, and the remains of our marines are beneath your sandy toes," Richard replied with growing impatience. He wondered if their relationship would, or even could survive the so-called 'Fourth Crisis.' Until now, politics had been a thing of play between the couple. Suddenly, however, even though not unexpectedly, the topic had become as confrontational as the international mood. As much as Richard respected Jade, he saw her as he does most Chinese: insulated from reality by a government-controlled machine spewing propaganda under an Orwellian sham passed off as journalism. Despite living and studying abroad, Jade had promptly bought a satellite dish to pull in China Central Tele-Vision and shunned all other sources of news. Richard wondered how an otherwise academic mind could accept such one-sidedness. He blamed years of indoctrination, what he termed: 'slavery of the mind.' He sighed, took his last bite of lunch, and turned to view the enthusiastic teacher surrounded by a semi-circle of young students.

The teacher closed his mock Lincoln speech with, "…government of the people, by the people, for the people shall not perish from the Earth."

Jade and Richard stopped talking, both staring blankly into the distance, and Richard looked to his watch. Even though he still had time to spare, he announced he had to get back to the office. Jade grabbed his sleeve to keep him with her.

"I'm sorry. Do you hate me?" she asked. Although she seemingly batted her eyelashes, her eyes reddened and swelled with tears.

"Do I hate you? No. We just need to be careful with this stuff. You know, agree to disagree. Otherwise…" he raised an eyebrow and put an arm around her.

"If there is war, your country will send me home," she said resentfully, and swallowed the lump in her throat.

"If yours doesn't call you back first," Richard added. He shook his head, wishing his choice of words had been more compassionate. He sighed again and hugged Jade. Despite not really believing it, he continued, "There won't be any war." He kissed her and started down the Memorial steps. Time to get an early jump on his afternoon of work.

Richard cancelled their dinner date, so he could work late into the evening. The secretary of state had to brief the Senate Foreign Relations Committee on the origins of the Taiwan conflict. As specialists at CIA scrambled to organize, Richard had already established himself as the subject matter expert. Unknown to most, Richard's ethnicity was Hakka, aboriginal Austronesians that had inhabited Taiwan long before the arrival of the Han Chinese. Like most Hakka, his blood was now mostly Han, but loyalties and knowledge of the unique island culture remained undiluted. He finished the report and headed for the secretary's office.

Secretary of State Georgiana Pierce stood at the window, watching a cop ticket a car and a public works employee clearing a storm drain outside the Old Naval Observatory. Light from the early-evening street lighting subtly flickered and flooded the office through rain-spattered bulletproof windows. It added bluish highlights to the roundness of the secretary's face. At Secretary Pierce's wide back, the office was an eclectic mix of African idols and retro furniture. As the direct descendant of a slave, Pierce's traced her family tree back to a man taken from the African port of Benguela to the American colonial dock auction at Charles Town.

His bill of sale hung on her office's wall. Dated July 20, 1750, the framed document transferred ownership of the teenager, from a French ship captain to a local landowner, a Mr. Pierce. Tattered and yellowed, the document had taken money, time, and power to acquire. She was proud that, centuries later, the descendant of this slave now filled one of the world's most important positions. While she could never know it, Secretary Pierce had the same big moist brown eyes as her ancestor. They had the same shape and glaze as the eyes of that scared boy who stood clapped in irons on the docks of the New World. Those old eyes could lull as the secretary's rapier intellect and wit skewered. Her love of country and American history was matched only by a passion for Creole cooking, a hobby that had contributed to her girth. As she looked out at the west side of the capital, Pierce saw Richard reflected in the office window and smiled. He had recently completed a tour of the Pacific Rim in her company. This meant he had spent untold hours inside 'the bubble' of her political life. He had broken bread on Special Air Mission aircraft that whisked the secretary and her entourage around the globe where she walked the balance beam on behalf of the United States. Secretary Pierce wiped the smile from her face before turning to greet Richard.

Pierce went to a stainless carafe, poured a cup of coffee, and offered it to Richard. He accepted, and took the saucer by two hands. He smiled with the realization that she had come to like him. Sipping the hot, black brew, Richard watched as she poured her own cup and added cream and sugar before stirring the concoction quietly. Pierce thanked Richard for staying late and for all his recent work. He blushed and muttered that he had already forwarded his notes to the Under Secretary for Political Affairs. She chuckled at his modesty, and then grew seriously quiet. Richard squirmed and sipped his coffee.

"I'll be blunt. I was raised on Ivan the Terrible, not Ming the Merciless. I'm going to need you in my ear on this one," she confided. Richard laughed.

"Ma'am, Ming the Merciless is the villain in Flash Gordon. But the Mings actually were a Chinese dynasty." He giggled. However, he then saw it was time to answer properly. "Secretary Pierce, I appreciate your faith. I am at your disposal."

"Good. Now, go home," she said, and turned to the windowpane to again address the diplomatic chess game that played in her head. Richard got up to leave, and, hopefully, salvage what was left of an evening with Jade. "You know…" she said to the window.

"Yes?" Richard turned, but not sure he wanted her to continue.

"There were some who didn't want to trust you with this one." Her voice had grown husky. Richard had to think.

"Who? Why?" He replied, his voice cracking.

"Some. And, if you think about it, you already know the 'why' part." She let that hang and fell quiet again. The rain took an ovation and tapped at her reflection. "Goodnight, now."

Goodnight, ma'am," Richard replied. As he walked down the hallway, past the portraits of former secretaries, Richard realized he knew the answer to the 'why' all too well.

General Zhen sat before China's president and the men of the Central Politburo of the Communist Party. His head was high, and his chin jutted like a shelf from between bulldog jowls. The president directed the supreme political body to vote. A majority of the hands went up, and Zhen's was proudly among them. 'Operation Red Dragon,' the invasion of Taiwan, was on.

Zhen and several other non-permanent members were then dismissed. The general was last to leave the golden chamber. He strutted through the colorful mural-lined halls and snickered. Then, as he strutted farther from the guarded door, the snicker morphed into a gruff laugh.

2: RED DRAGON

"The art of war is of vital importance to the State. It is a matter of life and death, A road either to safety or to ruin."—Sun Tzu

At Datong Air Base outside Beijing, Operation Red Dragon began just after midnight, local time. Two People's Liberation Army Air Force H-6 Huan medium bombers held at the threshold of Datong's main runway. Copies of Soviet Badgers, the twin-engine Chinese warplanes featured long, sleek fuselages with swept-back wings, and were painted off-white, with big, red pennant numbers just behind airliner-style cockpits. Massive red stars embellished the bombers' tall empennages and declared for whom they fought, while tail cannons warned of a very painful sting. Ungainly birds, the Badgers sported double chins housing radar, huge air inlets at the shoulders, and antennae blisters covering the long, thin, tapering fuselages. Despite appearances, the formidable warplanes, when coupled with advanced standoff systems like the six bright red Dong Hai-10 'East Sea' land-attack cruise missiles slung from each of the bomber's wings, the Badgers proved as ferocious and sneaky as their namesake.

The cockpit radio crackled, and Datong's controllers transmitted clearance for departure. The lead bomber's young Chinese pilot shifted and looked to his copilot, who raised a bushy eyebrow in amazement. After being roused from sleep, they had found their bombers in the hanger, armed and fueled. The aircrews had asked questions as to the mission, and naturally assumed they were going to hit Taiwan. Over breakfast and guarded conversation, they guessed their target to be the Sky Spear missile base on Taiwan's Dongyin Island, the installation that had fired at Fuzhou. Air Force General Piao had then arrived. He ended their meal and their suppositions with sealed codes and orders, and commanded them to go to their bombers. Hangar doors rolled open, and the old planes were kicked out of bed.

Taxiing in the moonless night, the Badgers rolled over the yellow chevrons of Datong's runway blast area, and held at the threshold. With gloved hands, the lead Badger pilot gripped two big throttles and nudged them forward. Nestled where the wings met fuselage, two massive turbojets spooled up and shook the large airplane. The long runway's green centerline and white edge lights shimmered in the rattling windscreen.

"Release brakes," the pilot ordered. With a squeal, the Badger began to roll on its oversized tires. Even though encumbered by a heavy load of both fuel and weapons, the Chinese bomber accelerated quickly. Their speed increased. Marking the end of the runway, red lights appeared and drew nearer. The Badgers were loaded to slightly above maximum take-off weight, so the copilot anxiously watched the ground-speed indicator before announcing 'V2'—take-off safety speed. The runway-end marker lights rushed at them, with the Badger still hugging the ground.

"We're heavy. Pull back now," the copilot urged, while tugging at his duplicate control column.

"Stop pulling. I am flying this airplane," the pilot yelled. He had decided to get a bit more speed before rotating skyward. The nose wheel breached the runway-overrun area and the pilot pulled back,

hard. The Badger's main gear trucks approached the end of the strip.
Beyond they could see only grass and a horizontal metal bar of marker
lights. Just in time, the spinning tires left the ground. With hydraulics
whining, they folded and tucked into the bomber's belly. The doors
sucked closed. The Badger was aerodynamically clean now and
generated more lift. Blasting thick black ribbons of smoke, the lead
Badger lumbered out as the second Chinese bomber began to roll.

The Badgers linked-up and banked south. They accelerated to
480 knots and climbed to 38,000 feet, just above standard commercial
cruise altitude, and transmitted the electronic tags of passenger jets.
The Chinese bombers settled into filed commercial flight-paths bound
for Shanghai International Airport. Soon thereafter, both Badgers
went electronically silent and dove toward the East China Sea.

The controller at Shanghai saw two transponders go dead on
his radar screen. He rolled his chair to another display, where two
blips reported rapidly decreasing altitude. He was about to call the
airplanes, but his supervisor and a man showing military credentials
told him to ignore the readout. The controller stammered for a
moment, but complied when the military man's eyes grew wide with
warning.

With the Badgers now nose-down and shedding altitude fast, it
took both pilots to pull each of the clumsy, fragile machines out of
their dive. The plane was a hog at high-speed, barely answering
frantic throttle and stick inputs, kicking and bucking all the while.
They'll bite you, too, if you're not careful, the lead pilot thought as he
felt his airplane trying to pitch over. He counteracted the force
expertly. Chosen for their ability to control the Badgers, the Chinese

aviators used radar altimeters to settle just 200 feet above pitch-black water and race east. Inside each cockpit, pilots opened their orders, revealing launch points and target coordinates. A somber quiet came over the Chinese aircrews.

In the windscreen, the rising sun outlined several islets on the horizon. The pilots used them to correct for deviation over the long-distance flight. The now-low altitude bombers screamed over a trawler, drawing curses from the deckhands tending their nets. They hoped they had not been recognized, or, worse, reported by these foreign fishermen. The lead Badger's copilot flashed wing lights to tell his trailer they were nearing position.

In the bombers' cockpits, tucked behind the flight crews, weapons officers played their instruments like mad musicians. They programmed and warmed up the load of East Sea land-attack cruise missiles. Now wing-to-wing, both Badgers began a slow, unified climb to 500 feet.

"Hurry, we're visible," the lead pilot said and shifted within the tight confines of his harness. The Badgers were as stealthy as the Kremlin Church and had probably just appeared on radar screens across the region. The bombers shuddered as East Seas departed wing pylons and dropped into the slipstream. Booster packs ignited, pushed the missiles up to cruise speed, and, when burned out, fell to the sea. Then the East Seas' stub wings deployed, inlets opened, turbofans started with a belch of black smoke, and small satellite dishes in the nose sniffed for signals. The American Global Positioning System and European Galileo constellations were now limiting their standard positioning services over the western Pacific, so the East Seas instead found the Chinese Compass and Russian Global Navigation Satellite systems. The twelve Chinese land-attack cruise missiles now knew where they were, where they were going, and the path of avoidance to get there. Their faceted skin, draped in radar-absorbent material, made them nearly undetectable. The East Seas sprinted away. Relieved of their load, the Badgers turned back. One of the cruise missiles malfunctioned and tumbled into the pink sea, but the rest of the swarm flew on.

◊◊◊◊

A leviathan traversed Pacific deeps, the Chinese nuclear attack submarine *Changzheng 6*, nearing the end of her long march. Captain Kun had taken *Changzheng 6* from China's Hainan Island, past a Vietnamese patrol, and out into the Philippine Sea. Steaming just above crush depth, the submarine's hull groaned with strain. *Give me the heaving, nauseating surface over this silent, steady crush*, Kun thought. The other half of his brain surveyed the panorama of instruments indicating *Changzheng 6*'s health. A pressure tone resonated through the submarine's metal bones. Kun's eyelids twitched. Worrying the tic was perceptible, and in an attempt to hide it, the captain gulped the last of his jasmine tea to block his face with the clay cup. Then he cleared his throat.

"Sonar post: Tell me your targets," Kun ordered. The sonarman reported his screen was clear, and recommended a clearing of the baffles, the acoustic blind spot behind the submarine's bow array. The executive officer nodded in agreement. Captain Kun took dice from his jacket pocket and rolled them on the chart table. He would let the universe decide the direction of his next turn. The pips added up to less than six. Kun announced, "Make your turn to starboard." Adapting the Soviet 'Crazy Ivan' tactic, *Changzheng 6* leaned and began to circle back on its original course, to listen for anything that might be following. The attack center's collective eyes rested on the sonarman, who scrutinized his scope, adjusted dials and knobs, and squeezed the headphones against his ears.

"All clear, sir," the sonarman reported. *Good*, Captain Kun thought, and licked his warrior chops, as secrecy and surprise were the order of the day.

"Coming back on original course," the chief officer reported. The submarine leveled off again. "Steady as she goes." He leaned in close to Kun and whispered, "Captain, we are ready." Kun signaled affirmation and then ordered that the boat be taken up to launch depth. The hull popped as it expanded. The attack center floor pitched up. Captain Kun stepped to the periscope pedestal. He drew a deep breath.

"Forward compartment: Immediately load tubes one through six with East Seas. Chief Officer: hover the boat at 20 meters," the captain said with a firm, emotionless affect. The order was acknowledged. In the submarine's weapons room, six waterproof canisters holding East Sea land-attack cruise missiles were winched from their storage racks and loaded into torpedo tubes. The chief officer confirmed the submarine holding steady at a standstill just beneath the glassy surface, and Kun ordered that the periscope be raising the periscope, which climbed from its hull well, poked from the submarine's sail, and pierced the surface. Kun unfolded the periscope's handholds and leaned into its viewfinder.

"Dawn has broken," the captain noted as he scanned the horizon, adding, "Surface clear of contacts." Kun snapped the handholds closed, and ordered, "Down periscope."

"Sir," the chief officer said, "forward compartment reports all tubes are loaded." Captain Kun surveyed *Changzheng 6*'s young submariners. They fidgeted with excitement, blissfully ignorant of all that could still go terribly wrong.

"Shoot," Kun ordered. The technician complied, and pushed an illuminated button on his weapons console. One after the other, missile canisters blew from the submarine's bow. The canisters raced toward the sea's surface; each swaddled in bubbles.

The Pacific Ocean lived up to its name there: peaceful and calm. A bubble rose to the surface and disturbed the still waters. Where it popped, a boil erupted. The boil spit a missile canister from its foamy center, a canister that leapt into the air, peeled apart and opened like a flower, a flower whose pistil was an East Sea cruise missile. The missile's upward momentum stalled, and its booster ignited, pushing the missile into the sky. Six more such blooms occurred and the canister petals fell onto the gently undulating surface of the Pacific.

A Soaring Dragon flew high above the Pacific. A stealthy Chinese unmanned aerial vehicle, it sailed on a pair of long wings joined at their tips. Sneaking from the mainland and out to sea, the Soaring Dragon's radar detected a large group of surface ships that had entered the theater. This aircraft transmitted the group's coordinates up to a satellite that bounced them to a People's Liberation Army ground station. Chinese command then relayed them to an HY-1 Hummingbird reconnaissance satellite parked over the ocean.

The Hummingbird focused its sensors on the area, and narrowed its field of view. Digital cameras captured several ships that surrounded a goliath ark. These ships snaked east, trailing white wakes eminently visible to Hummingbird's high-resolution cameras. The Chinese satellite then sent the data back home, and the intelligence became target coordinates for the People's Liberation Army's Second Artillery.

Southwest of Shaoguan—in Guangdong, China—a gravel-covered clearing, one of many ensconced, hid within thick forests. Two enormous ten-wheeled ballistic missile transporter-erector-launcher trucks sat at its center. The TELs had long cylinders across their backs containing anti-ship variants of the Dong Feng 'East Wind' intermediate range ballistic missile. A Chinese soldier paid out control cable from a spool.

He strung the cable from the TELs to a silvery tent pitched at the edge of the forest. Within this fire-resistant enclosure, an artillery officer opened a metal suitcase and plugged the cable's lead into the control panel inside. With the click of a single switch, the panel came alive with lights and power gauges. The Chinese officer turned a dial, and the missile trucks awakened.

Diesel engines turned over and chugged, headlights flashed and strobed, and horns blasted repeatedly to warn the unwary. Legs extended from the TELs to lift and level their substantial load. The missile cans elevated until they stood on end and pointed to the few stars that still clung to the morning sky. On his control panel, the officer powered up the missiles, punched in target coordinates, donned a gas mask, and inserted and turned a key. A charge ignited at the base of the first missile canister.

Rapidly expanding gas puffed the big ballistic missile up and out, 'cold-launching' it clear, and the main engine ignited with a loud bang. A cyclone whipped the command tent, and a crackling bawl reverberated through the forests of Shaoguan as the ballistic missile climbed out. Then the second East Wind popped out and thundered skyward on its tail of fire. It powered through willowy high-altitude clouds. Other missiles departed adjacent launch sites, and the deadly flock headed up and over the ocean.

The tropical paradise of Okinawa rose from the sea floor to form part of the Ryukyu island chain that stretched from Japan to Taiwan. Wiped clean of vegetation in the WWII battle called the 'Typhoon of Steel,' the island had since healed and was again verdant, though troubled memories lingered like a bad dream, and the ghosts of over 150,000 American and Japanese men remained forever restless. Sprawling Kadena Air Force Base served as the nucleus of American Pacific airpower in that theater.

Kadena sat next to the Okinawan town whose name it shared. Salient among its hardened aircraft shelters and runways was the base's control tower. At its top and behind tinted glass sat and stood American airmen who scrutinized intermittent radar tracks on their screens.

"Unknown," a young tech read what his computer told him.

"Got to be seabirds or something. Maybe wave tops?" the supervisor suggested. However, he ordered an airborne patrol to check it out.

Two American F-15 Eagles peeled off and dove at the gleaming East China Sea. Mottled shades of grey, their twin engines opened up and spat fire, pushing the heavy fighters supersonic.

Kadena's tower controller anxiously watched the Eagles race across his screen, toward the unidentified contacts. He quickly calculated distance and speed in his head and concluded the Eagles were going to be late. Now the controller got a solid radar reflection on the unknowns. Spinning and clicking a control ball, he zoomed in on the radar plots.

"High-speed; Low-altitude; Solid tracks now," he mumbled to himself. "Has to be small airplanes...or cruise missiles." He decided to stop second-guessing himself. The controller fell back on training and called out: "Vampires. Vampires. Cruise missiles inbound." He jumped from his chair and smacked a big mushroom-shaped button. Outside, the base klaxon wound up to a deafening shrill. Kadena's surface-to-air missiles began to sweep the horizon with their acquisition and targeting radars. A series of networked tractor-trailers inside one of Kadena's old hangars housed the base's air defense controllers.

"MPQ-65 has lock," a young woman said, declaring the radar had acquired the low-flying targets. "Targets approaching minimum engagement range." She turned and looked to her colleagues with concern. Across the airfield, a PATRIOT—Phased-Array Tracking Radar to Intercept On Target—missile burst from its launching station's transporter-erector-launcher. The long black, red, and white interceptor roared skyward.

Kadena's tower operators watched the missile pitch over and dive.

"Damn," somebody uttered.

Unable to distinguish the lead enemy missile from surface clutter, the PATRIOT had missed and plunged into the water, disintegrating on impact.

"Targets now inside PAC-3 envelope. Switching to I-HAWKs," the tech in the air-defense trailer announced.

Delta-finned HAWKs—Homing All the Way to Kill interceptors—ripple-fired from a sandy revetment at Kadena's seaward perimeter. Based on 1950s technology and tweaked to bring down medium- and high-altitude targets, the HAWKs had little hope of intercepting the low-level stealthy threat.

The Badger bomber-fired East Seas cast shadows as they crossed the clear shallows, the sandy beach, and green dunes of Okinawa's eastern shore. The Chinese land-attack cruise missiles leapt coastal Route 58. Startled by the noise and red blurs overhead, a panicked Japanese motorist swerved his car.

"Curse those Americans. Could they fly any lower?" the motorist asked his wife. She checked the children in the backseat. Although shaken by the radical maneuver, the kids were fine.

The East Seas switched from satellite to terrain recognition guidance. Their digital eyes recognized Kadena's perimeter fence and runways, and utilized these landmarks to refine their flight path to within one meter. The flock of cruise missile hopped over the base's tall outer fence, and, as programmed, divided and flew down the center of each of the 12,100-foot parallel runways. Fairings on the lead four missiles broke away.

A cargo of bomblets then released and showered the runways, ripping gaping craters in the asphalt and concrete. Softball-sized munitions then scattered over the damaged area, forming instant minefields that would impede engineers and their repair work. More East Seas arrived and continued their advance on the American air base's flight line.

Kadena's sirens shouted a sorrowful wail. Airmen, ordinance vehicles, and fuel bowsers danced about, as if the curtain would fall at any moment. Big, dark grey KC-10 Extender aerial tankers served as the backdrop, their third tail engine and tucked refueling booms high above the tarmac. A clutch of Strike Eagle fighter-bombers powered up to escape, and an E-3 Sentry AWACS—an airborne warning and control system aircraft with a large rotating saucer on its back—moved along Kadena's apron.

Watching from the base's tower, the controller lowered his binoculars, shaking his head in disgust.

"They've caught us with our pants down," he said. Unable to resist voyeurism of the coming carnage, he again raised his field glasses.

The Chinese cruise missiles began final dives, and crashed among the American airplanes. The resultant explosions shattered windows in nearby Kadena Town. A firestorm engulfed the scattered, shattered remains of aircraft, buildings, and people. Japanese ambulances and fire trucks emerged from hospitals and stations in neighboring Chatan, Kadena, Okinawa, and Yomitan. They sped for the main gate of the American air force base.

◊◊◊◊

East Seas skimmed the wind-whipped waves southeast of where the Chinese submarine *Changzheng 6* had fired them. Ahead of the cruise missiles was a palm-covered, hilly island that had emerged from behind a dark wall of tropical showers.

Drenched Andersen Air Force Base occupied the northeastern plateau of the American Pacific Territory of Guam, glistening in the emergent sunshine. Andersen was one of the US Air Force's Bomber Forward Operating Locations and played host to the gamut of American strategic bombers: B-1 Lancers; B-2 Spirits; and, those 'Big Ugly Fat Fuckers,' the B-52 Stratofortresses. Having ridden out the tropical deluge, a Lancer supersonic strategic bomber held short of Andersen's main runway.

Cloaked in a subtle blend of dark green and grey paint, the Lancer was an obvious speedbird, with a long, tapered fuselage, blended swing-wings, boxy engine inlets and distinguished moustache canards. The Lancer's slats and slotted flaps dropped from fully extended wings, and, with clearance to taxi, brakes released. The four turbofans throttled up and rolled the big bomber toward the puddled runway's threshold. Moving behind the Lancer's large cockpit windscreen were the shadows of four American airmen readying for flight.

The pilot/aircraft commander turned the nose wheel's control and steered for the runway. Seated to his right, the second pilot/mission commander was happy to be rolling again. He programmed the flight computer. Crammed in behind them were the defensive systems officer, the offensive systems officer, a small oven, and a chemical toilet. Something in the windscreen caught the second pilot's eye. Several silhouettes had popped-up from behind the shore cliff and headed for the runway. He removed mirrored sunglasses and squinted against the glare. Then he tapped the busy pilot.

"Is that inbound traffic?" he asked, as he pointed out the window. The pilot adjusted a sunshade and agreed he saw what looked like small fighter planes coming in low. "Holy shit, those are missiles. Raid. Raid," he yelled and drove the throttles forward. The Lancer surged forward and leaned hard. It made a fast turn onto the runway, found the centerline, and roared down the runway in full afterburner.

Raw fuel pumped into hot exhaust, burning like a blowtorch. Pushed by this controlled violence, the Lancer bounded up to the sky. Vortices streamed off wingtips, and moist tropical air enveloped the American bomber in a veil of contrails. It climbed out steeply, turned, and doubled back. The second pilot warned Andersen's tower, as the pilot slid the Lancer over the base. Like a helpless, agitated bird watching its nest pillaged by the neighborhood cat, it began to orbit.

Lounging in Guam's warming sun was a review of American bombers, fighters, tankers, transports, and, within several inflatable air-conditioned hangars, bat-winged strategic stealth bombers. The Chinese cruise missiles flew down Andersen's long single runway. Two climbed briefly and then dove into the pavement. The combination of inertia, left over kerosene, and 1,200 pounds of high explosives excavated huge craters from the concrete. The rest of the

East Seas advanced on Andersen's flight line, arriving over the parked American aircraft and dropping their bomblets. A KC-46 tanker was hit, inundating adjacent airplanes and structures with its load of burning jet fuel. Black smoke billowed and climbed in a whirlwind of hot air. Over the carnage, Andersen's lofty beige and red-striped control tower peered.

Choking on thick fumes and fly ash, and with the remains of the tower's windows crunching beneath their feet, airmen attended to an injured person. A controller pointed out a single cruise missile that jumped Andersen's outer fence. The lagging East Sea had ascended the sloping beach, pitched up sharply to clear a cliff, and then dropped level again. It lined up with the runway centerline and, like a flying telephone pole, skimmed over the smoldering craters that divided the airstrip into useless halves. The East Sea recognized the outline of Andersen's tower and turned for it, putting the landmark dead ahead. The tower controller surveyed the burning field, losing the red cruise missile in thick, black, sooty smoke. Then, the black bank swirled and spit out the East Sea.

"It's got a bead on us," the controller shrilled. Some that operated the tower's functions had the presence of mind to dash for an exit, although most of them failed to move. A Humvee halted in the shadow of the tower, and an air policeman jumped out and reached for a Stinger man-portable air defense system. He brought the anti-aircraft missile to his shoulder and its reticle to his eye. He led the fast-moving East Sea and waited for a tone from the weapon. When a buzz like an electric razor indicated the seeker had locked-on to a heat source, he squeezed the trigger. The small blue interceptor leaped from its tube and ignited. It streaked for the East Sea, but blew right by, missing the Chinese cruise missile before careening toward one of the hot ground fires. A tardy HAWK interceptor also plummeted from the sky, nose-diving into the pavement, and sacrificing itself to the pyre. The East Sea approached Kadena's control tower.

The Chinese cruise missile crashed through the tower's concrete wall, penetrated to an interior stairwell, and exploded. The tower burst, and the upper floors hung weightless for a moment, before telescoping down into a cloud of grey dust. Debris fell on firefighters and the damage control teams that dashed around. The thunder of an orbiting airplane drew nervous glances skyward until relieved personnel recognized its outline as friendly.

The Lancer's second pilot contacted Guam's naval base, transmitting imagery of the raid. A few minutes later, the Lancer received orders from command, instructing them to meet a tanker over Thailand before continuing on to their original destination, Diego Garcia in the Indian Ocean.

◊◊◊◊

The *Ronald Reagan* carrier strike group passed north of Wake Island on its westward odyssey. The supercarrier's hull buzzed with speed, her lower decks warmed by Pacific waters. Startled from a disturbing dream, Lieutenant Pelletier showered again and walked to one of the commons' video phones where she waited with shipmates to contact family and friends. Pelletier watched a Marine typing a familygram and a pimpled sailor chatting and smiling in front of a small screen. Each had a three-minute allotment to communicate with home. Her turn came, and she sat down at a terminal, logged-in, and saw her dad already online. He answered her video call immediately. Pelletier combed her hair with her fingers and leaned into the camera. Her father's stuttering face tiled with interference as they made their greetings through limited bandwidth.

"How's Hobbes?" Cindy asked. She'd had that damn cat since he was a kitten, sharing an almost psychic link with the no-good, lollygagging, mollycoddled rabble-rouser. Besides her dad, that damn all-terrain feline flea transporter was all she had known. She remembered her dream: Old Hobbes was gravely ill, yellowed with jaundice, and crying a pathetic meow for help.

"Uh... he's fine," her dad lied. "Hey, you won't believe who called."

Cindy let her father off the hook about the cat, allowing him to change the subject.

"Who?"

"Robby. Robert Gerardi. Can you believe it? He wanted to know if you were part of the fighting, and..." Pelletier's father continued, although his voice was drowned out by the music in her head. For a moment, she flashed back to high school and the night of her prom. She was looking at the boy with the broken heart, the husband that might have been. Seeing his little girl taken aback, Pelletier's father wrapped up the conversation with: "Give 'em hell," and the usual, "I love you. Be safe." The video screen went black. Pelletier sat for a moment. A sailor waiting to use the kiosk cleared his throat. Pelletier gathered herself and got up.

She made her way toward the fantail through the twists and turns of *Ronald Reagan*'s cramped corridors. The inescapable, maddening hum of machinery was louder than usual. She needed a moment of peace. She swung open a final hatch, felt the blast of cool air and tasted salt. Pelletier stepped out onto a wide balcony.

The balcony hung low to the water, roofed by the flight deck, and covered with equipment and catwalks. A sailor balanced to replace a bulb in the instrument landing system, the T-shaped set of lights Pelletier and the other aviators used during landings to judge the motion of the ship. Another working sailor saw Pelletier and threw his cigarette overboard, then returned to the jet engine he had strapped to a test stand. He saluted. Pelletier waved it away. He took this to mean he could light another cigarette. Pelletier went to one of the two close-in weapon systems that protected *Ronald Reagan*'s rear end from sea-skimming missiles.

She perched herself under its barrel-shaped radar and rotary cannon, and swung her boots from its base. Several stories down flowed the black water. Churned by the ship's four gigantic propellers, organisms phosphoresced and laid a neon carpet that was both wondrous and worrying, a big, glowing arrow that pointed right at the American supercarrier. Pelletier glanced at the sailor. He had stopped pretending to work on the engine. Smoking again, he looked thoughtfully to sea. Pelletier got a tight feeling in her stomach. She decided it was time to go back to bed.

Stationary above the western Pacific, an American Defense Support Program satellite performed a graceful orbital pirouette. Squinting through a telescope, its infrared sensors detected the heat plume of ballistic missiles rising from Chinese soil. The satellite alerted the 460th Space Wing in Aurora, Colorado, which informed Strategic Command at Offutt, Nebraska.

In the war room deep below Offutt Air Force Base, a bearish four-star general—an old WWII Mustang pilot— studied the computer-generated missile plots presented on the bunker's screen. *My hibernation den for the coming nuclear winter*, he thought. "Take us to DefCon 3," the general growled. On a colorful countdown board that went from DEFCON 5 to DEFCON 1—Armageddon—the big green number '4' changed to a yellow '3,' and the armed forces of the United States increased their defense readiness condition. Security zones around Midwestern Minuteman III inter-continental ballistic missile silos doubled, strategic bombers were loaded with nuclear cruise missiles and gravity bombs, and Trident missile subs— 'boomers'—were alerted that they may be needed.

"Get SBX on this. And cue Beale…" The general ordered the beams of Sea-Based X-band radar, and the big pyramidal radar in California, swung toward China. "Those missiles could be headed our way." The general grumbled, as he crossed thick arms.

Off Midway Island's shallow barrier reef, an old Japanese Val bomber rested on the sandy bottom. Upright, it sat in the water, as though still being flown by a spectral pilot. However, the old warplane dripped with rust and colorful fish congregated in its nooks and crannies. SBX floated above it on twin torpedo hulls. As if teed up for King Neptune himself, the converted oil rig had in place of its drilling tower a giant white ball. From inside this weatherproof dome, an antenna bounced powerful radio waves off the ionosphere, bent them around the curvature of the Earth, and found the boosting Chinese ballistic missiles.

Pulling in SBX's data, US Strategic Command analyzed trajectories with superfast computers, and confirmed that the Chinese launch was intra-theater rather than intercontinental. Impact zones were projected. They were located within the Philippine Sea, the current operating area of the *George Washington* carrier strike group. Word was forwarded to Hawaii, and then on to the American supercarrier.

◊◊◊◊

White Pacific dolphins frolicked in the supercarrier *George Washington*'s bow wave. They vaulted acrobatically and led the gargantuan warship and its procession through the Philippine Sea. Some of *George Washington*'s anti-submarine warfare helicopters, early warning aircraft, and fighter-bombers perched on the deck. Just beneath their beefy landing gear was a dimly-lit and chilled environment better suited to electronics than human beings: the combat information center, or CIC.

Vibrations from aircraft landing and launching overhead transmitted down bulkheads. The sounds melded with the murmur of sailors speaking into headset microphones while seated at computer terminals. The combat information center's Kevlar-lined walls were covered with flat video screens that displayed anti-air, anti-surface, and anti-submarine tactical data. A strike controller communicated with planes coming and going from the ship, as four different tactical action officers watched respective warfare teams. Cold, hostile stares stayed glued to perpetually refreshing data, and each waited and watched for any threat to the *George Washington*.

The air defense officer brought up a large graphic of the western Pacific on his screen. Parabolic lines represented several missile tracks reaching from China and advancing toward a large diamond that represented the carrier strike group. The officer in charge lifted a telephone and notified *George Washington*'s command.

The carrier's executive—a rear admiral with a face like an old sea chart—stood from his flag bridge chair and ordered the strike group to battle stations. Aboard ship, hatches closed and locked, and damage control parties reached their ready stations. The anti-air warfare commander observed the menacing advance of the Chinese ballistic missiles.

"It's up to *Lake Champlain*," he said.

Like Pallas Athena—the goddess of warfare and truth—the American guided-missile cruiser *Lake Champlain* bore her own buckler. Her protective shield was not of tightly woven gold tassel. Instead, it bristled with electronics and kinetics. *Lake Champlain*'s Aegis combat system included networked radar, powerful computers, and capable weapons. Aegis could track 100 targets out to 100 miles. Under the supervision of seasoned sailors, Aegis controlled the cruiser's vertical launch system—the VLS—a grid of lid-covered cells on *Lake Champlain*'s after and forward decks. Each cell contained Tomahawk cruise missiles in the anti-ship and land-attack variety, or a Standard Missile—the US Navy's primary long-range surface-to-air missile. Several third-generation Standard Missiles had been loaded at Pearl onto *Lake Champlain*. Each Standard lofted a sophisticated lightweight exo-atmospheric projectile, or LEAP, able to kill ballistic missiles at the fringes of space—a bullet to hit a bullet. *Lake Champlain*'s crew hustled to general quarters. Captain Ferlatto departed the bridge and rushed below to the cruiser's combat information center.

The Chinese missiles advanced within range of *Lake Champlain*'s radar, their steady approach shown as white lines on the CIC's big blue screens. Ferlatto joined several sailors huddled around the glowing panels.

"Update," the tactical action officer demanded.

"SM-3s are targeted and ready for launch, sir," the weapons officer reported.

"Shoot," the officer barked. Buttons were pushed at the fire control terminal.

A sheet of crackling flame vented from between *Lake Champlain*'s five-inch deck gun and her forecastle. The first Standard Missile lifted away. It roared skyward on a pillar of fire and white smoke. Aegis contacted the interceptor and guided it out. Another SM-3 fired, and then a third. An unnatural fog wrapped *Lake Champlain* as her surface-to-air missiles dashed for the Chinese ballistic ones.

The East Winds skirted the upper mesosphere, pointed back toward Earth, and started their plunge at the ships on the Pacific. Along with the warheads, polyhedral decoys released from the East Wind's booster buses. They would generate heat and reflect radar, confusing and drawing away the American interceptors, while the real warheads used their aerodynamic shape to generate lift, and used actuating chine tabs to swerve during their charge at the American ships.

A sprinting Standard Missile closed with an East Wind. However, it blew across the sky and, seemingly pushed by a gust, missed. A second Standard Missile passed its target and another flew into a Chinese decoy.

The winds purged launch smoke from around *Lake Champlain*'s bridge. Captain Ferlatto raised binoculars. He trained them on *George Washington* a mile to starboard. The supercarrier had sped up, he noticed. Awesome nuclear power shoved her through the sea. The precipice of *George Washington*'s bow rose like a speedboat's as her endless hull planed. She was a stampeding elephant. *Best not to get in her way*, Ferlatto thought. He reminded the helmsman to mind his course. Another sailor slammed down a telephone. The sound drew the captain's attention.

The sailor's Adam's apple bobbed up and down in a dry swallow. He struggled to announce, "Sir, all SM-3s failed to intercept. The admiral has ordered the group to disperse."

The helmsman spun *Lake Champlain*'s wheel and the cruiser heeled in, her deck plates vibrating with increased power to the turbines. Captain Ferlatto returned his magnified gaze to *George Washington*. Announcing a turn with a blast from her horns, the supercarrier's flight deck leaned to angles not seen since her shakedown cruise rudder trials. The other ships of the group added to the racket as they, too, made coordinated maneuvers. *Lake Champlain* and the destroyers scattered waywardly, and the group's attack submarine, *California*, went deep and sped off into the gloom, distancing her from a possible thermonuclear explosion at the surface. *Lake Champlain* established a course perpendicular to the other warships, her turbines slammed to full power. She turned again, leaning top-heavy hard. Captain Ferlatto clamped down on his cigar, shaking his head with concern and frustration.

"Goddamn it," Ferlatto lashed out, pounding a fist on a panel. He stared out again at the immense yet vulnerable *George Washington*. Networked to and controlled by *Lake Champlain*'s Aegis, the destroyers *Mahan* and *Paul Hamilton*, and the frigate *Rodney M. Davis* ripple fired a last ditch fusillade of Evolved Sea Sparrow Missiles. In the name of self-preservation, *her escorts were shunning George Washington*, leaving a naked behemoth. The frigate bolted like a spooked horse that broke for blue hills. *Lake Champlain* turned hard again, her hulk bent and leaned as waves smacked her long sides and washed over the gunwale. *Mahan* and *Paul Hamilton* turned their sterns to one another and dispersed. The supercarrier's airborne aircraft went high and sped from the area.

George Washington—her flight deck clear of aircraft and personnel—wept. Her fallout wash-down system pumped seawater through hundreds of deck- and island-mounted sprayers, enveloping her in a salty mist. Water cascaded from her vertical sides. The American supercarrier became the pot of gold at the end of an ironic rainbow, her sun-baked steel cooled by the wash-down. This reduced the heat signature presented to enemy weapon's sensors. At the very least, her captain reasoned, the water might suppress any fires. Blast, flame, and watertight doors closed, and damage control and firefighting teams stood ready. Overhead, consecutive sonic booms ripped the clear blue sky. Over 5,000 American men and women awaited their fate.

The Chinese warheads were now hypersonic, shoving through the troposphere. They pierced and shoved aside dense air, their ablative skin glowing and flaking off. Onboard targeting systems contrasted the hot ships against the cool sea. The warheads zeroed on the largest of the thermal signatures.

"Brace. Brace. Brace for impact," shouted *George Washington*'s public announcement system. Everyone grabbed a wall or crouched to lower their center of gravity. An unusual quiet permeated the nuclear supercarrier and her crew.

The outer casing of the first Chinese warhead separated. Tungsten flechettes, released from inside, fanned out and showered *George Washington*. The flechettes ignited as they ripped into the antenna tree and domed radars that crowned the supercarrier's seven-story island. Then they entered the island and pierced PRIFLY— primary flight control—before continuing through to the next level: flight deck control. Even running out of energy, they kept going, then deformed and came apart, spraying the supercarrier's navigation and flag bridges with their burning remains.

George Washington's island became a frappé of torn metal, flesh, and bone. Surviving equipment lost power. Fires started and the ship's alarms sounded. The American rear admiral glared at his gushing gut and stared at the headless sailor slumped beside him in a chair. Then he collapsed and crashed to the vibrating steel deck. Mustering his last energy to move a thumb, he touched his beloved *George Washington* for the last time. The sky cracked again.

The second surviving Chinese warhead slammed headlong into the American supercarrier's flight deck. Crashing through its non-skid rubber and thick steel plate, it burrowed through the gallery and three-deck, all before it dropped into the hangar. Within the hangar's open expanse, the warhead felt itself speed up, and the 660 pounds of high explosives contained by the armor-piercing jacket was triggered.

George Washington's stowed aircraft were consumed in the detonation, and one massive blast door jumped its track, pancaking other airplanes like a junkyard compactor. The eruption exhausted at the supercarrier's elevators and fantail, shooting out fireballs and parts of men and machines to the sea. *George Washington* shuddered. Black smoke spurted from air vents and portholes, and flame licked up the blackened sides of the ship as she lurched and started a dead wheel turn. The broken island's communication with the ship became disengaged, and auxiliary steering initiated from deep within the hull. To the tumultuous din of a cycling alarm, power to the shafts was reduced. *George Washington* straightened out and slowed down.

◊◊◊◊

Below hilltop apartments, in a field not far from the Taipei Zoo, a double perimeter of razor wire surrounded a Taiwanese air defense site. Within the berm that surrounded the site were PATRIOT surface-to-air missile launchers, antenna masts, and a radar unit. Heavy cables connected everything to a shipping container that housed an engagement control station. Inside it, Taiwanese airmen watched the skies on consoles.

A bland, concrete condominium overlooked the site. Just one of many, inside the building, at its sixth floor, was a small but expensive apartment where a man ate a breakfast of cold rice and salted fish.

The man listened to the radio, and to the sorrowful cries of a pipa—a four-string Chinese lute—it delivered. He drenched the day-old food in soy sauce and looked to a kit-cat clock on the wall whose eyes and tail swung back and forth, as it ticked to the top of the hour. This lone man had lived in Taipei for years and held a simple job at an electronics factory. Despite the innocuous façade he had erected, the man at the breakfast table was in fact a member of the People's Liberation Army Special Operations Forces; an 'operator' in military parlance. This operator chewed his fish and spun the radio dial. He left behind the lulling pipa it broadcast and settled instead on a station full of static. The radio clicked. The white noise cleared.

A woman began to broadcast numbers in Chinese. Her voice enunciated each as though reading a love poem. The operator's specific identifier block was spoken, and was then followed by an activation and verification code. Momentarily stunned, he abandoned the table, went to the closet, and removed a trunk from behind piles of clothes. He lugged and set the trunk upon the sofa and unlatched it with a resounding snap.

The operator emerged from behind wafting curtains and stepped onto the apartment's balcony. Wearing dark protective goggles, he emerged with a loaded rocket-propelled grenade launcher, and surveyed the enemy's air defense site from on high. Several bulbous reloads of grenade-tipped rockets, he hastily tossed onto the balcony's chaise lounge. He then rested the RPG on his shoulder and raised the weapon's metal sighting rail.

The rail included four drill holes. The Chinese operator settled its central one on the air defense site's radar set. Then he angled the weapon up and re-centered the radar on the next drill hole down, to compensate for distance. Happy, he squeezed the weapon's trigger bringing forth a familiar, satisfying and friendly surge. Hot gas kicked out the launch tube and ignited the apartment's willowy curtains. The first rocket-propelled grenade shot away.

Fins that sprang from the grenade's control column stabilized the missile as it flew over the fences and outer berm of the Taiwanese PATRIOT missile site, before it hit the radar dead center, shattering it with explosives and fragments. With the living room engulfed in flame behind him, the Chinese operator clicked another rocket into the launcher. A neighbor peeked around the balcony partition, choked on smoke and covered his mouth and nose before retreating from the nightmarish scene. The Chinese operator braced himself against the balcony railing and fired another grenade at the site's control center. It hit, exploded, and tore into the trailer. After a millisecond delay, the trailer burst, its metal skin peeling back in sheets to vent the overpressure within. With a dark giggle, the operator reloaded and sent another round.

This one went wild, slamming into the air defense site's berm. Dirt and rock bounced. He cursed and clicked another rocket into the launcher. This one connected with the nearest PATRIOT missile station and consumed it in a massive fireball, swallowing it and the truck-mounted launcher and interceptors it contained. Elated by the spectacle of his work, the Chinese operator loaded again and fired.

The rocket-propelled grenade whooshed away, and impacted the concrete beneath another missile station. It cooked off an interceptor that broke free and, uncommanded, shrieked toward the hillside building before it pitched up and corkscrewed into the sky. Accepting it as a salute to his masterful destruction, the Chinese operator paused to watch the missile dive and slam into the ground some miles away. Despite the raging fire in his apartment, the screams of fleeing neighbors and the sirens in the distance, the operator—high on adrenalin and rocket fumes—laughed. He did not see the puff of concrete dust kicked-up behind him.

"Right and high one meter," the Taiwanese sniper's spotter told him.

The sniper lay across the roof of a Humvee inside the air defense site's perimeter. He had seen the RPG's smoke trail that led his attention straight to the apartment balcony. He then had used this trail to guide his magnified scope and settled it on the center of mass of the perpetrator. He settled the reticle of the high-powered rifle on the man's chest. Then the sniper clicked the scope's dials to compensate for the breeze, bullet drop, and range.

"Send it," the spotter said.

The sniper rifle barked and bucked.

700 grains of lead punched the Chinese operator in the chest, tearing through his breastplate before fragmenting. The shards of lead from the broken bullet then spread out and bored through flesh— muscle, lung tissue, and the Chinese man's superior vena cava. Thrown backward, he fell to the floor inside the roaring fire. To be alive just a few more moments, all he was able to summon was a

twisted chuckle. He realized he had landed beside his favorite chair and a picture of his mother. A cracked, melting frame was his last blurred image. He died quickly, thereafter. His purpose was done. His duty, complete. It was time to sleep.

Along with this lone, wasted soul, other Chinese sleepers had awakened that day. He and his comrades had conducted an orchestra of mayhem at Taiwanese surface-to-air missiles sites, radar stations, and critical communications nodes.

◊◊◊◊

North of the Mall's Reflecting Pool, next to the stark Vietnam Memorial, Constitution Garden was a serene respite. It captured the city's dirt and noise in a hedge of mature maples that swished in the early-evening breeze. Jade and Richard sat on a bench where they listened to birds twitter about their day. Richard had had the idea of sharing some dinner before her night class. He pulled two foil logs from a plastic bag and declared them 'the best burritos in all of DC.'

"It's huge," Jade marveled at the 'little donkey's' girth, and accepted it with hesitation, placing it on a napkin. Intimidated by the burrito's heft, she grabbed for a greasy tortilla chip instead. "My parents want me home," she said with a crunch. Richard took a big bite in hopes of escaping the need to answer. "Would you ever come back to China with me?"

"I would love to see the place someday," Richard mumbled.

"You know what I mean," she continued, and shoved an entire chip into her mouth. Richard wondered if that was her idea of a marriage proposal. He shifted uneasily.

"Jade, this is my home." Richard looked to the garden's small lake and the island that memorialized the 56 signers of the Declaration of Independence.

"You do not belong here. You are Chinese," Jade persisted.

"No. I am Chinese-American. Don't confuse the two."

"You're not white enough to be American," Jade stabbed. Richard rolled his eyes.

"Look. Being American is a state of mind; a culture of liberty. It's not about race. Don't let a few ignorant people confuse you. You can only pity and try to educate them," Richard lectured. Jade believed he was referring to the drunken college student they had encountered, but he actually spoke of her. There was a long silence. In that moment, Richard realized the crisis might break them. Already full, he took another bite of the burrito to occupy his mouth. Somebody nearby cursed their cell phone and a car horn blared.

They both squinted into the low sun. Richard saluted to block the blinding glare. A black sedan honked again and weaved across grass and sidewalk, drawing curses from the after-work crowd. The car raced at Jade and Richard and then halted before their bench. A man in black with slicked-back hair and sunglasses leapt out. He greeted Richard by name, flashed credentials, and apologized for the interruption.

"Please come with me, sir," the US Secret Service special agent told Richard. Richard wondered if he had missed a call, and took out his cell phone. It had no reception. "*Now,* sir." Richard stood and apologized to Jade, saying he would see her at home. He was then nudged through the car's back door. Jade watched the car swerve on the grass and speed off again. She placed the unfinished remains of their picnic in a trash bin and started a lonely walk back to campus.

Instead of going up 23rd Street, the car turned onto Constitution Avenue. Richard realized they were not going back to the State Department. He asked the driver where they were headed. The agent spoke to the rearview mirror, stating they would arrive at their destination shortly.

"Destination?" Richard checked his phone again. There was still no signal. "Hey, who's your cell carrier?" he asked the agent. This time there was no answer at all. They neared the White House. Richard cursed to himself and straightened his tie. The car passed protestors from both sides of the Taiwan issue who hurled insults at each other and the mansion. A thin blue line of police separated them.

The car turned up Executive Avenue and approached one of the White House's gates. The agent directed Richard to prepare identification as they stopped at the Park Service guardhouse. The window came down and the air-conditioned car quickly filled with muggy air heavily scented by fresh cut grass and roses. Richard sneezed. Continuing up the semicircular drive toward the East Wing, Richard noticed several marines on the building's rooftop. The car pulled into the shade of the porte-cochere and stopped at an ornate pillared doorway.

Richard and the agent passed through a metal detector built into the door frame, and entered the East Wing's lobby. Another Secret Service agent asked if Richard was armed, though he did not wait to start patting him down. Satisfied, the agent pointed to the far door. Richard began a silent, escorted walk. An old African-American butler gave a nod and continued to wind a centuries-old grandfather clock. Richard passed an office where he noticed several computer screens that displayed Andy Warhol's 'Mao.' The colorfully abstract Chinese Communist leader smiled back at frustrated American staff that repeatedly pushed Crtl-Alt-Del on their keyboards. With a pat on his shoulder, the escort pushed Richard along, inducing him to an elevator guarded by two marines in full dress.

After a recheck of credentials, one of the marines inserted and turned a key, and the waiting elevator opened. The Marine's bright-white gloves pointed the way. Surprised to be proceeding alone, Richard hesitated and then entered. The elevator descended slowly into the city's bedrock before it stopped with a gentle bounce. The doors slid open at the arched basement level where Secretary Pierce waited.

"Read." She shoved a file at Richard. Just three lines of the Chinese action summary were enough to visibly awe the young man. She pulled him along as he continued reading, bumping him into a four-star army general as they all pushed into the Presidential Emergency Operations Center. PEOC's heavy vault door clanged shut as senior staff settled around an oval table flanked by large video screens.

Secretary Pierce took her seat among the group that included the president, several of the joint chiefs, and the assistant to the president for national security affairs, better known as the national security advisor. Richard found a chair among the other civilian and military aides. Settling in, he continued to read. Richard felt eyes upon him and looked up to find the army general staring. Richard nodded cordially, though he also recognized the suspicion in the man's look. He has fought Asians before, Richard thought, probably Koreans and Vietnamese, maybe even Chinese, too. We all look the same to him. Loathing simmered beneath the general's thin, politically correct crust. That crust had been cracked today, blown open by Chinese missiles. Richard looked away from the suspicious glare of the man he had sized up. A map of the Pacific theater came up on the screen with red marks on Guam, Okinawa, and in the middle of the Philippine Sea. Pictures of the damaged supercarrier *George Washington* appeared, along with still and video shots of the wrecked island air bases. The Chairman of the Joint Chiefs—a silver-haired admiral—began the meeting with continuity of government protocols.

"Mr. President, NAOC has departed Omaha, and Vice President Campos is at Mount Weather. Air Force One is standing by at Andrews. Marine One is four minutes out," the admiral said. "We'll have to keep this short."

"What do we know, Nathaniel?" President Keeley asked of his national security advisor.

"Well, sir, before we lost contact with the Taiwanese, they were claiming the missile launch that started this whole thing was initiated from within Communist China. Their people discovered some virus that had sat dormant and undetected before activating in their defense network. A Trojan dragon, if you will." The advisor saw the president's tired eyes glaze over, and decided to keep it simple. "Mr. President, just after sunrise Pacific time, the Chinese hit Andersen and Kadena Air Force Bases with cruise missiles. The bases sustained heavy damage. We have suffered large losses of both lives and equipment. The *George Washington* was also hit with ship-homing ballistic missiles. She is limping to Manila. The supercarrier *John C. Stennis* was sailing from Oahu, when her reactors' cooling pumps shut down. They got them going again, but not before the cores overheated and vented, contaminating most of her engineering spaces. *Stennis* is adrift and awaiting tugs.

"How the hell?" the president wondered, aloud.

"Hacked. Someone apparently had gained access to the ship's network and got into power plant control. We assume it was the work of People's Liberation Army information warfare units. Analysis of the attack's digital exhaust points in that direction. It could have been much worse, though, sir. *Much* worse." Everyone pictured two nuclear cores melting through the bottom of the supercarrier and exploding on contact with seawater; an atomic disemboweling. "*Ronald Reagan* is the last flattop we have in the Pacific right now. Hers will be the next carrier strike group to arrive in theater. On top of all this, we have experienced distributed denial of service cyber attacks on the White House and Department of Energy, and, as of five minutes ago, the cities of Boston and Atlanta have lost electrical power. It's doubtful these blackouts are coincidence, especially since cellular service is also down on the eastern seaboard. Finally, one of our 'recon' satellites was blinded as it passed over China, likely hit by the ground-based laser at Tianan. We're re-tasking other satellites to fill the gap, but we don't have much in the way of regional reconnaissance right now," the national security advisor lamented.

"We have an SR-92 Blackburn departing Nevada as we speak. It'll be over China in half an hour." He explained that, because with its hypersonic speed and that it would be flying against the rotation of the earth, it wouldn't take more than that. The president turned to the secretary of state. "Get our people out of Taiwan," the president ordered.

"Done. Sir, I recommend you establish communications with Beijing as soon as possible. Use the red phone," Secretary Pierce advised.

"Not until you're safely in the air," the army general interjected. The president sighed, deeply. The gravity of the situation weighed heavy in the room.

"Secretary Pierce, have the Taiwanese made any formal requests of us?" the president asked. She frowned, and gestured to the national security advisor.

"Mr. President, we are unable to contact their government, or their Ministry of National Defense."

An aide answered a flashing telephone. He ran to an air force general and spoke urgently into his ear. The general's eyes widened, and he stood.

"Mr. President, a second Chinese launch has been initiated."

"At us?" The president demanded.

"It's too early to tell if it's intercontinental, sir. Mr. President, it's time to get the hell out of Dodge,

Secret Service agents entered the bunker in numbers, signifying the president's helicopter was touching down on the White House's South Lawn. The agents surrounded the president, and, with feet barely touching the floor, the leader of the free world was bundled to his aircraft. The meeting was over.

◊◊◊◊

Rocket brigades of the People's Liberation Army's Second Artillery unleashed hell. East Wind ballistic missiles lifted and climbed out from fixed silos and big trucks, and East Sea and Long Sword cruise missiles departed shore launchers. The high-low missile swarm journeyed across the Strait. Taiwanese air bases, air defense sites, marshaling areas, naval depots, power plants, telephone exchanges, and railway junctions were all on the menu.

Among Taiwan's northern island chain was Tungyin the site of a Long White early warning radar, planted into one of the island's weathered hillsides. The radar spotted the massive Chinese missile launch. Command in Taipei alerted, Taiwan's 'Plan Monastery' initiated.

Military police deployed into Taiwan's major cities. Radio and television stations broadcast the locations of shelters, and reiterated the recall of all reserves and military personnel, and cancellation of all leave. Carrying last-minute shopping as they dashed home, civilians scurried about the cities, and stranded foreign tourists huddled in their hotels or at embassies. The Chinese missiles advanced. Taiwanese civilian and military air traffic control isolated over 272 radar tracks. Commercial airliners landed or diverted. Military planners calculated impact points. Taiwan's combat aircraft came off ground alert and scrambled for the sky. Horns bellowed at Taiwan's air force bases. At Chiayi, the bawl of the horns was followed by the base klaxon that wound up to a continuous shrill.

"Air raid," blared from the base PA. Major Han and the other pilots lowered their Fighting Falcons' bubble canopies. Han initiated the jet fuel starter, and the single afterburning turbofan reached self-accelerating revolutions and ignited. Cockpit screens energized and flight instruments appeared as avionics booted up. Han flipped several configuration switches between his legs. He checked oil and turbine pressures; both within limits. The radio crackled as the group started checking in. With the base klaxon just reaching its crescendo, the order for a scramble departure was broadcast by the base's tower.

Han advanced the Fighting Falcon's throttles and accelerated his aircraft toward Chiayi's wide runway. The rest of the squadron's nine fighter-bombers fell in and followed. Han turned onto the runway threshold. He swung the Fighting Falcon's sharp beak and pointed it down the black runway's centerline. The airplane curtsied with brakes. Two other Fighting Falcons lined up either side of Han. The helmeted pilots saluted. Han pointed to the sky and spun his hand. Exhaust nozzles opened as turbofans throttled-up. Han made a fist and held it high. Then he unclenched and flattened his hand. The first of Chiayi's Fighting Falcons started a unified take-off. Three more warplanes immediately took position at the line and started to roll. Han's three-ship launch rotated and powered out on afterburner. Barely off the ground, surface-to-air missile warnings blared and flashed in the cockpits as Chinese radar painted the Taiwanese warplanes.

"We have SAM activity. Probably S-300 and 400s; Favorits and Triumfs," Han transmitted. The Russian-made surface-to-air missiles had engagement envelopes that extended well into Taiwan.

All too aware of the omnipresent threat, Han and the rest of Taiwan's air force would use geography and tactics to mitigate the threats. Ground controllers coordinated a mass movement of aircraft to assembly areas off the east coast of Taiwan. Like a flock of migrating starlings that reeled and wheeled to avoid the predator, most of Taiwan's combat aircraft headed for the Philippine Sea. Han and the rest of the 21st did the same, turning their Fighting Falcons east.

Taiwan's central mountains grew larger and closer. Han lined-up with the summit of Jade Mountain, pulled back on the stick, cleared the craggy peak, and then dropped the Fighting Falcon down the mount's eastern face. The cockpit threat receiver stuttered and ended its chorus as Chinese radar beams were stymied dead by the highlands. Once behind the island's rocky carapace, Taiwanese aircraft planned to refuel and reorganize to counter raiders. Han wondered if the Chinese had gotten an air defense ship to this side of his island, though he concluded this was a matter for their navy. Dots filled his radar screen in neat clusters. In the upper right of the display, Han saw the orbiting tankers that would refuel him and his friends. Han looked left to his wingman, a captain and dear friend. They leveled out, booked over Taiwan's east coast, and went 'feet wet' as the Americans say, when leaving land for sea.

A black limousine with diplomatic plates sped down Washington's C Street. It turned into the State Department's porte-cochere and stopped abruptly, with a squeaky lurch. Two Chinese soldiers in smart suits got out and scanned the area, taking in potential threats. With a rap on the limo's tinted glass, an older, balding man with thick black glasses was assisted from the car. He scampered into the Truman Building with his heavily, though discretely, armed bodyguards in tow.

"Good morning, Mr. Ambassador," the State Department doorman welcomed Ambassador Fan Wei, showing the entourage into the foyer. The diplomat's own security could go no farther. Expecting to be greeted by the secretary of state herself, the ambassador hesitated to proceed. Looking around, Ambassador Fan gave a disapproving grunt and looked to an American security guard.

"Third floor," was all the guard would say to the ruffled dignitary.

Secretary Pierce sat by her office window, warming her face in beaming sunshine. She closed her eyes. *Why go meet him?* She asked herself, though it was more a statement than a question. *The cultural and diplomatic faux pas will make clear my disdain for the circumstances*, Pierce schemed. She chuckled and absorbed more rays. She had sent Richard to wait by the third floor elevators. *The ambassador would take a lonely and unceremonious walk and elevator ride, and be met by one of my subordinates*, Pierce hatched. She smiled wide, her closed eyes twitched as though blinking.

Richard watched the elevator indicator, which rang and lit up with every floor the ambassador passed. He ruffled his hair and loosened his tie. *A nice touch*, he thought. *The secretary would approve.* A final ding and the elevator doors slid open. Richard greeted the fuming ambassador, and extended his hand in welcome, though it was left hanging.

"Take me to Ms. Pierce at once," the ambassador growled. Richard's hand went from shake-ready to pointing the way. The ambassador stomped off, and Richard shadowed him. When he reached the secretary's office, the ambassador turned to Richard and told him to wait as if an obedient hound. Richard obeyed, but stayed within earshot.

With fingers interlaced and eyes locked on her oak desk, Secretary Pierce did not stand as the ambassador entered. She refused to speak first. After a moment of silence, the ambassador yielded.

"Good day, Madam Secretary," he uttered.

Her eyes finally came up to meet his. "No. Not a good day, Mr. Ambassador." She gestured for him to sit.

"I regret the circumstances of my visit," he pronounced, and dropped into the chair. "My purpose is to give a message to your president."

"I would be happy to deliver it," Secretary Pierce said, her hands still clasped as though in prayer. Ambassador Fan took out an envelope. He held it out to the American secretary of state, who did not budge. "As I said, I would be happy to deliver it." The ambassador sat up and cleared his throat. *He has practiced this*, Pierce concluded. *And here it comes…*

"Madame Secretary, the People's Republic of China has been attacked by one of its own renegade provinces. In measured and legal retaliation, China has begun reunification of its lands. I have been instructed to make absolutely clear that my government views this matter as an internal security matter and will tolerate no intrusion. The United States has persisted in arming, emboldening, and defending the

Nationalists, and, with this continued arrogant interference, China has now been given no other recourse than to defend itself by eliminating the tools of this interference. The People's Republic also reserves the right to resist should the United States escalate the affair…"

"Affair?" Secretary Pierce scoffed. "Ambassador Fan, this is not a lover's spat. This is a very dangerous game your government is playing. Over 700 Americans are dead with hundreds more injured. Two of our aircraft carriers have been knocked out and you have attacked us without provocation." Smiling smugly, the ambassador opened his mouth to speak. Pierce stood, leaned across her desk, and continued: "The president has authorized me to deliver a message to your government: A de facto state of war exists between our two countries. Tonight, he will formally recognize the Taipei government-in-exile and the independence of Taiwan. You and your staff are hereby ordered to leave the country. All further communication must be by red phone. Good day, Mr. Ambassador." The secretary sat again, lowered her head, and stared at the desktop. The insulted ambassador stood and exited. Richard offered to escort him out of the building.

"Stay, mutt. I know the way," the ambassador snarled. Richard shrugged and entered his boss's office.

◊◊◊◊

Taipei's sky crackled with manmade thunder. Peering up warily, Senior Master Sergeant Li reasoned that the sound was that of sonic booms. Dull thuds of distant explosions echoed through neighborhoods and rebounded off Hill 112. Masts of black smoke rose from the southeast and northwest. A blaze flared where the capital's telephone exchange and an electrical substation once stood. Li raised binoculars and focused on the airport he was tasked with protecting. Songshan was quiet. Its air force jets were already aloft and remaining commercial airliners were stowed in hangars. Li panned toward Jhongjheng District—the civic soul of the Taiwanese capital and nation—and fixed his magnified view on the legislative Yuan, Taiwan's parliament.

The parliament was housed in a brick building draped in red, white, and blue bunting. A portrait of Chiang Kai Shek dangled from its tall central tower. A sandbag wall snaked through the surrounding street. Soldiers and armored vehicles loitered beneath swaying palm trees. Li focused his binoculars and wondered what had become of his government. Before the missile raid had muzzled radio and television broadcasts, journalists were reporting targeted assassinations and kidnappings, though the parliament was still able to meet and approve a declaration of war against Communist China, as well as formal independence for the island nation. Remaining legislators, along with the president and other members of Taiwan's executive branch, reportedly have fled southeast, escaping the island to establish a government-in-exile.

A breeze licked Hill 112. Li lowered the binoculars to savor it. Air raid sirens belatedly sounded around Taipei. Firehouse and police station bells joined the frightening cacophony. The city was sobbing, Li reflected, and then thought of his little girl. One of Hill 112's airmen ran from the bunker and saluted. He reported to Li that several targets had entered radar range.

"They appear to be tracking on the airport." The two men ran together, swallowed by the hillside bunker.

Inside, it was cool and dark. Several airmen sat at terminals, their dour faces lit green by radar screens. They monitored Hill 112's tranche of sky, controlling the site's anti-aircraft guns and surface-to-air missiles. Li strode to a flatscreen that displayed strategic air, land, and sea domains. The picture it presented was fearsome: hundreds of Chinese missile tracks reached for Taiwan like skeletal fingers seeking a deadly embrace. Li shifted his concerned gaze to a tactical screen.

"Tell me," Senior Master Sergeant Li instructed one of the air-defense technicians. The man pointed at his screen. A cluster of low-altitude plots moved south and followed the meander of the Danshui River.

"Cruise missiles or low-level jets. A whole lot of them, sir," the tech said. Several of the computer-generated plots disappeared as they impacted their targets or were shot down within the capital's layered defenses. Li thought the Chinese were driving down the field deeper than they should have been able to. Eastern Taipei and Songshan Airport were the goal and, Hill 112, the goalkeeper—the city's deepest node of guns and interceptors. Three radar plots survived the ground fire. One turned east along the Keelung River. It was now Hill 112's responsibility. Li moved to the Sparrow surface-to-air missile terminal and examined its dedicated screen. The radar beam's path swept around, beeping as it displayed a single blip. The technician used a wax pencil to trace the targets' progress along the superimposed geography of the river.

"Sparrows cannot get lock;" the frustrated airman pounded his panel. Li ordered the anti-aircraft guns activated. Called Super Bats—Super Fledermaus in German—one of Hill 112's three Swiss-made GDF-006 anti-aircraft guns swung its twin cannons. The gun's coaxial camera and Skyguard targeting radar aligned with the trajectory of the threat. Li studied the Super Bat's indicators and realized that, by firing into the valley at such a low angle, they would not have long before the anti-aircraft gun was throwing shells off axis.

"Skyguard's hot. Super Bats are ready," the gunner informed. On the bunker's video screen, the gun camera tracked the cruise missile and the freeway it followed. Civilian traffic was thick, a panicked rush from the capital that had stagnated into a honking morass of stuck vehicles. The gunner looked to Li with concern. The hill's errant 35 millimeter rounds would very likely impact the highway and rip into the civilians. Despite this likely collateral damage, Li cleared the weapon technician to engage the enemy cruise missile.

The Super Bats' barrels fired alternately, at a high rate, barely recoiling before the next round was sent. The Chinese Long Sword cruise missile skimmed over freeway signs and gawking drivers. A string of incendiary tracers squirted at it from Hill 112. They fell short and sprayed cars with burning metal shards that slaughtered the unlucky, leaving them belted into air-conditioned coffins. A minivan was shredded, bouncing and splitting open. Airbags deployed and the lacerated driver slumped forward, resting her mess on the now-deflating pillows. Another car exploded and jumped from the pavement. Li's blink was long. When he opened his eyes again, the inadvertent butchery continued on the screen.

Homing pulses left the Super Bats' Skyguard radar. They tracked both the outgoing rounds and the target, adjusting fire to marry the two. The fire slapped the Chinese cruise missile down, exploding it in a tumbling fireball that expelled burning propellant and wreckage into a riverside park. A cheer went up in Hill 112, but it was quickly stifled by a triple sonic boom that reverberated through the bunker's heavy ceiling. A new and rapidly approaching threat presented itself: Chinese ballistic missiles. Li hopped back to the surface-to-air missile terminal. The Sparrows were ready and Li ordered them released. The white interceptors flittered from the hilltop.

"Sir, several enemy warheads are projected to impact within three meters of our current position," a seated airman exclaimed.

"Sparrows approaching targets," the missile technician reported in monotone fashion, his voice exposing a lack of confidence in the surface-to-air missiles. "They missed." Everyone looked to Li.

"Get ready," was all he could offer. Shadows shifted in the dimness, sliding from terminal chairs to the cold, coarse floor. Some put on steel pot helmets and tightened down chinstraps, while others claimed cover beneath wooden desks. Li crouched among his cowering men. "Here they come," the last man in his seat cried out, before leaving his screen to dive to the floor. The jungle went silent and then a rush of air brought two Chinese warheads to Hill 112.

Five thousand five-hundred pounds of high explosives came to the hilltop as the missiles slammed into the air defense site's cross-shaped platform. Surrounding trees cracked and toppled, and debris flew into the empty streets in Hill 112's shadow. Tucked beneath a shelf of limestone, Hill 112's bunker cradled Li and his men, keeping the explosive overpressure at bay. Li shook his head to clear deafness and lingering shock. The flatscreen, though cracked, still worked. It showed symbolic Chinese ballistic and cruise missiles merging with targets around the island. Taiwan's command and control took several debilitating blows. Strongnet blinked off the air.

◊◊◊◊

Major Han and his wingman circled off Taiwan's east coast, awaiting their turn at the tanker. Other friendly aircraft were also nearby, stacked, packed, and racked over the sea. Hearing a beep, Han looked to the console between his knees. A menacing text message from ground control scrolled across a small screen: BANDITS. LRG ENMY FORMS, FUJIAN. It meant vast numbers of enemy aircraft were assembling in mainland skies with the largest congregation over the Chinese province just opposite Taiwan. With the enemy refueling now over their territory, they would charge in behind a wall of surface-to-air missiles. *Their fighters will come first, surely to be followed by strike aircraft*, Han reasoned. Taiwan had picketed the Strait with Aegis destroyers to thin out the onslaught. Then they will have to deal with me, Han bristled. He positioned the Fighting Falcon behind the big tanker and followed its director lights to close the distance.

A prone airman in the tail of the tanker expertly guided the fuel transfer boom into the receptacle behind Han's canopy. The nozzle mated with a clunk and Han heard the reassuring sound of flowing fuel. A grey wisp streamed by Han's canopy. He realized it was not fuel spray, however. He looked behind and downward. Smoke blew from Taiwan's bases and cities, gathering and thickening at all flight levels. The transfer boom disengaged, and Han backed off, his bird satiated, His wingman moved in to suckle at the tanker. With both jets topped off, Han and his buddy made room for a thirsty delta-winged Mirage 2000. They left the gas station and met up with a third Fighting Falcon. Ground controllers then vectored the refreshed fighter-bombers to a quadrant of sky over Taiwan's west coast. The three warplanes pointed northwest and went supersonic.

The three Taiwanese Fighting Falcons hopped through a pass on Snow Mountain, and slid down its western side. Chinese radar and surface-to-air missile warnings warbled again. Han's three-ship pressed on and arrived over the island's west coast at Taichung City. The sun was blindingly low in the sky. *It will be behind the Chinese. Good planning*, Han lamented. He lowered his shaded helmet visor and considered the first Chinese warplane they were likely to meet in mortal combat: the formidable J-11 Flanker.

A kit-built Russian heavyweight, the Flanker air superiority fighter featured two big afterburning turbofans that cranked the airplane up to Mach 2. Han ran through memorized specifications: operating range: 3,200 kilometers; ceiling: 18,000 meters at 280 meters per second climb-rate. Armaments: several air-to-air missiles, including short-range infrared-guided PL-8 Thunderclaps, and beyond visual-range, radar-guided SD-10 Lightningbolts, and also an internal 30 millimeter cannon. *A prickly pear indeed*, Han mulled. It was time to rally the group. He clicked his radio to the designated frequency and mashed the transmit button.

"Defenders of Taiwan: Aerial combat has always been about the warrior in the cockpit—his aggression and skill—not the number of machines facing off. Your experience and training are superior. We act in defense of home, family, friends, and freedom. Flight leaders... report."

"*Chi.*"

"*Choa.*"

"*Chiang*," came back on the radio. The 21st Squadron's Halberd, Hammer, and Spear flights had checked in.

Han's *Pam* (Shield) flight banked with him over the buildings and farms of Cingshuei Township. Immediately apparent was Ching Chuan Kang Air Base throwing up a wall of flak and tracer fire as several Chinese cruise missiles closed on the airfield and the power plant nearby. The robotic onslaught tore into the air base's shelters, runways, and fuel tanks. East Seas overflew the power plant, and dropped metal strips on its tangle of high-voltage lines, substations, and transformers, that then overloaded with brilliant flashes. Taichung City and its environs went dark. Ching Chuan Kang's burning aircraft, buildings, and fuel belched choking black smoke that wafted into town.

A solid tone sounded in Han's cockpit, and a panel indicator flashed: SAM. Chinese surface-to-air missiles had been fired; Favorit and Triumf interceptors were on the way. To prevent dominance of the air by China, Han and the Taiwanese air force had to survive this first broadside, as the missiles would be followed in by Chinese fighters carrying long-range air-to-air missiles. *We must get in close with the big Chinese jets; Close enough to take advantage of the Fighting Falcon's superior climb and turn rates*, Han reasoned.

"Twenty one. SAMs terminal. Your sector," a ground controller announced. Enemy surface-to-air missiles were now entering the 21st's area of responsibility.

The setting sun loomed as a giant orange ball on the western horizon. Han blinked to clear the purple spot burned into his vision. He looked down at his radar screen. A blip showed a rapidly approaching Favorit. Han caught a flash in the sunset's corona, then distortion from the long cone-shaped missile's superhot thrust. The three-ship of Fighting Falcons commenced well-rehearsed defensive tactics, dropping chaff canisters that blossomed into radar-reflecting clouds of zinc-coated glass fibers, and then rolling the warplanes into a steep inverted dive. Han's G-suit inflated, squeezing blood from legs and lower torso, forcing it back to organs and brain. The threatening grey veil of unconsciousness pulled back and Han's vision cleared. Feeling his neck would snap under the nearly hundred-pound strain, he struggled to lift his heavy head to keep eyes on the enemy missile. Han's jet rocked and rattled. A Chinese surface-to-air missile had exploded among his chaff, though his cockpit radar warning continued to blare. Han looked to the cockpit screen and yelled orders into his oxygen mask.

The Fighting Falcons dumped more chaff and shot off perpendicular to the axis of attack, to get behind the seekers of the Chinese surface-to-air missiles. There would be no respite. Chinese Flankers fired their Lightningbolt radar-guided air-to-air missiles. They sent three to charge Han's three-ship. More chaff pumped to the wind, however the sophisticated missiles ignored the chaff and zeroed in on the smaller but stronger radar reflections that bounced off the Fighting Falcons. The Chinese air-to-air missiles bent into an inhuman turn to follow the Taiwanese warplanes.

"More chaff…" All three Taiwanese jets inked the sky. "Break." Han pulled straight up. His wingmen banked left and right. One missile went left as its associates stayed with the decoy cloud left by the splitting jets. The left missile flicked terminal radar at the Fighting Falcon, matching moves as it slithered in. The Lightningbolt's proximity fuse sensed the fleeing aircraft and triggered its fragmentation warhead. The blast took a bite of wing, hot; jagged barbs piercing the Fighting Falcon. The machine hemorrhaged vital fluids as the hands of the dead pilot dropped from the stick. Assuming its Falconer stricken, the airplane's avionics took over and put it in straight and level flight. The damaged wing dragged, pulling against the computer's attempt to counteract the force. An aileron moved, spitting the last of the dark-green, life-sustaining hydraulic fluid from its actuator. The Fighting Falcon entered a flat spin. A sickly crack, and the spar let go, freeing the wing to somersault away.

"Come on, come on, eject," Han pleaded with his colleague's corpse. He spotted another inbound missile, and snap-rolled. More chaff and a steep climb. The roaring engine clawed at the sky. The Chinese air-to-air missile stayed with him. Han selected the external fuel tank and unlocked it. He rolled the Fighting Falcon upside down and pitched into a dive, releasing the teardrop tank as the airplane plunged. The near-empty container was weightless for a moment and wobbled from the sloshing avgas still inside. To the enemy missile, one radar return became two. This gave Han a 50-50 chance. *We are The Gamblers.* He grimaced, as he struggled against self-induced Gs. The Chinese air-to-air missile turned for the fuel tank. Han won the bet and got a kick in the pants as the Lightningbolt obliterated the decoy. Han let out a cheerful howl. Disoriented by chaff and seemingly unsure of its purpose, the last Chinese air-to-air missile passed high and flew off. Major Han called out to his wingmen to reform. Only one Fighting Falcon arrived on-wing as new symbols appeared at the upper edge of the radar screen.

"Flankers now 10 miles out. They're supersonic," Han told his friend.

"Let's get them, major," Han's wingman had also tasted the poison of loss.

"AMRAAMs," Han responded. The Taiwanese selected their advanced medium-range air-to-air missiles. The computer locked them onto targets. "My lead," Han said. "Pam One: Fox Three." He squeezed the stick's trigger and the Fighting Falcon shook. The large air-to-air missile flashed from beneath the wing and raced into the orange sky on puffy smoke. Then just a dot, and then a silent fireball expanded and contracted in the distance. Smoking debris fell from within its fury, and a rolling smoke ring rose above. *One down, three to go,* Han counted. The Taiwanese light warplanes dashed at the Chinese heavy ones. They merged at a combined 2,000 miles-per-hour.

"Take them down the left," Han ordered. "We'll turn in tight. Stay with me."

The enemy jets appeared, dots at first that quickly grew to intimidating silhouettes. Han heard the wind they drove, and then the fearsome roar of big, angry engines. As the Chinese Flankers approached and passed, time and speed slowed for Han. He made out the Flanker's unique nose, the red star on the pilot's white helmet, and the enemy jet's wide shoulders and rear radar housing that poked from between twin-engines and tails. Violent buffeting snapped Han back, his chest vibrating from the powerful thrust. Han banked into the turn. The G-force meter shot up to nine, and the suit inflated. "Ten G's." Han's view of the instruments went hazy and started to tunnel. Through distant echoes, he heard his wingman's repeated request to slacken the turn. Han backed off, clearing his vision in time for a cognitive glance at the radar. A wheel of airplanes turned in the sky, and the little Taiwanese fighter-bombers gained position. One of the three Flankers split off and dove.

"Stay with these two," Han ordered. However, it was too late. His wingman had been tempted out of position. "*Gan*," Han swore and kept his Fighting Falcon with the two Flankers. The Chinese cut in hard and wobbled as their low-camber wings stalled. An explosion and a hail of bits pitter-pattered on Han's canopy.

"Pam Two?" Realization came instead of an answer: his wingman—his friend—had just died. In that distracted moment, the Flankers popped speed brakes and slowed down so fast that Han almost flew right between them. Han instead threw the Fighting Falcon away. Although ramming the enemy might be effective, it was his job to live long enough to send at least 15 Chinese pilots into the afterlife. With his two wingmen dead, that responsibility now became

45. A midair collision seemed less acceptable than racking up such numbers, Han supposed. Too close to use the cannon, Han relaxed the turn to gain some distance. He looked to the infrared-guided Sky Sword air-to-air missiles mounted on his wingtips, and made computer inputs to wake them up. A glowing green crosshair appeared in the heads-up display, and an anxious trill flooded the cockpit. Han maneuvered and centered the floating reticle on the silhouette of a Flanker. The trill changed to a solid tone as the Sky Sword acquired the enemy's hot engines.

"Pam One. Fox One." The Sky Sword streaked off to take a swing at the heavy fighter. Han saw the Flanker fold in half. Its rear fuselage separated and exploded as the canopy blew off the tumbling forward section. With the cockpit coming apart around him, the Chinese pilot ejected and parachuted into the Taiwan Strait over which the dogfight had wandered. With one Flanker left in his windscreen, Han wondered about the one he could not see. "Where are you?" he asked aloud. Han selected his last air-to-air missile. It locked and begged for release. Han pulled the trigger and the missile was a shooting star in the purple sky. Firing and forgetting, Han dropped the Fighting Falcon's nose and hit the afterburner. He had to quickly regain his airspeed. Speed was life.

The missing Flanker landed on Han's six—it fell in behind his tail—and sent a spurt of cannon fire that whipped by. Han evaded and cornered at a high bank angle, came around, and saw the big Flanker again. Its engines were torch blue in the night sky. Han jerked the nose up to an extreme angle-of-attack, fired his own cannon, and sent sparkling tracers at his foe. The Fighting Falcon swayed in its unnatural position, its thin wing no longer generating lift. A whooping filled the cockpit. Then a female electronic voice affectionately known as 'Bitching Betty' announced the stall. The Fighting Falcon spun and toppled hard, slamming Han against the canopy. He purposely released the side stick and let the avionics take over. Several disorienting pitches and yaws, and the Fighting Falcon automatically recovered and returned to level flight. Han grabbed the stick and took back authority.

There was a near flash. A Chinese Thunderclap—a dangerous heat-seeker based on stolen Israeli and Russian technology—was on the loose. Han dropped flares to offer an alternative to the Fighting Falcon's hot engine and leading edges. Then he spotted his adversary on radar. He craned his neck to the twinkling stars, caught the Flanker's silhouette among them, backed off the throttle and dove. The Thunderclap ignored the string of hot flares and chose instead to snuggle with the warm Fighting Falcon.

"Pull up. Terrain," Bitching Betty expressed with her monotone synthetic voice. Han saw the black ocean. "Pull up. Terrain," Betty repeated. The altimeter spun toward zero. Han yanked the airplane out of the dive and dropped flares like turds of fright. The Thunderclap followed unerringly. Han pumped more flares and jerked the airplane into a plumb ascent, his slamming into the back of the seat. He felt his midsection flatten as his organs squirmed and oozed into new gravity-induced shapes. Han rolled the Fighting Falcon and looked down. The red streamer of missile thrust continued toward his falling flares. He watched as, one-by-one, the flares snuffed in the sea. The Thunderbolt's tail fire disappeared as it impacted the water.

Shifting from defense to offense, Han changed radar modes for a broad sweep and found the Flanker watching from a cloud perch on high.

Detecting Han's radar, the Flanker locked its own on the Fighting Falcon, and swooped back in. Han put his nose on the enemy. A spear of flame erupted from the Fighting Falcon and a ribbon of tracers reached for the Flanker. The Chinese warplane jerked away in a barrel roll, escaping the stream of explosive bullets. Approaching from behind, another airplane appeared on Han's radar.

"Pam One. Bo Two. On your six," the radio crackled. An identification friend or foe code identified the radar blip as friendly. The Chinese pilot was now outnumbered—an unfamiliar and uncomfortable first—and bugged-out due west. Han realized he was soaked with sweat and shaking. He shifted in the restraints. Like its optical illusion namesake, a Mirage 2000 belonging to the 499th's Cobras appeared beside Han's Fighting Falcon.

"Nice to see you, Bo Two," Han transmitted.

"Proceed to ALS 260." The Mirage driver was all business. *He has lost friends today, too*, Han understood, all too well.

"Your lead," Han acknowledged. Han settled the Fighting Falcon behind his compatriot, and they both turned east toward their alternate landing strip, a six-lane highway that ran down the middle of Taiwan.

Secretary Pierce shivered in what she called 'the tomb,' her dedicated bunker deep beneath the Truman Building. Fourth in line for presidential succession, hers was one of many fortresses under the American capital. From this continuance of government shelter, the secretary communicated with leadership and her ambassadors, embassies, and consulates around the world. Pierce adjusted her colorful blazer against the chill. The secretary of defense and the national security advisor were before her on a video screen. She leaned across the table to adjust the small camera and microphone.

"Better?" she asked the screen. The secretary of defense nodded. Carrying papers, Richard Ling entered the bunker. He took a seat far enough away to remain off camera.

"Secretary Tillison. Dr. Westermark," Pierce greeted the men. "How are the Taiwanese holding up?"

"The Chinese have air superiority over the Strait, but most of Taiwan's air force has survived the first blows," the secretary of defense initiated.

"Are we helping?" Pierce prodded. The national security advisor jumped in to explain that, with damaged air bases on Guam and Okinawa and the *George Washington* carrier strike group out of action, the options for assisting Taiwan had become quite limited. "How long to get Andersen and Kadena cleaned up?" Pierce asked. The secretary of defense responded that engineers were repairing the runways, and they would be reopened in about five hours.

"The Chinese could hit them again, though," the secretary of defense said, lifting both eyebrows. He then, more cheerfully, added that the 31st Marine Expeditionary Unit was departing Japan, and that all available fast-attack submarines were being surged into theater.

"How's the *GW*?" the national security advisor inquired.

"Afloat." Defense gave the short answer, before elaborating that *George Washington* was combat-ineffective, unable to do what she did best. He said the supercarrier had made it to Manila, and Mobile Diving & Salvage Unit One had flown in to crawl over her from stem to stern. *GW*'s escorts—the cruiser, destroyers, frigate, and submarine—had since formed the new Task Force 16. Although two littoral combat ships—agile, stealthy, corvette-sized surface combatants—had since headed out of Singapore to join them, these paltry ships represented the only American naval assets currently near Taiwan. Pierce and the national security advisor shook their heads in disbelief, and the secretary of defense rubbed bushed eyes. "On top of all this great news, the Chinese are massing ground forces along the Taiwanese Strait, as well as near Xinjiang and Tibet," he added.

"They're making sure the Indians don't get any fancy ideas," Pierce offered.

"Georgie, is this little island chain worth starting a world war over?" the national security advisor asked Secretary Pierce, as his digital image tiled and flickered.

"It is," Pierce declared. "Taiwan is a democracy. China is a dictatorship. This is not about cheap products or tiptoeing around a creditor. We have fought many times to do what is right by our beliefs and values. Isn't that so, Dr. Westermark?" she asked the grandson of a Holocaust survivor. Richard watched intently, more impressed with her than ever. He had had his doubts when the new administration had come to town and appointed an old political ally to head America's diplomatic corps. Although, now, watching Secretary Pierce get all fired up and hearing the passion in her arguments, he realized she was no simple crony. Both men smiled on the video screen.

"Okay, okay," the national security advisor conceded. "Glad you're on our side, Madam Secretary." Knowing her department's stance was clear, Pierce informed her colleagues that the Japanese had decided to sit this one out, and officially viewed the attack on Kadena Air Force Base as an attack on American soil. Their ambassador, however, had iterated his government's policy of allowing combat operations to be launched from Japanese air and maritime space.

"Good." The secretary of defense welcomed the news of Japan's acquiescence. "Taiwan needs airpower. If China dominates Taiwanese airspace, the cost of us getting back in there goes up. Anything more from State?"

"Yes, but only by other means," Pierce responded sternly. The men nodded understanding.

"Right then…" On the video screen, a Pentagon emblem replaced the secretary of defense, and VC-25B' centered on color bars took the place of the national security advisor, ending the teleconference.

3: CENTERS OF GRAVITY

"Let your plans be as dark as night, then strike like a thunderbolt."—Sun Tzu

Richard strolled to Jade's school, hoping to make up for lost time. He planned to surprise her outside class and treat her to lunch at the campus café where they could smooth things over.

Richard peeked through the little window on the classroom's door. Attentive students filled the amphitheater's lecture hall. One sneaked out a few minutes early, and Richard put his foot in the door to listen.

"...Renaming Taiwan 'Takasago Koku'—Highland Nation—Japanese rule of the island waffled from oppressive to paternal, and then plagued by resistance and violence," the professor orated. Like many Asians, the professor harbored ill memories of Japanese wartime behavior. His voice trembled momentarily, revealing his latent hatred. "During the Second World War the Imperial Navy home-ported the South Strike Group on Taiwan. With America, China, and the other Pacific allies finally pushing the Japanese back to their home islands, the Imperial garrison surrendered to Chiang Kai Shek and his Nationalists in 1945. With the common enemy defeated, Communist and Nationalist Chinese immediately fell back to fighting each other, reigniting the interrupted Chinese Civil War. Since no official Chinese government existed to legally claim or administer Taiwan, the territory was placed under American stewardship. The Treaty of San Francisco--" The hall bell cut the professor off. Released from the gate like spirited race horses, a throng of young people erupted from the classroom and into the hallway. Richard flattened himself against the cold, brick wall to protect himself from the human swarm. Not seeing Jade's shiny black hair among the bobbing heads, he peeked back inside the room.

Jade stood at the professor's podium, where she accepted a padded envelope that she nonchalantly tucked into her purse. Feeling Richard's gaze, she turned. Jade did not exhibit the look of innocent joyful surprise. Instead, Richard realized, she was startled. Jade collected herself, pasted a smile on, and thanked the professor.

"What are you doing here?" she asked, as she went to Richard.

"I thought we could get some lunch," Richard said, eying the professor who now erased the day's lecture notes from the whiteboard. Jade walked one step ahead and kept speed walking. Richard followed.

"What, are you boinking your teacher?" he half-joked. She stopped and turned. As usual, his joke had fallen flat. He thought their incompatible sense of humor was cultural, but she thought he was just a rude American. "Can I buy you something to eat?" Richard tried again.

"Sure, *Dick*."

In the early morning and stillness of dark at China's Jinan Air Base, three thousand Chinese paratroopers marched on the flight line.

"*I-erh, I-erh*," they counted, one-two, one-two. The men belonged to the 43rd Airborne Division, an elite formation that traced its proud heritage back to the Korean War's Battle of Triangle Hill.

General Zhen presided over the awesome congregation, standing on a command vehicle. The base's commander sat in its driver's seat.

Like a proud father watching three thousand sons, Zhen surveyed his tools for victory. Proudly, he returned salutes as they passed. The men of the 43rd were destined for Taipei's Songshan Airport. Other airborne divisions would drop on Chiang Kai Shek International Airport as well as other smaller airfields that dotted the Taiwanese capital and its outskirts. *Once these strategic positions were in Chinese hands, Taiwan's entire 6th Army will be pinned*, Zhen thought. Then the airborne divisions would break out and seize control of the island's northern third. Zhen smirked and nodded. A sniveling emanated from the otherwise silent ranks, disturbing the general's mental machinations.

Zhen looked to the base commander, who called for the formation to halt. Zhen jumped from the vehicle, wearing a concerned look and, pushing through the phalanx, moved for the sound. He closed in on the racket, hearing other men as they urged the culprit to stop. The sniveling became a sniffling mumble. Finding the source of the disturbance among the engineers, Zhen pulled the young man from the line.

"What is it, my boy?" The general put his arm around the young man with the boyish face. Zhen felt the teenager tremble.

"I have family where we are going," the engineer pleaded.

"Oh oh oh, yes, yes, I understand," the general pulled the dissenter in tight as he drew a pistol with his free hand. In a fluid motion, he placed the gun beneath the engineer's jaw and discharged it with a loud report. Despite the bang and grotesque spray, the other men stood perfectly still. Zhen removed a handkerchief, wiped brain matter and fluids from an adjacent paratrooper's face, pocketed the bloody mess, and returned to his vehicle. He climbed up and scanned the ranks, studying the men with a remorseless scowl. This lesson had been well learned, Zhen ruminated. He yelled at a passing tractor driver to clear the body from his sight. The aircraft technician, visibly shaken by the strange order, went about lifting and transporting the warm corpse. General Zhen nodded to the base commander, who ordered preparations to proceed. Zhen crossed his arms and watched the renewed dance of men and machines. He returned his concentration to Operation Red Dragon:

The 43rd Division was tasked to fly south and form up with the 44th and 45th over the Chinese coast at Wenzhou. The entire 15th Airborne Corps would then meet its escort of fighter-bombers—glossy dark-grey delta-winged J-10 Vigorous Dragons. The Vigorous Dragons would spearhead the transports, clear the sky of any last Taiwanese fighters, and attack remaining drop zone air defenses. General Zhen cracked a crooked grin.

Paratroopers lined up at the rear cargo ramps of big propeller-driven An-12 Cubs. The division's light tanks, airmobile artillery pieces, and infantry fighting vehicles drove into the bellies of voluminous Il-76 Candids—strategic transports with hunched, swept-wings, four big turbofans, towering T-tails, and noses freckled with observation windows. Zhen squirmed with excitement. Despite his age and political status, the general had convinced the Politburo to let him join the division's second wave into the drop zone. Ignoring the risk, General Zhen insisted his place was with the soldiers of the republic where he could lead from the front to instill courage, discipline, and morale. His bravado inspired the old men that ran the country, who then gave reluctant support.

◊◊◊◊

Senior Master Sergeant Li's breakfast was a boxed meal-ready-to-eat. He noted with ironic amusement that it had been manufactured in the People's Republic of China. Finishing the MRE, he considered the cigarette it included. Li stood, stretched, and exited Hill 112's command bunker to smoke. A passing airman gave him a light. The Chinese tobacco was stale; it popped and hissed with each draw. This was the first cigarette Li had had in months, and it made his heart pound and throat sting. Li surveyed what was left of his air defense site.

About midnight the night before, a platoon from the 6th Army had towed a new Sparrow launcher and radar up the hill. The soldiers stayed to reinforce the garrison and better protect the high ground from air or ground assault. The Sparrows were set up on the platform's remains, just beside the site's one remaining operational anti-aircraft cannon. Hill 112's airmen and soldiers had cleaned up most of the mess overnight, cleared fallen trees, and used the wood to buttress new perimeter trenches. A dump truck came up before first light, too, and poured its load of coarse gravel in revetments for the hilltop's mortars and heavy machineguns. Li crushed the cigarette and raised light-enhancing binoculars from around his neck. Piercing the dimness, Li peered into the valley.

Taipei Songshan had been built where Matsuyama Airdrome—an Imperial Japanese airbase—once stood, and had evolved into a modern mid-size commercial airport. Li and the air force knew that Songshan's proximity to the government center meant it was integral to Chinese invasion plans. So far, Li assessed, Songshan looked unscathed, and, despite surrounding blacked-out city blocks, emergency power flowed to the airport. A subordinate hurried from the bunker and gestured for Li to rejoin them inside.

In Hill 112's bunker, a crowd had congregated around a radar terminal.

"Tell me," Li ordered

"Senior master sergeant, this airman is tracking six mid-altitude fast movers, with another 15 high-altitude targets trailing them. Both contact groups are inbound from the northwest and bearing on our relative position," the seated technician reported. Two blips appeared on the radar screen. The technician pointed at them. "Those are our fighters climbing out of Songshan. They are climbing to meet the raiders, he proudly deduced." Everyone huddled in the green glow of the radar.

Two Taiwanese F-CK-1 Ching Kuos powered their way into the sky. Underpowered kludges named for a former president, the Ching Kuos raced headlong at the Vigorous Dragons. Taiwanese air controllers sent a Mirage to help even the odds.

"Ready a Sparrow," Li ordered. Hill 112's new surface-to-air missile quad box-launcher elevated. Dots on the radar screen represented Chinese and Taiwanese aircraft as they converged and flew about, playing out a dogfight. Intertwining puffy trails appeared in the dawn sky. Thunder echoed around eastern Taipei. Ruined Chinese and Taiwanese aircraft crashed into neighborhoods and splashed into the rivers. With both Ching Kuos down, the Taiwanese Mirage heeded a low fuel warning, dove, and turned for the east coast. More Chinese Vigorous Dragons roared over downtown, their crackling engines echoing among the nervous streets. People crouching in the heights of Taipei 101 felt the skyscraper vibrate from the close fly-by.

"Okay, our sector is clear of friendlies. Weapons free," Li directed. The radar technician reported that high-altitude targets were coming in from the north. Some were slow, others moving fast. With only four surface-to-air missiles and limited ammunition for the anti-aircraft cannon, Li decided to engage the fast-movers with the Sparrows, and then switch over to the cannon to fire at the slower targets, what he assumed to be enemy troop transports.

Hill 112's surface-to-air missiles bolted from the launcher and flew off. Its lone anti-aircraft cannon tilted up, and let it rip. Tongues of flame shot from its barrel and smoking brass clinked to the concrete.

Explosive rounds zipped among the big Chinese Candids and Cubs as they entered their drop zone. Hill 112's anti-aircraft fire struck a Cub transport hauling enemy paratroopers, and then an old An-2 Colt observation biplane that carried the drop coordinator. Smoking pieces fell, as the damaged Chinese airplanes veered from the formation.

"Fast movers are still inbound. Sparrows are closing," the missile technician declared as he watched the surface-to-air missiles ride the radar beam toward their targets. Half the control screen suffered from electronic noise, turning it a blinding greenish-white.

"Enemy jamming." Everyone watched as the blips that represented the Sparrows began to divert, turned from the true path.

Two Vigorous Dragons screamed down the river with impunity, the Chinese warplanes dwarfed by the hollow mountains of downtown Taipei. The Chinese fighter-bombers hauled two 1,000-kilogram gravity bombs. They hopped over bridge wreckage and then turned east to follow the highway. A whip of glowing cannon fire stretched from one of the hilltops ahead. Then the Chinese flight leader spotted a puff of launch smoke and ordered chaff.

The Vigorous Dragons continued to drive on their target. Contrails erupted from their canards, as the pilots pulled their machines into an abrupt climb. With afterburners ablaze, they lobbed their big bombs at their aim point: Hill 112's bunker entrance. Hill 112's Super Bat spit its last few rounds. The explosive projectiles bit into another Chinese transport.

"Incoming," Li screamed. The Taiwanese dropped to the bunker floor and hugged whatever furniture and equipment they could grab. Hill 112's army platoon scurried inside, huddled near the ground, and awaited the inevitable. Twin, massive explosions drove the bunker into blackness. Half the structure collapsed with a sickly tearing sound. Everyone inside not instantly killed was left bleeding and unconscious.

Senior Master Sergeant Li awakened to a mouth full of grit. Dry blood crusted his ears and nose. Even with his arm broken, he was luckier than the poor mangled fellow lying next to him. Crafting a splint for his twisted arm, Li touched his aching head and felt the large bump under his greasy, matted hair. He stood and swayed, and then grabbed for the steadiness of a wall. He shuffled along it as he checked on his groaning men. The hum of enemy transports infiltrated the bunker's bent door.

Flying in 'vics'—inverted v-formations of three planes each—the Candids and Cubs filled the sky, casting shadows that snaked over Taipei's buildings, parks, and streets. Coordinators peeked out the nose windows of their transports and alerted jumpmasters that landmarks had been spotted. The aircrafts' side doors opened. Jumpmasters, whipped by the slipstream, spotted the memorized curve of the river and the appropriate marker bridge. They turned to their cargo of nervous men.

"Stand in door," a Cub's jumpmaster barked. The paratroopers stood and lined up. Each attached his parachute's static line to a cabin rail before they waddled into position. A green light flashed, and then stayed lit.

"Go," the jumpmaster said, smacking the back of the lead man, who hurled himself out, arms and legs splayed. The static line yanked the parachute from its bag, deploying it to drift like a jellyfish caught in the current. The roar of Candids that also arrived over the area drowned the Cub's whirring propellers.

The big jets lined up with Songshan's single east-west runway and sank rapidly toward its expanse. Forming a long line, the Candids configured for landing, deployed huge flaps, and dropped multi-wheeled landing gear trucks. Around Songshan Airport, Chinese paratroopers hit the ground, cleared their parachute harnesses, and went to their gear. Little groups assembled around weapons canisters, and the Chinese paratroops got fully armed and dangerous, spreading out to establish a security perimeter. The first Candid flared and settled its bulk on the concrete.

The Candid carried the first of the Chinese mechanized forces: tracked Chariot infantry fighting vehicles that carried an anti-tank missile launcher, 30-millimeter cannon, and a squad of troopers. Other Candids swooped over Songshan and flew parallel to the runway at low altitude. Tail ramps yawned open and drogue chutes yanked cargo pallets from inside. Chinese Dragon Turtle light tanks with half-egg shaped turrets deplaned first.

Main chutes deployed, decelerated the loads, and the pallets bounced along the ground and skidded to a halt on the runway's grass apron. Paratroopers ran to their tanks, freed them from restraints, crawled through hatches, and started them up billowing curls of black exhaust smoke. A fuel truck drove up to the armored congregation and gassed everything up, as a flatbed truck moved about, dispensing ammunition with its integral crane.

Chinese paratroopers swept through Songshan's passenger terminal. In the ticketing area, next to a bar and bookstore, Taipei Police and a small contingent of soldiers made a brief stand, but were quickly quieted by concentrated gunfire and tossed grenades. The infantry fighting vehicles and light tanks moved to the airport's fence line to cover the airlifters that continued to land and disgorge cargo before turning right around for scramble take-offs. One big Chinese transporter landed and taxied to an isolated corner of the tarmac, its ramp lowered and under heavy guard. A truck bearing a large wooden crate sped for one of Songshan's remote hangars. With the airhead firmly established, the airborne forces expanded their perimeter.

An anti-air warfare team set up next to Songshan's flight line. Snipers established overlooks on airport building rooftops. Atop the terminal, two paratroopers paid out wire from a spindle, unfolded a small satellite dish, adjusted it to a specific point in the sky, and attached the wire. A squad took up residence on the terminal's overhang and erected a tripod to steady their Red Arrow anti-tank missile launcher. A heavy machinegun crew settled in behind a wall of newly placed sandbags, training their weapon on the airport boulevard. Chariot infantry fighting vehicles and paratroopers fanned out to the airport's fence line while Dragon Turtle light tanks assembled on the tarmac. Chinese fighter jets circled overhead as the last of the big transports climbed out from Songshan, and a double-deck jetliner broke from behind Taipei's northern hills.

The four-engine wide body showed its livery: Air China, and displayed the calligraphic phoenix of the national carrier on its giant tail. The jet executed a high-speed bank and lined up on Songshan's runway. It sank fast and kicked up smoke when 20 tires met the ground. The double-decker's weight settled and the nose dropped, putting the front wheels down with a screech. Spoilers flipped up. With a deafening roar of reverse thrust, the jet raced to the end of the runway, turned around, and stopped. Two airport staircase tractors raced over and aligned with the airliner's lower cabin exits. Doors swung open and Chinese soldiers disembarked in two long lines. When the last man stepped off, the staircase tractors backed away and the airplane's running turbofans spun back up. The airliner's doors were still swinging closed when it started to roll again.

Two companies of People's Liberation Army regulars formed up on Songshan's flight line. Dividing into platoons, they scattered to reinforce the several hundred paratroopers already manning the outer fence. Another jetliner—a 'China Eastern' twin-engine wide-body—came out of the northwest, a dedicated Flanker on its wing. The airliner carried General Zhen, his squad of bodyguards, and teams of special forces.

Zhen pressed his face to the airplane's small oval windows. It was the first time he had seen the urban expanse of Taipei. He watched vortexes swirl off the descending airplane's winglets. As the fighter escort pulled up and away, Zhen buckled his belt and squirmed like an excited child on a first flight.

◊◊◊◊

South of Songshan Airport, Taiwanese Brave Tiger main battle tanks rumbled up Min Quan Road and marshaled for a counterattack. Souped-up Vietnam-era American Pattons, the Brave Tigers belonged to the army's 542nd Armored Brigade. The Taiwanese tanks held shy of the airport, hiding in nearby alleys and parking lots as they awaited infantry support.

"They're late," the Taiwanese tank commander again checked his watch. When they get here, he mentally planned, we will break through the airport fence and destroy the enemy aircraft and armor on the airfield. The infantry will then swarm the airfield and secure key objectives around the property. Every moment the tank commander waited exposed his tanks to ambush, and the longer the Chinese held Songshan, the more equipment and men they could deliver. The tank commander looked at his watch again and got on the radio to plead for infantry. His face betrayed disappointment as he put down the headset.

"They're not coming," he said to the gunner who squirmed in the confines of the Brave Tiger's hull. "They were caught in the open by enemy aircraft and cut down in the street." The tank commander took a deep breath and scratched his crew cut. "It's up to us." The gunner swallowed hard. Changing the radio to the formation's frequency, the Taiwanese commander transmitted to the other tanks. Silence ensued as the Taiwanese tankers shared a moment of collective doubt. Despite quality of machine and advanced training, they knew that to attack without infantry support would be very risky. "Start up," the commander broadcasted.

On rubber treads as quiet as paws, the Brave Tigers emerged from hiding, and lined up on the road. Scanning the area with his fire control imaging system, the tank commander swiveled the turret and main gun.

"Now," he ordered. The driver leaned on his throttle and lurched the lead tank into a charge. The rest of the Brave Tigers followed. Shadows moved on Songshan's terminal roof as the Taiwanese tanks materialized on the airport's main boulevard. A flash emanated from the terminal's overhang.

A Chinese Red Arrow anti-tank missile arrived and hit the lead Taiwanese tank between turret and hull, stopping the tank dead. A second Red Arrow flew into another Taiwanese tank, penetrating and detonating stored ammunition and fuel, and incinerating the crew and machine in a multi-colored blaze. A third Red Arrow reached out to the next Brave Tiger, impacted, and shredded its track. Despite being immobilized, the tank's turret swung toward the missile's source and fired its cannon.

The shell ripped into the airport terminal roof, with the impact and explosion sending up a cloud of brick shards and concrete dust. The tank's hatch clanked open, and, burnt and bleeding, a Taiwanese soldier shimmied out. He cocked the pintle-mounted machinegun, and sprayed the airport fence with bullets. A final anti-tank missile arrived to perform the coup de grâce on the crippled man and his machine. The remaining Taiwanese tanks escaped the killing ground. They retreated for the cover of nearby shops and apartment buildings, but were then ambushed and slaughtered a block away by Chinese paratroopers armed with rocket-propelled grenades. Thick black smoke from the burning Taiwanese tanks screened Chinese movements at Songshan.

Chinese Chariot infantry fighting vehicles massed near the main gate as Dragon Turtle light tanks joined up with infantry on the airport's tarmac. General Zhen strutted around the congregation, motivating and/or filling with fear those he approached. He went to the airport tarmac where an officer called the men to attention and saluted the approaching general. Zhen climbed onto an ammo crate.

"My sons, you have your objectives," he boomed. Zhen jumped down and strode to an antenna-covered armored infantry fighting vehicle, entered the rear hatch, settled inside, and strapped himself in. For the umpteenth time, he studied a map of east Taipei, as he pondered tactics and fretted over the urban terrain that precluded the launching of a single thrust toward the civic center. *Against better judgment, I must divide my force*, he posited. *I will send one column south and another to the southwest to seize the objective. The Chariots will speed ahead, survey routes, and provide information and reconnaissance for the slower infantry. The Dragon Turtles will follow the infantry fighting vehicles and overwhelm any enemy resistance.*

The rail terminal, Presidential Building, Legislative Yuan, and Ministry of National Defense had all been circled in red. *Objectives I will soon hold,* Zhen judged. The ground trembled as the machines started up. The Chinese infantry fighting vehicles departed first, speeding south down freshly paved Dun Hua Road and followed by a cavalcade of 3,000 Chinese paratroopers and soldiers led by light tanks. As the procession made its way through the streets of Taipei, those Taiwanese brave enough to peek from windows received only polite salutes.

The leading infantry fighting vehicles pushed aside parked cars while blasting Taiwanese Military Police Command roadblocks with cannon fire. Infantry and tanks turned east, splitting into two columns: one headed for the Ministry of National Defense and the Presidential Building, and the other for the train station and parliament. Intelligence said that elements of Taiwan's 6th Army—including the feared 152nd Dragons and 178th Tigers infantry brigades—guarded these strategic objectives. A last minute update showed infantry fighting vehicles from the 351st Armored Infantry Brigade among the Taiwanese defenders.

Zhen's Chariot pulled into an alley between low buildings. A Dragon Turtle, with its thicker steel shell, lingered to shield the general and his infantry fighting vehicle. Nestled between the alley's sheer walls, Zhen choreographed by radio the final push on Taipei's civic center. When his colonels reported they were in position, Zhen uttered the single code word that would invoke The Chinese God of War and unleash his force on the government buildings: "*Kuan Ti.*" And the attack commenced.

Three Vigorous Dragon fighter-bombers rolled in and dove on Taiwan's Ministry of National Defense, breathing fire from their cannons, spraying the ministry's windows and wavy concrete roof with explosive bullets. Several such softening runs preceded the Chinese vehicles that then moved in on the fortress. The Taiwanese shook off the air strike and opened fire from the building, claiming a Chinese light tank and two infantry fighting vehicles with TOW anti-tank missiles. Explosions rocked the ministry grounds as Chinese engineers blew the tunnels that linked the building to sewers and the subway. Taiwan's Ministry of National Defense was now surrounded and cut off from reinforcement and supply.

Chinese Chariots peppered the ministry building with heavy machineguns, as Dragon Turtles blasted holes in its sides with their cannons. With smoke belching from windows, the Taiwanese return fire waned. General Zhen lowered the ramp of his command vehicle and stepped from its confines. Crushing a cigarette under his boot, he looked to the battered, pockmarked building.

"Seize it," Zhen ordered a colonel, who saluted and ran off to supervise the final attack on the ministry. Breach teams stacked up at doorways, and Dragon Turtles fired tear gas rounds through torn building openings. Chariots opened up with their machineguns and hosed the upper floors with deadly fire. Explosives detonated and blasted steel doors from hinges. The breach teams rushed in.

Several muffled explosions ensued, accompanied by small arms fire. Soon thereafter, the colonel reported to Zhen that the building had been taken. Happy with progress so far, Zhen watched two Cub transports fly overhead, dropping more paratroopers over key sites in the city; mainly bridges and intersections. Zhen climbed back into his command vehicle and ripped paper from a printer. It said the 44th Airborne Division had seized Chiang Kai Shek International Airport, and the 45th was mopping up the last resistance at Hsinchu City's airfield to the southwest. It added that the Republic of the Philippines had offered to host the Taiwanese government-in-exile, though the former president of Taiwan, his cabinet, and remaining legislators reportedly remained on the island, operating out of the southeastern city of Manjhou. General Zhen ordered the Chariot driver to take him back to Songshan Airport.

With Beijing and Taipei 13 hours ahead of Washington DC, Secretary Pierce and most of the Executive Branch had taken to spending noon to midnight, local time, at work. Richard and the secretary's staff also adhered to the new schedule. Obviously tired, Richard appeared in the secretary's doorway. He clutched a mug of coffee and looked at the school supply clock that hung in the secretary's office, set to Beijing/Taipei time. It is high noon in the Middle Kingdom, Richard pondered. He rapped lightly on Pierce's open door. Although he tried to speak coherently, and despite the infusion of caffeine, he made little sense. The stream of briefs, reports, updates, dispatches to ambassadors, and calls to allies on behalf of the secretary had taken their toll.

"Get some sleep," the secretary ordered him. "I need you crisp."

Too tired to deal with the train, Richard decided on a cab ride home. Alighting across the street from his brownstone, he noticed a shadowed figure leaned against the gnarled trunk of an old maple tree. "Richard," the shadow spoke in an ominous, but familiar tone. Richard smiled.

"I was just thinking about you," he confessed.

Jade jumped out with a giggle and hugged him tightly. With her tantalizingly devious smile, she asked if she could come in.

"You live here too," he reminded her.

"I still want you to invite me in."

"Well, my lady, please do come in." Richard swept his hand toward the door with exaggerated graciousness. Jade batted her eyes, raised her chin, and walked in.

They stole a kiss in the brownstone's foyer. Richard grabbed her ass and whispered, "I want you." She smiled as though she already knew it. They began to climb the long stairs to the first landing.

Richard's landlady was at their apartment door, scrubbing the raised wooden panels. She stopped her frantic cleaning when she noticed the staring couple.

"What are you doing?" Richard asked. He signaled her to lower the towel that she was using to block their view of the door. She lowered it and mumbled apologies about not getting it done in time.

Across the door, emblazoned in red spray-paint, was the word: 'CHINK.' The landlord made promises of security cameras and the installation of new locks. Richard fished his keys out and paused to read the graffito one more time. He nudged Jade into the apartment and the door slammed behind them. He did not notice the red paint staining Jade's thumb. As the landlady was about to go, Richard re-emerged to pin a small American flag over the epithet. The door slammed again and latched with a resounding click.

"Sorry," the landlady said to the empty hall before slinking back to her own apartment.

Richard approached his computer and sat down. The screen woke up when he tapped the keyboard. Prompted for a password, he typed it in and clicked [Enter]. However, the password box popped up again. He typed harder and faster, and then mashed his fists on the keys. Soon he picked up the keyboard and banged it on the desk.

"Richard," Jade said. "Give it a rest." Richard huffed, and then forced a smile. He watched as she slid off her shirt and sprawled across the bed. He relaxed with a giant sigh and went to his girl. She reached for him. He took a deep breath of her natural perfume and put his mouth to one of her dark, hard nipples. She arched her back and moaned. His hand pushed against her toned stomach and slid down, where he found her soft, wet place, and he eased two fingers inside.

Physically and psychologically exhausted from the unwanted welcome at his door, he soon fell fast asleep. Richard slipped into a dream: a mushroom cloud rising over a burning city.

A debate raged in the command bunkers of the American capital. Civilian and military leaders argued various measured and total responses to the Chinese attack. The president absorbed the recommendations and, with substantial Chinese nuclear forces to consider, decided on a response that respected the escalation ladder. Conventional strikes will destroy the Shaoguan missile base that had launched against the *George Washington*.

Shaoguan's bunkers contained a huge store of China's DF-21D East Winds. American leadership concurred that these specialized anti-ship intermediate-range ballistic missiles had to be taken out, and such a plan made crystal clear American willingness to hit the Chinese homeland. With the course of action set, US military leaders turned their attention to making the president's order happen.

A stealth bomber raid was the first proposal. The B-2 stealth bombers could destroy a dispersed and forested base in exceedingly hostile air space. However, the military and political cost of losing an aircraft and its crew made that choice less than acceptable, and, with the nuclear option off the table, they settled upon a cruise missile strike. An admiral proposed the nuclear guided-missile submarine *Ohio* as the perfect instrument of destruction.

◊◊◊◊

Steaming out of Washington State, *Ohio* had already sped to the western Pacific. After three days of high-speed transit under the protection of a nuclear attack submarine, *Ohio* now held steady on station 100 miles south of the Korean Peninsula. A gargantuan hole in the water, the 560-foot submarine hovered just beneath the swelling surface.

Aft of *Ohio*'s tall sail was a swimmer delivery vehicle—a midget submersible attached like a lamprey to her steel casing— obviously not necessary to this mission. However, the sub also featured there, a field of missile tube hatch covers. A former 'boomer' on doomsday watch, *Ohio* no longer carried Trident nuclear missiles. She had instead been converted and loaded out with conventional Tomahawk land-attack cruise missiles. Trailing her extremely low frequency antenna, *Ohio* pulled in an encrypted message from command that was deciphered and delivered to the officers in the control room.

The emergency action message raised eyebrows, but also brought satisfied grins to *Ohio*'s submariners. By whispers and mumbled conversation, the crew learned the mission before the captain could make his formal announcement: *Ohio* was going to fire on China.

"Battle stations, missile," the captain barked. The periscope raised, *Ohio*'s commanding officer leaned into its eyepiece. He did a quick scan of the horizon. "It's raining topside, he muttered.

The mast receivers also assessed the electronic environment. "Multiple transmitters. Lots of radar. Nothing localized," the executive officer announced. The captain then ordered the scope lowered, and strode to the weapons station. He scanned indicator lights and the status board, and watched as the seated missile technician finished programming the Tomahawks. The tech input *Ohio*'s current position, multiple waypoints along the flight path, and individual target coordinates, including corresponding digital landmarks. Completing his task, the tech reported missiles one through 70 were ready in all respects.

"Conn, sonar. Report all contacts," the captain ordered. The sonar post reconfirmed the scope was clear, with no surface or subsurface contacts. "Very well," the captain said. He scanned the young faces that looked to him with anticipation and a touch of fear. The captain milked the moment and paused as he smiled wryly. "Weapons, conn. You have permission to release the weapons." *Ohio*'s weapons officer took the trigger in hand, swallowed hard, and gave it a squeeze.

Despite its immensity, the American guided-missile submarine quivered as Tomahawks ejected from her steel body. For four long, vulnerable minutes, *Ohio* vibrated from the mass launch. Taught to whisper, gently close hatches, and never ever drop a thing, *Ohio*'s crew cringed at the racket. The captain stared at the deck as he suffered the long launch. If he had done his job well, no enemy submarine had sneaked up on them. If he had not, now was when *Ohio* would take some torpedoes amidships or astern. When the shaking stopped and the panel lights went green, the weapons officer announced the last missile as away. With that, the captain ordered the submarine secured from launch configuration and into the deep.

Ohio's Tomahawks tore above the ocean's rippled surface. The cruise missiles wore a dark-grey, energy-absorbing coating, and their noses and bodies were faceted to reflect radar. They passed an invisible marker, the first of their GPS waypoints, and turned to the southwest. As the Tomahawks neared the Chinese coast, they maneuvered again to minimize exposure to densely layered air defenses. Once over the beach, the cruise missiles dove in and out of valleys and jumped through mountain passes. One Tomahawk's engine failed, and it careened into trees, surfing along the canopy before degrading into segments by thick branches. In the darkness, a startled Chinese shepherd glanced up and watched a flight of many unidentified flying objects passing overhead.

At Shaoguan missile base, an artillery officer checked on security patrols that emerged from dense trees. He scolded a soldier for an unbuttoned tunic, but then his attention was diverted to a rushing sound. Then, an anti-aircraft battery peppered the sky. Flinching at its reports, the officer spotted the first of the American cruise missiles.

The Tomahawks swept in at treetop level. They peeled off for individual structures, and, one-by-one, slammed into command bunkers, flew into missile shelters, and lit off fuel tanks. A siren serenaded as the Chinese base was laid to waste. The surrounding woods were drought-dry and would burn for days.

◊◊◊◊

US Navy Task Force 16 rounded Shihmen Point at the northern tip of Taiwan, the Taipei metropolitan area off to port. Placed under the command of Captain Ferlatto, TF16 was short an aircraft carrier. It consisted of the cruiser *Lake Champlain*; the destroyers *Paul Hamilton* and *Mahan*; the littoral combat ships *Coronado* and *Fort Worth*; and the nuclear attack submarine *California*. *California* sped ahead of the task force's surface ships, and then drifted and listened, ready to destroy anything in TF16's way. Soon, *California*'s sonar heard the surface ships' thunder as they approached. *Lake Champlain* powered up her phased array radar, and soon Ferlatto was awed by the juicy choice of airborne targets populating the ship's combat information center displays.

"Who do you want to shoot first, skipper?" The commander's cocky question was redundant as Aegis had already prioritized the plots and had decided for them. Ferlatto folded his arms and stepped back into the shadows, allowing the anti-air warfare officer to do what he did best.

Two Chinese Badger bombers cruised on maritime patrol west of Taiwan. Belonging to the People's Liberation Army Air Force's 4th Bomber Regiment, they were loaded with East Sea anti-ship cruise missiles. They swept ahead with chin-mounted radar and found weak reflections on the horizon. The Badgers turned in and readied their missiles.

"There," *Lake Champlain*'s electronic warfare technician pointed at the radar screen. "Weak signal, low on the horizon." The flickering dot became solid. "Inbound contact. Two on the same bearing." On the screen, four small dots were born from two big ones. They sped toward the task force. "Vampires. Vampires. Fast movers inbound."

"Tracking four," another sailor added. Four dots appeared on his tactical screen, and began skipping toward the ships.

Deck mortars sent canisters aloft from the American ships. The canisters burst, and spread radar-spoofing metallic clouds over the task force. The destroyer *Mahan* fired at the Badgers, while *Paul Hamilton* shot at the inbound cruise missiles. One East Sea was taken out by an Evolved Sea Sparrow Missile, however the other three Chinese anti-ship missiles locked on target, with two tracking *Lake Champlain*, and the other, *Mahan*. The East Seas got in close fast.

Lake Champlain brought one of her SeaRAM turrets to bear. Rolling Airframe Missiles burst from the box launcher, and zoomed off over the water. They collided with two East Seas. *Mahan*'s Phalanx Gatling guns built a wall of tungsten before the last enemy missile. The East Sea slammed into this wall and exploded, creating a shockwave that rocked *Mahan* to the keel. *Lake Champlain* guided Sea Sparrows into the Badger bombers, tumbling them from the sky, to disintegrate in high-speed impacts with the water and sprinkling their bits to the bottom. The American cruiser's combat system re-prioritized the 33 enemy targets it tracked over Taipei, and assigned each a weapon: a Sea Sparrow or the longer-ranged Standard Missile. The task force readied for a massed launch.

Over Taipei, flashes and sparkling showers showed where 29 Chinese aircraft had been blotted from the sky. Doing the hit and run, Ferlatto ordered Task Force 16 to wheel east and increase speed. In addition, he read orders that would send the task force's nuclear attack submarine off toward the west.

California slipped silently through the water. Her shrouded propeller made turns for seven knots. In the vacuum of space instead of the black crush of Earth's oceans, *California*'s command and control center would be the bridge of a starship. Its science was far from fiction, however, and the bank of video screens that wrapped the long room showed environmental, navigation, power plant, sonar, and weapon systems, not galaxies, cloaking devices and warp drives. American submariners manned their outward facing terminals, and, out front and surrounded by dedicated screens, were two young men in bucket seats who drove the boat with joysticks: *California*'s planesman and helmsman. Commander Wolff ordered that a bathythermograph sensor be launched from the submarine's ejector tube.

The sonar watch supervisor reported a thermal—a sound-reflecting boundary between upper warm and lower cool water—at 100 feet. Wolff planned to take advantage of this acoustic membrane and bring his boat up to run just below the layer. *California*'s burly, tattooed chief-of-the-boat paced behind the center's seated submariners. He was, in turn, overseen by the officer-of-the-deck. Wolff and the XO leaned over the tactical table that displayed a line, marking the boat's course and summary data, including bearing, course, depth, and speed.

Sonar arrays mounted along *California*'s long lateral axis, and on her sail and forward hull, pulled in sound for the submarine's sonar system and, along with the big active array in the bow dome, could map the seafloor, localize minefields, pin-point the quietest of enemy submarines, and track far-off ships in transit. The computer heard something, and a red light blinked on *California*'s sonar station console. The sonarman leaned in to scrutinize the display. Called the waterfall, it showed all ambient noise in the form of cascading bars that represented bearing, frequency, and range of a sound's origination. The sonar technician reported the contact to his supervisor, and began the classification and identification routine.

"Conn, sonar," the sonar watch supervisor broke the control center's quiet. "Faint, submerged contact bearing three-one-zero. Designate: Sierra One."

Wolff and the XO moved to the sonar station. The officer-of-the-deck wandered over, too. The computer compared the new noise with a catalog of known signatures as the sonarman tried his best to discern a blade count.

"What do we have?" Wolff prodded his sound team.

"The screw sounds Russian to me; blade tip imperfections. No pump noise. Could be an SSK running on batteries, sir." The sonar technician had deduced they were listening to a diesel-electric submarine.

"Water beneath the keel?" Wolff asked.

"Two hundred, thirty feet," The XO replied. "Someone's in a hurry," he quipped. The contact, though quiet, was on a speed course and sacrificing stealth for speed. If it was a diesel-electric boat, its passive sensors would be degraded, making it harder to hear *California*.

"He's rushing right at us," Wolff licked his chops.

"Hey, that's fine with me," The XO countered. He preferred his enemies careless.

"Put us in a hover," Wolff told the XO. "And bring us just above the thermocline. Do it smartly." Wolff's glare said it all: you will be in a world of shit if they hear us.

"Conn, sonar. Sierra One classified as diesel-electric attack submarine," the sonar supervisor announced. "She's making turns for 18 knots."

"Fire control, begin localization and tracking," the officer-of-the-deck ordered. The tracking team began their target motion analysis.

"Sierra One is bearing three-one-five; course one-eight-zero; depth holding at 200 feet; range now 3,000 yards," fire control reported.

"Conn, sonar. Sierra One identified as *Kilo*-class diesel-electric attack submarine. Redesignating Sierra One as Kilo One."

"Steady as she goes." The chief-of-the-boat watched the helmsman and planesman level the boat at 70 feet. Now above the thermal layer with her acoustic cloak in place, *California*'s propeller turned lazy and quiet, just enough to maintain steerage in the current, and creep her long hull along. Her course zigzagged. This action enhanced bearing rates and ranging on the plot. Wolff readied to joust with his counterpart, and ordered *California* to battle stations, torpedo. The chief-of-the-watch sounded the general alarm. Crewmen scurried to their posts.

"Skipper, we have a firing solution," the XO informed.

"Very well, input presets."

"Fire control, Conn. Make selections for Mark 48 ADCAP, and input presets," the executive officer ordered. "Weapons, make tube one ready in all respects." The chief-of-the-boat repeated the orders and made sure they were followed. Beneath their feet, the submariners in *California*'s torpedo room sprang into action.

Four stout hatch covers lined the torpedo compartment's forward bulkhead, and racks of dark-green Mark 48 advanced capability heavy torpedoes covered its curved walls. A torpedoman

134

hoisted one of the weapons from its cradle and lowered it to a track. He removed a protective cover from the torpedo's blunt, black nose as another man unpinned the rammer that would slide the Mark 48 into the open launch tube.

"Pin out," the torpedoman observed. The torpedo began to move forward and slide into the open tube. "Good speed," he noted. From a dispenser at the torpedo's tail, the technician attached the Mark 48's umbilical to the submarine. The tube breech was sealed, and the hatch closed and locked. The tube's indicator placard was turned around, changed from 'Empty' to 'Warshot Loaded,' and a report went to the center that tube one was ready. *California*'s computerized combat system talked to the torpedo and readied the weapon to swim.

"Firing point procedures, tube one," Wolff ordered.

"Solution updated." The boat was ready for combat, the chief-of-the-boat reported.

"Weapon and tube ready, sir," the weapons officer confirmed.

"Okay," Wolff acknowledged. He had trained for this moment all his life and he savored it. "Match bearings and shoot, tube one," Wolff ordered. A button was depressed on the fire control panel and *California*'s air turbine pump drew in seawater to squirt the Mark 48 out. Shutter doors closed behind it, and, free of the hull, the American heavy torpedo accelerated to 55 knots. Trailing its umbilical, it rose above the thermal layer. *California*'s fire control technician used its seeker as an off-board sensor to update the firing solution.

"Fish is on the wire; running straight and true," *California*'s fire control supervisor reported to Wolff. The sonar and fire control team confirmed the enemy submarine was maintaining course and speed, seemingly unaware of the weapon now closing on their bow.

"Bring the torpedo below the layer and activate," Wolff told his executive. Instructions went down the wire to the Mark 48. The torpedo nosed down, penetrated and passed through the thermal convergence, and activated. High frequency sonar pinged away as the Mark-48 slowed to 40 knots.

The Russian-built Project 877 Paltus (Turbot) diesel-electric attack submarine's new Chinese owners had named her *Yuanzheng 65* in honor of the main character of the fictional historical novel, "Romance of the Three Kingdoms." Designated by NATO as belonging to the *Kilo*-class, *Yuanzheng 65* had raced out of the Taiwan Strait to intercept the US Navy's Task Force 16.

"Torpedo dead ahead." The announcement turned Chinese blood cold. *Yuanzheng 65*'s captain ordered ensonification bubblers. The noisemakers shot from *Yuanzheng 65*'s hull as she began to rise above the thermal boundary. Cursing himself for allowing his boat to be jumped, the Chinese captain wondered if he had made his last mistake. *Yuanzheng 65*'s sonarman believed the active weapon to be an American heavy torpedo. The captain sweated, and leaned against the pitch of the hull. Still on the wire, the American torpedo was told to ignore the noisemakers. It angled up and homed on *Yuanzheng 65*'s soft round belly. Then the torpedo knocked at the door.

"Conn, sonar. Large explosion to the south," *California*'s sonarman announced. "I have breaking up sounds from Kilo One's last position." The shock wave arrived and shook *California*. A young submariner hooted. He was quickly silenced, however, by stern

136

glances from the more experienced crew. Commander Wolff strolled over and pressed his weight on the respective man's shoulders. Forced down into his seat, this petty officer regretted the impulsive and unprofessional sound.

"That was pure luck. Exploitation of a careless skipper," Wolff whispered, although everybody in the silence of *California*'s control center heard his words and took them to heart. The admonished man stuttered acknowledgment. Wolff stood and ordered, "Take us up. We must share our good fortune." *California* leveled 60 feet beneath the chop.

Three masts poked through the surface and rose above the sea-spray. High-resolution cameras on *California*'s photonics mast looked for surface contacts while the electronics mast scanned for enemy radar and the antenna mast transmitted to *Lake Champlain* and ComSubPac Commander, Submarine Force, Pacific Fleet. In less than five seconds, *California* had taken in the world above, talked to Task Force 16, reported a kill to Pearl Harbor, and pulled in updated intelligence and orders.

Wolff read the transmission, and handed it to the executive officer. The XO unfolded reading glasses with his teeth and took a look. *California* was to be pulled from direct support of the task group and make a stealth approach to the outer channel of Dinghai Navy Base, home to the People's Liberation Army Navy's East Sea Fleet headquarters. The XO looked down at the computer-generated chart that Wolff had already brought up on the tactical table. Once on station, the XO continued reading, *California* was to execute her primary objective: placement of a minefield in the waters adjacent to the enemy base; with a secondary objective of reconnoitering vessel traffic, and eavesdropping enemy communications.

"Take us down, Tom," Commander Wolff muttered.

◊◊◊◊

The American supercarrier *Ronald Reagan* sailed with fair winds and following seas. Her group cut a broad cobalt path through international waters 200 miles east of Taiwan and 50 miles north of Japan's Ikema Island. On point and fresh from causing trouble were *Fort Worth*, *Lake Champlain*, and *Mahan*. They had rejoined the destroyers *Decatur* and *Gridley*, and the frigate *Thach* in a ring of steel around *Ronald Reagan*. With a shortage of submarines in the Pacific, the nuclear attack submarine *Connecticut* was sprinted to meet the newly formed carrier strike group. United States Navy Rear Admiral Norman Kaylo commanded the group from *Ronald Reagan*'s flag bridge.

Rear Admiral Kaylo was a rubicund, salty old seafarer with a sharp, stabbing glare. Standing over his own planning table, Kaylo noted his group had now moved within known range of China's East Wind missiles. Although strategic reconnaissance had confirmed *Ohio*'s Tomahawk strike had caused extensive damage to the Shaoguan missile base, American command still assumed that several of the enemy's specialized anti-ship ballistic missiles had survived. Kaylo went to the window and looked upon the sprawl of the supercarrier's flight deck.

An E-2 Hawkeye tactical airborne early warning aircraft held in position at the number one catapult. Enveloped in steam, the Hawkeye belonged to *Ronald Reagan*'s Black Eagles squadron. Its twin eight-bladed propellers hummed, and the large radar saucer on its back rotated. A 'green shirt'—a sailor responsible for aircraft launch and recovery—attached the Hawkeye's nose gear to the catapult tow bar as another green shirt displayed the Hawkeye's weight to the 'shooter.'

The shooter served as the aircraft launch and recovery officer, a proficient aviator who manned a small control room that stood proud of the flight deck. Based on the launching aircraft's weight, the shooter primed the catapult cylinder with steam. If the shooter were to set the wrong pressure—too much or too little—he would either rip the airplane's front wheel clear off or slowly drag the airplane into the sea. The shooter observed dials that indicated steam shunted from the reactors was building up. The Hawkeye's propellers reached a deafening roar as they tugged against the hold-back. The shooter saw the green shirt salute the Hawkeye's pilot. Then the green shirt crouched down and pointed along the short runway to the ship's bow. The shooter pressed a button. The catapult dragged the Hawkeye down the deck and flung it into the air. It sank momentarily, dipping below the lip of deck, and then powered out and climbed over the waves. Steam billowed across *Ronald Reagan*'s deck. Under the direction of a yellow shirted aircraft handler, a single engine twin-tailed F-35 Lighting II stealth strike fighter took position at the catapult. A 'Charlie' version of the US military's so-called Joint Strike Fighter; the carrier-borne version sported beefed-up landing gear and more wing area for improved low-speed handling.

The Lightning II was a haze-grey bird accentuated by dark-grey, saw-toothed lines, her only color a hornet and nest emblem on the twin tails. The aircraft's sharp lines and faceted sides were obviously stealthy in nature, and, nestled within the gold tinted canopy and wearing a sensor-covered helmet with a dark visor, the pilot appeared insect-like and alien. Her name, painted on the aircraft's side: LT. CYNTHIA 'CYNDI' PELLETIER.

CYNDI—Pelletier's call sign—was assumed by most to be an uncreative use of her first name, but instead stood for 'Check You're Not Dumping, Idiot.' The moniker stemmed from her first landing at sea. Pelletier had approached the carrier with her trainer's fuel dump valve wide open. With her trailing a stream of avgas, the carrier's captain had forever branded her. Now, Pelletier was in charge of the Navy's latest and greatest. The yellow-shirted deckhand formed an X with his arms, and Pelletier halted the Lightning II over the catapult's track.

A green shirt squatted beneath the airplane to ensure the landing gear tow bar was properly seated in the catapult shuttle. A water-cooled blast deflector popped up behind the Lightning II's big turbofan to keep its 41,000 pounds of thrust at bay. The green shirt re-emerged and gave Pelletier a thumbs-up. Completing final checks on the airplane, Pelletier touched the cockpit's single large liquid crystal display, and then looked up to confirm the attitude indicator was projected in the head-up display. She looked to *Ronald Reagan*'s short deck and the cold, unforgiving sea that lay beyond. She adjusted her back in the ejection seat and pushed her helmet against the rest. The shooter in the bubble went through final preparations.

"We're green." He confirmed the catapults were interlocked. "One at final, 23 forward."

The green shirt grabbed his wrist. "Good hook."

The shooter watched all deckhands get clear of the airplane. "Man's out."

The shooter was then signaled that the aircraft's power was at military and brakes had been released. Pelletier moved all the control surfaces. Happy, Pelletier locked her neck, placed her tongue on the roof of her mouth, and saluted. After final checks by deckhands for engine problems or leaks, they gave the shooter a thumbs-up.

"Winds?" The shooter checked the wind speed gauge, and confirmed gusts across *Ronald Reagan*'s bow were within tolerances. "Crosswinds are good."

The shooter confirmed that nothing was in the way of the airplane. "Clear forward."

He pushed the big red button on the console. The shuttle release bar broke and tons of steam pressure pulled the Lightning II along the deck, accelerating it to 170 miles-per-hour in two seconds flat.

"Gone."

Pelletier was sucked into her seat as the Lightning II shot airborne. The Lightning II accelerated, and climbed through a low cloudbank. Despite the deadly seriousness of her job, Pelletier giggled with excitement. She sucked dry air, pulled back on the stick, nudged the throttle, and rocketed skyward.

Moving at just past the speed of sound, the Lightning II settled at 40,000 feet, taking its place among *Ronald Reagan*'s combat air patrol. With her radar powered down to prevent detection, Pelletier linked her onboard computer with that of the Hawkeye, and tapped into the orbiting airborne early warning aircraft's sensors. This gave her a picture of the sky, and she noted a pair of friendly aircraft patrolling at a lower altitude. They were 'Rhinos,' she knew, Super Hornets nicknamed for the small bump on their nose. Pelletier listened in on ship chatter. Another F-18—an older Charlie version—sat waiting on the catapult. It could get airborne in seconds. Two more Rhinos were on Alert Five, and could also be airborne with just five minutes' notice. Time to check in, Pelletier thought. She clicked the transmit button.

"Stingtown One, on guard."

The morning sun peeked through the Jade and Richard's bedroom blinds. The dusty shaft of light climbed the mattress, crossed the folds and tucks of disheveled sheets, and then over Jade's feet. The beam reached Richard's face. His eyes opened.

Richard arrived at the Truman Building two hours later and hunkered down for another long day of work. With Secretary Pierce's increased reliance upon him, Richard had a whole new range of responsibilities, drawing jealous stares from co-workers. In the usually rigid hierarchy at State, the crisis had mutated the immutable. Richard had become the guy who floated around the organizational chart, a bubble that connected here and there, with dashed lines. Richard forewent a visit to the cafeteria and instead began to compile the morning reports provided by the Central Intelligence Agency and the Pentagon. He would glean data that came in from American embassies around the globe, compile and compress it, and write a summary for the secretary's breakfast brief. He thumbed through the documents and read about operations that had transpired as he slept:

The Chinese Arctic research vessel *Xue Long* (*Snow Dragon*) had been boarded and searched by an American warship, and a joint US-Panama operation had seized Chinese container facilities located at either end of the Panama Canal and found anti-shipping mines, likely thwarting plans to disrupt canal traffic. An American warship intercepted and halted the Chinese supertanker *Xin Pu Yang* (*New Port Ocean*) just outside Malaysian waters. Her belly was full of crude from Saudi Arabia, bound for Chinese refineries, factories, power plants, and vehicles. The sea lines of communication between the Middle East and Chinese shores were long, undefended, and traversed multiple chokepoints. Richard pondered this Achilles' heel as he began to type.

An hour later, the secretary of state closed her office door, removed a bran muffin and a double latté from a brown paper bag, and started to read Richard's report. With some food and caffeine in her, she went to work.

As midday in the American capital arrived, Secretary Pierce, Richard Ling, and several other aides and department heads again found themselves seated in the bunker beneath the Truman Building. Video screens displayed the deputy director of central intelligence and an army general. Secretary Pierce opened the meeting.

"Good morning, gentlemen. We, at State, have filed a resolution with the UN condemning the Communist invasion--"

"Won't the Chinese just veto it?" the general at the Pentagon interrupted immediately and with obvious contempt.

"Yes. Or abstain from voting. Despite a potential Chinese veto, we want the resolution filed. We believe this will help build diplomatic pressure on Beijing," the secretary continued. "Thailand and the Philippines have offered access to their bases, and the Japanese continue to be cooperative. As you know, the Australians have begun their own reconnaissance flights over the area, and are sharing their information. Thirty-seven American citizens—tourists and students mostly—have been evacuated from Taiwan via the American Institute, our de facto embassy. We have ordered all Chinese tourists and students out of the United States, and Air China has been denied landing rights within our territory. We helped move the Taiwanese government to Taitung City on the island's eastern shore, and have plans to spirit them to the Philippines should the need arise. How's the president holding up?" the secretary asked.

"Tired of hiding in the sky," the general said with a smile. "Okay. My turn. The *Reagan* carrier strike group and the 31st Marine Expeditionary Unit are approaching Taiwanese waters. We're beginning to implement our long distance blockade, and have stopped several of their tankers and cargo ships. They're calling us pirates, of course," the bearish general chuckled. "The PLAAF has secured an air corridor over the Strait, as well as superiority over the northern third of Taiwan. They have 33,000 men—three airborne divisions— already on the island, and hold major airfields at Hsinchu, Taipei, Taoyuan, and Yilan Counties." As the secretary listened, Richard slipped a political map of Taiwan in front of her and pointed out the counties in the north of the island. "Although Taiwan's army remains largely intact in the southern half of the island, anytime it tries to move north, bam, it gets turned back by Chinese air power. Right now, Taiwan's air force is scattered to highways and eastern bases, but retains substantial hardware and pilots. In the Taiwanese capital," the general grumbled, "the Commies are moving in on the civic center. We think they're attempting a decapitation, trying to get capitulation without having to occupy the whole shebang. We're seeing enemy preparations for a trans-Strait amphibious assault, too." The general rubbed tired eyes.

The deputy director of intelligence, dressed in a dark suit and his grey hair slicked back, leaned over his Langley office desk, and stated the Chinese amphibious assault would take place at Penghu County in the Strait, as well as at the strategic Port of Mailiao on Taiwan's western coast. He talked about resistance forming in Taiwan, and rumors of dissent within the People's Liberation Army and Politburo. "We are infiltrating agents into Taiwan, building resistance, and providing intelligence," he added.

The general—a man pulled fifty different ways—asked if there was anything else. The three executives realized they were done. After exchanging pleasantries, the video screens blued out.

Richard's cell phone beeped. A text had just arrived from an old college buddy, now over at the Department of Treasury. Richard shared the information he had just gained, with the secretary.

"There has been a massive sell-off in T-bills by the Chinese and Russians," Richard informed Secretary Pierce. "But the dollar seems to be holding steady, and the Europeans and Japanese are taking up some of the slack. Cell service appears to be back up, too." He held his phone up and smiled. Pierce put an arm around his shoulder, and asked Richard to join her for lunch. They strolled toward the elevator. When it arrived, Richard gestured for the secretary to go in first.

"After you," he smirked, revisiting a long-time shared joke, "it could be dangerous."

Pierce smiled and stepped in. The door slid shut and the cabin jerked, bouncing as it rose.

"How are things with your girlfriend?" Secretary Pierce asked. Taken aback, Richard tried to remember if he had ever mentioned having a girlfriend.

4: POUNCING TIGER

"Confront them with annihilation, and they will then survive; Plunge them into a deadly situation, and they will then live. When people fall into danger, they are then able to strive for victory."—Sun Tzu

General Zhen presided over Songshan Airport from his terminal office. He went over the timetable and tallied progress: the 43rd Division held Songshan Airport; the 44th: Chiang Kai Shek International Airport; and the 45th were dug in at Hsinchu Airfield southwest of Taipei. These elite units would not sit still for long, however. Zhen donned body armor and a helmet, and then headed for an armed Z-9 Haitun utility helicopter—a Chinese copy of the European-made Dolphin—that sat on the tarmac.

The pilot engaged the helicopter's main rotor and ducted fantail. A soldier in the open cabin offered a hand to General Zhen, and yanked him onboard. Whirring blades bit into the air, and the helicopter lifted from the asphalt, rising above Songshan. Zhen observed the capital beyond. Elements of the 44th were breaking out and blitzing southwest to the Toucian River on Taiwan's western shore. Explosions and fireballs reflected in the windscreen, lighting up the delighted General Zhen.

He watched as several Taiwanese Military Police units were swept aside by his forces. The Chinese armor and infantry surged toward the Toucian River. A brigade and regiment of his paratroopers had reached the shallow waterway that ran down the central mountains, flowing west to join the sea. Zhen would reinforce this line with army regulars that had poured into the captured airports.

The Toucian's pebbled bed was a no-man's-land, watched over by opposing trenches. On the northern bank, several thousand Chinese paratroopers and soldiers had assembled, now hiding in shadows and among buildings, crouching inside their infantry fighting vehicles and light tanks. Newly arrived Thunder Dragon main battle tanks roamed the captured city streets at will, and the Chinese had since humped in many light and heavy mortars, pointing their tubes south toward Taiwanese positions. Zhen contemplated his map.

Reconnaissance had said that two of the three bridges that spanned the Toucian were demolished—reduced to sagged wreckage—and only a freeway viaduct still crossed the river's gorge. Zhen knew he had to hold the river until amphibious forces could land on the island's south. The general looked up at the stars through the helicopter's whirring rotors. Unable to spare time or focus to contemplate their twinkling beauty, he sighed and considered: *Once the marines land, they will move north. I will push south, and pinch the Taiwanese defenders between my army and marines. Thusly, we will crush the Taiwanese in this sector.* General Zhen looked to the helicopter's cockpit console and the thermal image collected by the electro-optics bubble beneath the aircraft's nose. The view it showed panned along the river's southern bank. In the dark of early morning, there was little indication of what lay ahead.

◊◊◊◊

Elements of Taiwan's 6th Army now massed south of the Toucian River. These elements comprised elite armor, infantry

148

brigades, mechanized infantry, a special warfare brigade, and the 21st Artillery Command. An infantry division had also formed up in the urban area of Jhubei City. This division was oriented for the coming fray and ready to exploit breakthroughs or block enemy counterthrusts. In command of these forces and the coming counteroffensive was Republic of China Army Major General Tek Foo Chek.

Major General Tek sported a shaved head. His bulging arms sported tattoos with a leopard on one; and panda upon the other. These images rippled with every movement, and symbolized the duality of man, as well as the schism between Taiwan and the mainland. Tek looked hopefully to the gathering clouds. He knew the coming rain would break the humidity and conceal his army's movements. Tek scanned the far riverbank through binoculars. His deep-set eyes flickered with anger. The enemy occupied his land, and they would pay dearly for it. Seated cross-legged upon the ground next to Tek, a soldier specialist studied a small screen.

Its image came from a Hermes unmanned aerial vehicle that flew along the shallow river. Bought from Israel, the unmanned aerial vehicle's camera showed the body heat of a Chinese crew, manning a machinegun position. This targeting data was being shared with the Taiwanese artillery, helicopter gunships, and fighter-bombers assigned to frontal aviation. Loud and slow, the Hermes drew Chinese flak and soon disappeared from the sky. The soldier's screen blanked-out. Tek checked his watch, and nodded to the soldier.

"It is time," Tek decided. The soldier clicked a radio and transmitted a code phrase: "Pouncing Tiger."

Taiwanese field cannons—M-59 Long Toms, self-propelled M-110s, and towed M-115s—opened fire from beneath trees and camouflage nets. Truck-mounted multiple launch rocket systems joined the fray, in whooshing unison. Artillery rockets and shells screamed away and landed several miles to the north, detonating over Chinese infantry and mortars that dug into the riverbank. Positioned at the front, Taiwanese forward artillery spotters refined their fire by radio, making adjustments to where the high-explosive and phosphorus rounds landed.

Shells burst over enemy positions along the Toucian, spraying them with burning, sharp fragments. Those rounds that impacted lifted earth, rock, and flesh, and cascaded the mélange back down in a sickening rain. Illumination rounds washed Chinese armor, speeding troop carriers, and sprinting infantry with bright white light. A low thumping became discernible from the barrage's waning, rolling explosions. This thumping echoed in the distance, and then drew closer and grew louder. Suddenly, the Taiwanese artillery fire ceased as their attack helicopters came on scene.

Apaches: black flying tanks that kept low to the streets and spread out through the city, fluttering behind billboards and low buildings, and leaving only their rotor-top sensors to peek above such cover. The Apaches carried Hellfire anti-tank missiles on stub wings and a Chain Gun beneath armored fuselages. The lead aircraft slowed, reared to a stop, and hovered. Its gun swiveled, following the movements of its copilot/gunner's head as he scanned the battlefield. Before advancing to cause havoc, however, the Taiwanese Apaches would have to wait until their air force had knocked out Chinese flak cannons.

A lone Fighting Falcon swept in from the mountains, shrieking northwest along the freeway. Eight red stars adorned the Taiwanese fighter-bomber's fuselage; each representing a confirmed kill. There was a dent in the Fighting Falcon's empennage, a nick in its trailing edge, and a large repair patch beneath the squadron number and Taiwanese sun. The battle-worn jet carried two heat-seeking missiles, and two big cluster bombs slung beneath its wings. Where the external tank was usually mounted, the Fighting Falcon instead carried a night navigation and targeting pod. Major Han—Taiwan's first Ace of the war—was the Fighting Falcon's driver.

Anti-aircraft artillery had been spotted on the north bank of the river. Han's initial mission task was to take it out and then fly cover, protecting the ground hugging Apaches from marauding Chinese fighters. Han plugged data into the Fighting Falcon's impact point aiming system: air speed, bomb weight, and distance to target. He dropped the airplane through rain clouds. When they parted, the silvery sliver of the Toucian River showed in the canopy. Han used it to line up for the bomb run, and then kept the targeting computer's sliding indicators centered in the heads-up display. Flak started to burst around the jet, and Han saw muzzle flashes on the river bank. He weaved the Fighting Falcon through the fire and pressed on. The impact point aiming system showed two parallel lines that began to converge. When they met and flashed, Han pickled off the cluster bombs, a weapon his air force called 'Ten Thousand Swords.' There were two thumps. The airplane shook and, growing lighter, began to

151

climb. Han pulled back on the plane's stick. The Fighting Falcon's nose pointed skyward and the engine flamed as Han opened the throttle.

The spinning bombs dropped their casings and released a cargo of bomblets that dispersed and rained over the Chinese anti-aircraft emplacement, obliterating everything within a wide circle. Given the all clear, the Taiwanese attack helicopters went on the warpath.

An Apache hovered behind a parked seafood truck with a smiling fish on its side. The Apache showed only its rotor-top radar to anyone on the wide boulevard, where a Chinese main battle tank clanked along, traversing its main gun and sighting sensors. The Apache's pilot pulled back on the collective, and the helicopter rose from behind the cover, quickly firing a Hellfire anti-tank missile. The Apache dropped down again as the Hellfire skittered along the street.

The missile met the Thunder Dragon. Its tandem warhead bypassed the blocks of explosive-reactive armor that adorned the tank's squat, sloped turret and ripped into it. In the Chinese tank's crew compartment, metal spalled, ricocheted around, and tore everything to pieces. The Thunder Dragon's ammunition stores exploded. Blowout panels fluttered into the air. With its crew dead and much of its guts destroyed, the enemy tank lurched to a stop.

The Apache rose again from behind the truck, its gun and nose sensors swinging back and forth in search of threats. Looking for a new ambush position, and with a clear field-of-fire, the Taiwanese attack helicopter dashed over the burning enemy hulk. Several blocks away, another Apache hugged the riverbed. Its rotor's downwash blasted friendlies as they infiltrated the area.

Taiwanese army frogmen crossed the meandering shallows of the Toucian. With bowie knives and silenced gunshots, they neutralized several enemy soldiers, and disabled sapper charges set to blow the remaining bridge. Taiwanese armor surged north as a jet roared overhead.

Major Han exited his bomb run, and climbed over the river and out to sea. He pulled the Fighting Falcon into a loop and then settled back at 3,000 feet for another strafing run on enemy positions.

A Chinese paratrooper ran to the parapet of an apartment building's roof. He brought a Red Tassel anti-aircraft missile to his shoulder, and centered the Taiwanese jet in the launcher's reticle. The paratrooper flipped a switch on the launcher's pistol grip and locked the seeker on the Fighting Falcon's hot tailpipe, causing a bright flash as the Red Tassel launched.

Han saw a flicker in his peripheral vision and instinctively dropped flares, before snap-rolling the jet and climbing to escape. The Chinese missile swerved to the burning decoys and exploded. Han had no time to relax. A radar warning joined the tense chorus of cockpit sounds. A quick glance at the display showed two bandits approaching from the north. Subsonic and flying nap-of-the-Earth, Han surmised they were light bombers sent to silence the devastating Taiwanese artillery, and, if he was right, that meant enemy fighters could not be far off. Han swiveled his head around.

The rain had broken, and the cloudy, black sky admitted very little moonlight. Han turned the Fighting Falcon and activated the cannon, a gun site popping up in the heads-up display. Beside the projected site was '473,' the number of rounds left in his ammunition feeder drum. A new, intermittent high-altitude plot appeared on the radarscope. *That would be the fighter cover*, Han considered. He continued his charge at the Chinese attack aircraft, as they crossed the river: *Fantans*. The supersonic, single-seat warplanes with deeply swept broad wings had been named for the old game still played in the casinos of Macau. These particular Fantans were painted white and looked like bunnies as they hopped over the hills. Han noted that the Fantans hauled external fuel tanks and very big bombs.

"Pam One, Tally Ho," Major Han called out. He rolled in, lined up the crosshairs, and pulled the trigger. Flames erupted from the Fighting Falcon. From on high and behind, a shadow crossed the moon.

Arriving high above the battlefield, Chinese naval aviator Senior Lieutenant Peng observed the Taiwanese fighter emitting its tracer fire. Peng banked his big Flying Shark, and maneuvered to gain position on the enemy.

The Fantans took hits from Han. One of the light bombers careened into his wingman. Both spun into a hill and exploded in a fireball that lit up miles of city and sky. Han turned his attention to the Chinese fighter.

He toggled between radar modes, but found each one degraded by the weather. Han then slipped the Fighting Falcon into a dark, towering cloud. The cloud rattled Han's airplane, and droplets tapped the bubble canopy. Hypnotic grey mist rushed past. A momentary vertigo hit him, and Han's stomach protested with a wave of nausea. He looked down at his instruments. His head cleared and his belly settled, just in time for a blast of 30-millimeter fire from Peng's Flying Shark.

Peng matched every move the Taiwanese Fighting Falcon made. He twisted and rolled his Flying Shark, keeping his Taiwanese counterpart centered in the canopy-mounted infrared search and track system all the while. With his cover blown, Peng reached down and powered up his bird's radar.

The radar caution went off in Han's cockpit, quickly joined by a whooping missile warning. Han cursed. This meant that a radar-guided air-to-air missile was after him, likely the capable Chinese Lightningbolt. Han rolled the Fighting Falcon inverted, dumped chaff, and then edged over into a dive. Sucked into his seat, and with his eyes graying out, Han squinted to read the vibrating altimeter. *Fifteen thousand feet. Not good...* The missile alarm wailed again, the sound sending a now familiar cold chill down Han's sweaty back. He jerked the airplane left and right, chucked more decoys, and took the airplane supersonic.

Peng's missile veered from the metallic confetti of Han's chaff and pointed its nose back at the Fighting Falcon, closing on the hot fire of Han's engine nozzle. The Lightningbolt detonated and sprayed a cone of shot, small steel cubes that ripped into the Fighting Falcon's engine and stabilizers. The rear half of Han's airplane broke away and exploded. Slammed violently, he pulled the yellow handle between his knees.

Explosive bolts popped, and the canopy kicked free. A fist of air knocked Han unconscious. The seat harness snugged and the ejector rockets fired, lifting the seat and his limp body from the dead

155

airplane. A drogue pulled the main parachute free. The seat fell away, and a survival pack unrolled beneath Han as he floated gently toward the darkened town.

Peng's Flying Shark let out a contented snarl as it turned, but then Taiwanese ground fire harassed the Chinese pilot, throwing up a hail of sparkling fire. Peng climbed his machine to escape. Hanging high in a cloud, Peng saw the twisted wreckage of his vanquished foe burning in the city streets. He spotted a helicopter low over the Taiwanese lines. Tempted to roll in on it, a surface-to-air missile warning changed Peng's mind.

Taiwan's Major General Tek continued to observe operations from a Kiowa helicopter. Hovering just three feet off the ground, the Kiowa floated from behind an abandoned motor coach and provided Tek a thermal image of his main battle tanks and infantry fighting vehicles as they streamed across the bridge. *Although an Apache was lost to a rocket-propelled grenade ambush, the attack helicopters had served their purpose by taking a gruesome toll on enemy armor.* Furthermore, the artillery had devastated fixed Chinese positions, and with the enemy bloodied, Taiwanese armor had shown their stripes and carved out a bridgehead for infantry to storm the front.

"Move up," Tek spoke into the radio, and ordered the artillery to advance and gain a deeper reach into the city. For an entrancing moment, Tek watched the heavy rain that pelted the Kiowa's windscreen. Then he saw his Brave Tiger main battle tanks and eight-wheeled CM32 Cloud Leopard infantry fighting vehicles as they sped along the freeway. A rolling wedge, the Taiwanese armor dashed across the bridge. Tek told his pilot to move to the next vantage point.

The first Brave Tigers and Cloud Leopards sneaked across the span and fanned out. A missile tube emerged from a warehouse. It spewed a Red Arrow anti-tank missile that hit a Cloud Leopard, pierced the thin armor, blowing its turret and rear hatch off. The inferno vented, and a burning man stumbled out and collapsed. A Brave Tiger tank deployed a smoke screen and pointed its big gun at the warehouse.

"Sir, may I fire?" the Taiwanese gunner asked.

"For God's sake, shoot," the tank commander yelled, looking through his thermal site at the Chinese anti-tank crew as they reloaded their launcher. The tank's cannon boomed and lurched the heavy machine in recoil. Supersonic ball-shot stippled the warehouse housing the Chinese anti-tank crew.

"They're dead," the gunner morbidly observed.

A Taiwanese Brave Tiger tank punched through the smoke bank to push the wrecked Cloud Leopard infantry fighting vehicle aside. Another Cloud Leopard emerged from the smoke screen, sped to the first intersection, and dropped its rear ramp. The squad it carried exited, and the Chinese opened fire on them. Their muzzles flashed, illuminating the black windows of surrounding buildings. The Cloud Leopard opened up with its turret machinegun as the squad fought their way to a perimeter and secured the intersection. Beyond the river's southern bank, a small helicopter darted from behind a tree.

Major General Tek directed the helicopter pilot to gain a bit of altitude. The small Kiowa flew up to 100 feet. A roar overhead announced the arrival of a Taiwanese Mirage. The triangular jet dove through ribbons of rain and strafed Chinese infantry caught retreating.

157

Tek and his pilot shared a dark smile of approval at the slaughter. The pilot pointed to the screen. The heat signatures of several enemy tanks registered. A column of Chinese light and main battle tanks had rallied, and they were moving for the Taiwanese bridgehead.

"Gunner, main gun, tank," the commander of the lead Chinese tank ordered. "Identify CM11. Fire." A depleted uranium penetrator left for a Brave Tiger. With a shower of blue-yellow sparks, it pierced and killed the Taiwanese tank. A TOW missile arced in and serviced the Chinese main battle tank, its commander blown out the top. Two Apaches pounced on the rallying Chinese column and raked it with Hellfires. The lead tank was dead and burning, so the Taiwanese attack helicopters shifted fire to the column's trailing tank, trapping the rest between two shattered ogres. The Apaches then methodically butchered the rest. Although a Taiwanese Hellfire was already on the way to it, a Chinese main battle tank managed to get off a final cannon shot that ripped an Apache from the sky.

The last surviving Apache had run out of missiles. It reared, tipped, and banked away from the wasted enemy column. When the melee quieted, tree frogs again sang. *We have our foothold*, thought Taiwan's Major General Tek. He ordered his pilot to get him back on the ground.

◊◊◊◊

A summer storm had soaked DC, blowing off the stagnant humidity that had settled over the city, and replacing it with a dry, cool, steady breeze. Jade reclined on the couch, deep in study. Richard worked at his computer desk by an open window. He thumbed through papers as he researched potential diplomatic repercussions of a strike on a Chinese base in Sri Lanka. A muted commercial flickered on the television, and the 10 o'clock news started. Richard reached for the remote and turned up the television's volume.

News of the war led the program. Jade grunted with disapproval. The kettle whistling in the kitchen triggered Richard that it was his turn to brew the tea. He welcomed the distraction and obliged.

Richard returned with two steaming mugs and the day's mail tucked into his armpit. Jade accepted the cup from Richard, thanking him with a kiss. He returned to his desk, sipped his tea, and pawed at the mail. Pushing aside charity solicitations, furniture catalogs, and coupon clippers, he found a letter from Immigration & Customs Enforcement. The official letter bore Jiao Zhang's name, c/o Richard Ling. *It could mean only one thing*, he concluded. He spun in his chair.

"Hey, Jade?"

She quieted him with a finger to her lips, gesturing to the television and the breaking news it showed. Taiwanese citizens gathered before Taipei's parliament building, cheering and waving little red and gold flags of the People's Republic,.

"Look at this," she smirked.

◊◊◊◊

The midday sun blared. Chinese paratroopers were dressed in festive outfits and baseball caps, holding back loyalist throngs that had gathered outside the Taiwanese parliament. On a small stage preened General Zhen and Ai Bao Li, vice president of the People's Republic of China. Lined up on either side of the two Chinese officials was an apprehensive collection of Taiwanese legislators representing both the pro-unification and pro-independence parties. Of course most stood there under threat of arrest. Vice President Ai stepped to the microphone. It squealed, and the crowd quieted.

"My fellow Chinese," the Party man paused and gestured to the bright, clear sky. "The sun has risen on a new day in China's long and glorious history: the criminal separatist regime in Taipei has been deposed. It is, therefore, my pleasure to announce the new chief executive of the Taiwan Special Administrative Region of the People's Republic of China, Yao Ou Pei." Ushered by applause, whistles, and cheers from the carefully selected crowd, Taiwan's new Communist head of government emerged and strode to the microphone.

"Thank you, my fellow citizens, thank you." Chief Executive Yao bowed his head and waved sheepishly. "I," his voice cracked, "address the people of a united China, the world's greatest power, and also, our neighbors in the international community. My first directive as chief executive of Taiwan," his voice grew stern, "is an order to all military units of the former regime to cease hostilities against liberating forces of the People's Republic. Abandon your weapons and uniforms now. Compliance brings assurances that no further harm will befall you. Brave soldiers of Taiwan…go back to your families." The crowd roared again and the region's chief executive crossed his arms and smiled approvingly. Letting the applause linger, he theatrically raised a hand. The crowd calmed. "Effective immediately, Taiwan and its island territories comprise the 23rd province of the People's Republic of China. As head of government, I shall appoint all ministers to the legislative and executive councils. Like Hong Kong, Macau, and Tibet, Taiwan will enjoy 20 years of semi-autonomy. Finally, I entreat the international community— particularly the United States of America —not to interfere with this peaceful reunification. Leave the internal affairs of China to the Chinese people. As lovers of peace, we wish to cease hostilities, and rebuild a fruitful future with our foreign friends and partners. Citizens of Taipei, citizens of Taiwan, citizens of the People's Republic, it is indeed a glorious day. Long live China. Long live Taiwan. And long live the Communist Party." Chief Executive Yao raised his arms to the sky. Accentuating the moment, three Vigorous Dragons shrieked overhead, trailing red and yellow smoke from their wingtips. A Chinese news crew focused their lens on the joyful tears of a woman who clutched her child and patriotically squinted skyward. General Zhen, Vice President Ai, and Chief Executive Yao smiled and shook hands.

◊◊◊◊

"Unbelievable," Richard said, impressed by the political spectacle on his television. Jade had spotted the official-looking envelope among the junk mail. She tore into it with a manicured nail and read.

"They revoked my student visa," Jade choked. Realizing she was about to cry, Richard grabbed her hand for comfort. "I have one week to go home," she managed before she sobbed. Richard pulled her close and hugged her tight, feeling her slight but sturdy body tremble. Her warm tears dripped to his bare arm.

"They cannot do this to you," he cried. "It's unfair catching students up in international games." She looked up to him. Her face porcelain and her eyes, moist with tears, glistening like wet coal. Richard could smell her hair; floral and clean. He would do anything for her. He pulled her closer and shot a glance deep into her soul. He kissed her like it was their last kiss. When they parted, Jade smiled, though the smile quickly disappeared, replaced by the worry that permeated her. He knew he could not be without her. He admitted to himself what he already knew.

"I love you, Jade," he declared.

"I love you, too," she whispered, and sighed.

"This is going to be difficult." He held her tighter.

"More than you think. I'm pregnant."

◊◊◊◊

Senior Master Sergeant Li and his men huddled around Hill 112's only working radio, eating the last of their rations. Smoke from a small cooking fire vented through the shattered bunker's ceiling as moisture dripped down twisted rebar and collected in silted pools. The change of government ceremony ended, and the radio broadcast concluded with the national anthem of the People's Republic. A soldier snuffed the radio racket with a click. The men looked to the senior master sergeant who rubbed his injured arm. One asked if this meant the war was over. Another, if Taiwan had surrendered. Li realized he must act quickly to stem the confusion. Li scanned the apprehensive faces that awaited an answer. He stood and said:

"We have not surrendered, and we do not take orders from the Communists or their lackeys. Understood?" The response was hesitant and lukewarm. One soldier said he had not talked to his wife in a week. He had no idea how his children had fared. This caught Li unprepared and momentarily snuffed the flame that grew inside. *What of my own wife and child*? He wondered.

"Senior master sergeant, sir," an airman interjected. "For all we know, we're holding out for nothing. We've even lost contact with command."

"This is exactly what the enemy wants, doubt and confusion in our ranks. We are fighting for our country and our way of life. Are you willing to roll over so easily? Are you all strawberries like the Communists say? Does your liberty mean that little to you?" While he framed his words in questions, Li wanted no rebuttal.

"I don't want to die," a young conscript whined. Li, exhausted, sat back down. There was a long pause. A jet—probably Chinese—roared overhead. Unknown to the men on Hill 112, several sympathetic Taiwanese officers—Communist stooges in positions of command—had succeeded in disarming and dismissing major elements of Taiwan's army. Although the professional units did not succumb to this psychological operation, large numbers of soldiers had abandoned their positions and weapons. Li scanned the semicircle of men that surrounded him.

"How many of you wish to desert?" Li asked, with a cautionary choice of words. Several hands started to rise timidly. Li's first instinct was to grab his assault rifle and execute the traitors on the spot. He fought this instinct and, instead, said, "You are free to go."

Several airmen and soldiers stood, disgusting Li. Without making eye contact, he insisted they leave their identification and uniforms behind. Then, in a blur, a seated soldier raised his gun. Another man screamed for him to stop, but the soldier cursed and opened up on the deserters. The bullets propelled them backward into a dark corner of the bunker. While one man still twitched, they were soon all dead. With ears ringing and head swimming, Li saw the shooter splattered with magenta polka dots. The assault rifle exhaled a twist of smoke from its bore. Li grabbed his own rifle and hit the shooter with the butt. The shooter fell backward onto a rock that knocked him unconscious. In the still air of the bunker, gun smoke lingered in dancing layers. One soldier cried. Li covered the bodies with a rain tarp, collected himself, and stood before the remaining men.

"We are soldiers of the republic. We will hold until relieved or killed. Is that understood?" The men nodded, coaxed by the firmness of Li's voice. He pointed at the unconscious shooter. "This man is under arrest for murder, and will face a court-martial. These men are deserters, but they did not deserve to die like this. Li began to secure the unconscious shooter with handcuffs.

"Sir, the Chinese. They will be here any moment. How can we--" A sharp glance from Li cut him off.

"They'll overrun us. Kill us all," another man picked up where the soldier had left off.

"You are all strawberries," Li shouted. "They should have sent your girlfriends and wives, instead."

One soldier stood, and snapped to perfect attention.

"Senior Airman Hong Xu. I am ready for duty."

One-by-one, the Taiwanese air stood. Each stated their rank and name, albeit some reluctantly and halfheartedly. Nonetheless, Li was inspired.

"Sir, we need food. I suggest we journey into town. We can use civilian clothes," the senior airman proposed. Li smiled.

"We also need a radio; preferably a military one," Li said. The waning adrenalin had left him shaky. He put his face in his hands.

◊◊◊◊

From within his air-conditioned office that overlooked Songshan airport's tarmac, General Zhen reviewed maps and timetables. He rested a stubby digit on the map. It covered several small islands in the Strait that comprised Taiwan's Penghu County. On the largest isle were Magong City and its small airport. By the runway was a Taiwanese Sky Sword air defense site. *We must seize the airport and destroy the surface-to-air missile battery*, Zhen plotted. Operation Red Dragon called for the Chengdu Military Region Special Forces Unit—The Falcons, as they were called within the People's Liberation Army—to seize these targets. Zhen lit a cigarette, sipped some coffee, and rubbed his aching temple.

◊◊◊◊

A heat shimmer appeared on the Taiwan Strait's horizon. This mirage obscured a grey hull. The 150-foot Chinese landing craft *N7579* thumped through the moderate chop, her bow visor shielding the landing ramp from the sea. One mile southeast of the target airfield, the big craft approached the quiet Taiwanese beach and scraped ashore. *N7579*'s bow visor swung up and her cargo of Falcons streamed down the landing craft's ramp.

Carrying futuristic bullpup assault rifles, and wearing blue, white and black camouflage, the Falcons waded through waist-high water and stormed the beach. They dropped to the sand at a line of barrier dunes. A strolling elderly Taiwanese couple stopped to watch the commotion, and a Chinese officer politely urged them to leave. An invader stabbed a red signal flag into the dunes, now flapping in the shore breeze.

With the Falcons ensconced on the beach, a tracked ZBD05 Sea Storm amphibious infantry fighting vehicle rolled down *N7579*'s ramp. Painted shades of blue, the Sea Storm clawed up the dunes, and its 30-millimeter cannon and Red Arrow anti-tank missile launcher menaced the swath of shoreline. The Sea Storm led ashore a 6x6 cargo truck carrying ammunition, food, and water. The truck sank into the gravel, but then its powerful diesel engine coaxed the truck ahead. As the truck negotiated the soft sand, *N7579* reversed her powerful, ducted propellers, raised her bow ramp, and lowered her bow visor. Kicking up mud and sand from the bottom, *N7579* backed away from the beach. The Falcons bound inland under cover of the infantry fighting vehicle and its cannon and missiles.

Where rough shore road met the pavement of Penghu County's Route 204, the Chinese Sea Storm infantry fighting vehicle stopped at the airfield perimeter fence, and waited for the sprinting special forces to catch up. When the Falcons made it, the vehicle pushed down the fence, and raced onto the airfield and its rubber-streaked concrete runway. Followed by their supply truck, the Falcons made their way down the runway. They blasted and disabled a small Taiwanese helicopter, as well as a single Mirage already stripped of parts that had been abandoned in place. The Falcons dashed for the far end of the field. The speeding Sea Storm locked one of its Red Arrows on the primary target—the airfield's Sky Sword surface-to-air missile battery—and sent the anti-tank missile on its way. The Red Arrow impacted the Sky Sword's rectangular quad launcher and exploded the Taiwanese emplacement in an inferno of solid rocket fuel and high explosives.

The Chinese Sea Storm then rolled up and shredded the emplacement's radar antenna with cannon fire. The Sea Storm's hull ramp dropped and a breach team dismounted. Wearing gas masks, these Falcons burst into a small Taiwanese command trailer. Muffled gunshots and a small explosion followed, and smoke and gas vented from the trailer. A Falcon emerged. He made a fist, signaling, mission accomplished.

Then, with a sound like rocks knocked together, a firefight heated up between a Taiwanese platoon and a Chinese security detachment. Men had fallen on both sides, when the pops of gunfire subsided. The Falcons then shifted their attention to secondary objectives, including sabotaging several more aircraft and seizing airport vehicles, including fuel bowsers and cargo trucks. When the Falcons reported they had taken the abandoned terminal and the control tower, their commander, seated within the infantry fighting vehicle, transmitted an encrypted success code. Loitering over the Taiwan Strait, several Chinese airplanes received this code and turned toward their destination.

Eight minutes later, a single Candid strategic transport lined up on the captured airfield's runway, and entered a steep descent. The heavily loaded airlifter touched down, and the pilot immediately deployed spoilers, reverse thrust, and then brakes. Struggling to slow down and not overrun the short runway, the airplane wobbled along the runway's centerline and, with brakes smoking, the big Chinese transport stopped at the crux of concrete and grass. Using brakes on one side and engine thrust on the other, the Candid pilot skillfully spun his airplane in place, lined it up for a rapid departure, and then stopped. He 'kneeled' the big airplane, using its hydraulic lowering capability, as on some city buses. He then lowered its tail ramp. A machine growled inside its hold, announcing its presence.

Trailing a ribbon of black diesel smoke, a Thunder Dragon main battle tank rolled from the Candid's interior. It clanked off toward the airfield's small terminal, now called, 'The Falcon's Nest.' A self-propelled Favorit surface-to-air missile transporter-launcher was next to emerge from the Candid. It drove carefully down the ramp and headed toward a collection of hangars. Since the Candid was highly vulnerable while on the ground, and had already deposited its clutch, the big bird hurried to leave. Four turbofans unrolled a carpet of thick smoke, and the lightened Candid rotated and climbed into the sky. Once clear, another airplane lined up on the runway and began its descent, the first of three passenger airliners tasked to ferry Chinese soldiers to the small Taiwanese island.

With only four Taiwanese army platoons and some police at hand, the mayor of Magong City ordered his police chief to lower the flag flying above City Hall. In hopes of sparing the town and its citizens from violence, a white one was raised in its stead. Torn by the decision, the mayor stepped onto his apartment's balcony. He heard the pleas of his police chief again, and they echoed in his head. A low rumbling reverberated from Magong City's airport. Two Vigorous Dragons roared overhead. These Chinese aircraft shook the old building to its foundation. Heartbroken to see Communist jets roaming freely through Taiwanese skies, the mayor began to sob.

◊◊◊◊

With overwhelming airpower at its back, Chinese naval surface groups punched through the Taiwanese naval forces. With the cream of Taiwan's navy out of the way, Chinese amphibious operations commenced forthwith.

Painted orange by the late afternoon sun, the men and machines of China's 1st and 2nd Marine Brigades assembled off the west coast of Taiwan. The collection of landing ships, hovercraft, and troop transports sailed for the strategic Taiwanese ports at Mailiao, site of a petroleum terminal and tank farm; and to Kaohsiung, with its vast container facility. A third amphibious prong would hit the beaches of Liuqiu, a geographically important islet off the southwest coast of Taiwan's main island. At Kaohsiung, along with several other merchantmen similarly trapped in the Taiwanese port, the Greek bulk carrier *Himitos* lay at anchor.

Having watched missiles and airplanes crisscrossing overhead for two days, her captain enjoyed some momentary quiet on the bridge. Sipping a coffee and fingering a string of worry beads, he looked out over the ship's four big deck cranes, and then out to the port's breakwater and the Strait beyond. Squinting into the glaring sunset, the Greek spotted two inflatable raiding boats on the horizon.

A small Chinese flag whipped from the lead boat's radio antenna. A Chinese marine surveyed the port and spoke into his radio. The rubber raiders came about. Smoke generators started up and chugged thick grey smoke that concealed the port's entrance. The cloud lingered, and the sound of machines grew from within it. Air cushioned personnel landing craft rode inflated skirts, emerged, and sped into the harbor.

Each hovercraft docked at a tire-lined concrete wharf and disembarked its team of Chinese operators, who sprinted for the terminal's power distribution grid and fresh water manifold. Pushed by three ducted propellers, a huge hovercraft trudged past the breakwater, passing by a quay stacked with multi-colored containers waiting to be loaded on ships, trains, and trucks. Then the hovercraft lined up with a boat ramp. Big propellers reversed and blasted, slowing and stopping the Chinese hovercraft on the ramp. The craft's bow door opened. Crab amphibious armored personnel carriers and a Dragon Turtle light tank scuttled out and climbed the seaweed-covered incline. The two smaller hovercrafts turned and led the larger one from the harbor.

The Crabs and the Dragon Turtle sped for the main wharf; a concrete appendage sized to accommodate modern container ships, and positioned themselves by the wharf's travelling gantry crane. Assault squads dismounted. The all-clear was given and two big troop transport ships prepared to dock.

The ships came in fast for their size, and kicked up mud and sand as they slowed and paralleled the wharf. Lines were secured and gangways lowered. Beating their best practice time, 800 Chinese marines disembarked. At the port's southern perimeter, amphibious armored personnel carriers, light tanks, and infantry fighting vehicles swam ashore and scrambled their way up the muddy embankment. They fanned out and secured the flanks and the terminal's perimeter road, and established a strongpoint at Highway #71, blocking the major north-south artery, the most likely route for a Taiwanese counterattack. Vigorous Dragons swooped in and flew menacingly low over the water, making their presence known. They screamed over the Greek ship. The sound and spectacle sent her officers ducking again. Down the coast, the Chinese amphibious assault on Mailiao was equally successful. It was on the sleepy Taiwanese island of Liuqiu that unexpectedly fierce resistance was met, however.

Coastal Huandao Road overlooked the long beach on Liuqiu's eastern shore. Civilians—fishermen mostly—had been organized by the island's military police unit. It was on Huandao Road that they watched, peering out to sea through binoculars. With lawn chairs, smoky grills, and full coolers, the beach watch had become a social gathering where they discussed war and politics, and took turns scanning the calm horizon. Although Chinese ships passed frequently, none had yet turned for Liuqiu. Speaking his native Lamai dialect, one lookout reported all clear with a walkie-talkie and put his eye back to his hobby telescope. Sandy, serene beaches sprawled below the cliffs upon which he was perched.

They had been prepared with firing positions and ammunition caches. Announced and discussed in the town square, the plan for defense comprised a reaction force of men and weapons able to rapidly mobilize, deploy, and employ to counter an attack originating from any direction. The coastal road that circled the kidney-shaped island was perfect for getting the small force of trucks, tanks, and infantry to the right spot, while paths in the wooded hills facilitated ambushes and strategic retreats. Although the enemy could assault Liuqiu from any compass point, most expected a landing on the flat, open eastern beach. The lookout again focused the telescope, and noticed that several silhouettes had appeared on the horizon. They were small boats with hunched shapes aboard, he noted. He clicked his walkie-talkie and reported. The sound of motors arrived on the breeze.

Taiwanese military police, stationed in the nearby harbor, jumped into their vehicles and sped off. They then manned their trench positions and weapons, and readied heavy machineguns and anti-tank missiles. A single Brave Tiger main battle tank joined the deployment, clattering up the hill and positioning itself into a prepared revetment that protected its hull and provided a clear field of fire over the beach. Taiwanese soldiers and militiamen draped camouflage netting over the tank, and set machinegun crews and snipers, to over-watch on the flanks. Mortar crews elevated their tubes to predetermined settings. In a trench line that zigzagged, soldiers braced their rifles, pressing their butts into their shoulders. Having hurried, the Taiwanese now awaited that which became inevitable.

Chinese pathfinders weaved through the breakwater and came ashore in rubber dinghies, dragging their boats onto the sand. The Chinese marines spread out and dropped prone. With the area seemingly quiet, they fired a flare that climbed to the sky and arced. This signal invited the main force to commence landings.

172

The rumble of diesel engines arose from the darkened horizon. Packed with Chinese marines, a line of landing craft emerged from the dusk and sped toward the beach, their square bows smacking the waves. Within the open hold of one craft, a man vomited on the back of another, starting a chain reaction of puke. Chinese amphibious armor, bobbing on the rolling surface, followed these craft. Whistles were blown amid "Beach in sight" screams. The flat bottoms of the landing craft rode up onto the beach, crunching on rocks and sand, and bow ramps crashed down. The Taiwanese opened fire.

One of the rectangular craft became a flesh blender as Taiwanese heavy machinegun fire ricocheted within. Another disgorged screaming Chinese marines into the surf, and guns up on the bluff hosed them down. More landing craft scraped ashore, spilling men onto the beach. These Chinese invaders took several steps before the cliff-top machineguns traversed their way. Mortar rounds burst in the air and on the beach, showering the invaders with hot needles of metal. Men fell beneath this unnatural rain, and a sickly pinkish foam spread over the gentle surf. A few Chinese scampered to a beach boulder and fired blindly back at the wooded hill. A Chinese Dragon Turtle light tank dragged itself onto the beach.

The Dragon Turtle fired its coaxial machinegun, raking the dunes. A Taiwanese soldier at the edge of the woods aimed his tripod-mounted TOW missile at the front of the Chinese light tank and pulled the trigger. The TOW arrived and served the enemy tank with a shaped charge warhead that pushed high-velocity molten copper through the tank's dense steel shell, doing bloody murder within. The tank stopped and smoldered at water's edge. High above the beach, from the safety of its revetment, the Taiwanese tank fired its main gun and pummeled enemy landing craft with armor piercing rounds. It then switched to deadly ball shot to blast the Chinese marines. Those lucky or skilled enough to make it to the dunes ran into mines that exploded before them, scattering ball bearings and shrapnel, leaving only stained boots where men once ran. Shrieking across the beach, a Chinese Fantan strike aircraft dove in and strafed the overlook.

A Stinger missile shot from the forest canopy knocked off the Fantan's vertical stabilizer. The Fantan spun in and exploded on a shallow reef. Two more Chinese attack aircraft swept in to drop cluster bombs on the trench line. One dropped a laser-guided bomb on the Taiwanese tank as more Fantans came in low over the water and screamed over the landing craft and amphibious armor, tossing cylinders into the woods. Gelatinous gasoline—napalm—ignited and sucked the oxygen from the air, suffocating those it did not incinerate. The Taiwanese were stunned by the close air support during which several more landing craft had sneaked in and deposited marines on the beach.

Liuqiu's commander had suffered many casualties and his one tank had been destroyed. He initiated a well-practiced retreat. Under rocket and machinegun fire, the Taiwanese abandoned their positions. Snipers provided final cover fire as the last of the defenders melted into the woods or sprinted to camouflaged vehicles and sped away. With his remaining men safe, the Taiwanese commander jumped into a last pickup truck. He flipped open a cell phone, dialed a number, and pushed [Send].

Buried beneath the beach's sand was a 2,000-pound aerial bomb, connected to another cell phone. This cell phone rang and triggered the buried aerial bomb. Everything above the improvised explosive device disappeared in fire, sand and flesh raining back down. The flood tide quickly claimed the large crater as a pool. Beneath a small black mushroom cloud, the beach became momentarily quiet, and a seabird landed to pick at the carnage. Diesel engines rumbled once more as the Chinese landing continued. Amphibious armored personnel carriers, light tanks, and landing craft that carried trucks and marines arrived to claim the beach and cliff. They staked out the shore road and moved on to the nearby harbor.

The Chinese spread out and secured key junctions in town. The Chinese troop transport *Xuefengshan—Snow-peaked Mountain—* lingered offshore, where she finally signaled and turned for Liuqiu's small port. Twenty minutes later, *Xuefengshan* had docked and unloaded 200 marines, ammunition, light vehicles, supplies, and a Favorit surface-to-air missile battery that was hurriedly set up beside the harbor's riprap breakwater.

General Zhen picked at a dinner tray resting on maps arrayed across his desk. With scant appetite, Zhen instead poured another cup of coffee—his sixth so far today—and walked to the window. Songshan, now an efficient Chinese base, operated smoothly as airplanes and helicopters came and went, a line of MiG 29 Fulcrums took on fuel and weapons, and, bathed in yellow spotlights, paratroopers ate at a kitchen trailer. Knowing battle lay in front of them, they then cleaned weapons and rested on cots. Zhen took a shaky sip of coffee, stood, and went to a map pinned to a wall. On it he saw red markers, covering Kaohsiung, Liuqiu, and Mailiao. *With these ports secure*, he strategized, *we can shift from aerial to maritime supply*. Zhen removed a green pushpin from the mainland port of Xiamen and stuck it into the Taiwan Strait.

The pin represented the *Star of Peace*, a large commercial liner drafted into the service of the republic. Designed to carry 400 passengers, *Star of Peace* now managed 1,000 soldiers and their gear, crammed aboard. A tank landing ship sailed with the liner, and bore 200 men from the 164th Marine Brigade, their kit, artillery, and several light tanks. Although Zhen knew the air force and navy had sunk the last of Taiwan's capital ships, he worried about enemy submarines not yet been accounted for. These was why the liner and tank landing ship—both bound for the port of Bali at Taiwan's northern tip—were under escort of the frigate *Anshun*, as well as various small patrol craft. Zhen looked at his watch. In two hours, the ships would arrive and unload. Once marshaled in port, the marines and soldiers the ships transported would move through the occupied zone of the Taiwanese capital, secure the strategic intersection of Sun Yat Sen Freeway#1 in Wugu, and then establish a fire base in the parking lot of a shopping center next to the freeway's cloverleaf interchange. From this shopping center, Zhen's force would be able to police access to the city center and control downtown without actually having to occupy it.

Zhen was proud of his plan. He had studied many urban battles, especially the defense of Stalingrad by Soviet Georgy Marshall Zhukov, and therefore knew to avoid engaging the enemy in difficult urban warfare where tanks lost their advantage, and where his men

176

lacked experience and proficiency. Unlike Friedrich Paulus and the German 6th Army, Zhen would not be drawn into house-to-house fighting, but chose instead to bypass and choke off areas of resistance, much like the Americans when they fought Imperial Japan in the Pacific. *This standoff plan*, he reminded himself, *will minimize the impact of war upon the capital, on the local citizenry, and the Taiwanese economy.* Furthermore, this force would be available to relieve pressure on the Toucian River Front where his forces had seemingly stalled. General Zhen lit the first of his two traditional after-meal cigarettes, taking a long drag. He checked his watch. He was due in Beijing for a conference, but Zhen hated such bureaucratic distractions. *Perhaps the president might accept a videoconference?* His mind returned to a familiar place: the contemplation of strategy; and looked at a cluster of blue pushpins at the edge of the map. He growled contemptuously: "The American navy."

With the Taiwan Straits closed, the Malaysian-flagged container ship *Bunga Teratai Satu—Lotus Flower One*—steamed 60 miles east of Taiwan. A colored quilt of stacked containers, each full of automobile, computer, and television parts bound for Pusan, South Korea, covered her vast decks. The captain pushed the engines, steaming hard and fast to pass waters in turmoil. He noted the fuel readout and engine power levels, and cursed that they were burning twice as much fuel as usual for the run. The bridge officers reiterated the reluctant acceptance of safety over profit. Then, a blinding light filled *Bunga Teratai Satu*'s bridge.

The officers shifted nervously as the light grew brighter and a rumbling vibration swelled. The light extinguished and a jet roared low over the container ship's bridge, close enough that some of the sailors instinctively ducked. With a lighted US NAVY on its side, a Super Hornet passed again and wagged its wing lights at the mammoth merchantman. On *Bunga Teratai Satu*'s radar screen, at its outer edge, appeared a large green mass, surrounded by several other, smaller ones.

Twelve thousand yards to the north, the American nuclear supercarrier *Ronald Reagan* turned into the wind as she conducted night flight operations. Protecting the goliath were the destroyers *Decatur*, *Gridley*, and *Mahan*, the cruiser *Lake Champlain*, the frigate *Thach*, and the littoral combat ship *Fort Worth*. Besides having a combat air patrol up, the *Ronald Reagan* carrier strike group had two Seahawk helicopters out on anti-submarine warfare patrol. Furthermore, a Poseidon maritime patrol aircraft had flown out of Japan and, flying a mid-altitude racetrack pattern, watched over the vicinity. The American sub hunter, a grey and windowless military variant of the popular 737 twin-engine airliner, carried Barracuda torpedoes, mines, and SLAM anti-ship missiles, and could detect magnetic distortions with its tail boom. The Poseidon leveled out for the next leg of its search pattern. High above, a deuce of *Ronald Reagan*'s Super Hornets kept a weather eye open for bandits. Besides the Poseidon, *Ronald Reagan*'s anti-submarine picket included the destroyer *Decatur*. She sprinted ahead of the group, and then slowed to a drift to listen to the water with her towed sonar. In *Decatur*'s combat information center, the computer and sonarman analyzed the collected sounds.

Decatur's sonarman adjusted a dial on his console, and typed commands at a keyboard. Then he held his headphones tight to his ears. Among background noise and the slashing of the Malaysian merchantman's twin four-bladed propellers, he thought he heard a low thumping. However, the computer insisted the sound belonged to a fully loaded container ship. Although trained to trust technology, the sonarman's human ear told him there was something else there, something the machine had missed.

Beneath the keel of *Bunga Teratai Satu*, matching the gargantuan cargo ship's speed and course, the Chinese nuclear attack submarine *Changzheng 6* prowled.

"Sir, American surface group includes an aircraft carrier," *Changzheng 6*'s sonar station operator reported excitedly.

"Load bow tubes with wake-homing torpedoes. Fire control, get me a solution on that carrier immediately," Captain Kun ordered, and rocked on his heels. With hands behind his back, Kun announced tactics. His chief officer concurred and pushed the orders down the chain. *Changzheng 6* would ripple fire torpedoes, reload, fire again, and then run for the deep. The men had drilled for this, and had the procedure down to mere minutes, all without compromising safety. From under *Bunga Teratai Satu*, *Changzheng 6* shot six Sturgeon heavy torpedoes in a tight fan pattern. The tubes were then rapidly reloaded with cone-shaped Squall torpedoes. In the submarine's weapons room—a warren of pipes and valves—the supervising torpedoman reported to the attack center and clicked his stopwatch. He and the men had made record time.

The VA-111Shkval (Squalls) spit from the hull by a blast of compressed air. Tail fins snapped out and rocket motors ignited with a pop. Combustion gas shunted to the front of the weapon where it exited to form a bubble around the casing, a super cavity. Flying through water as though it were air, the Squalls quickly reached over 200 knots. From beneath *Bunga Teratai Satu*'s keel, *Changzheng 6* crash-dived into the abyss. Coming about in a sharp turn, her seven-bladed screw bit the black water to push her deep.

A red light blinked on *Lake Champlain*'s sonar station and green bands cascaded down its screen.

"Holy shit," the American sonarman exclaimed, as he was almost physically shoved backward by surprise. "Torpedo, torpedo, torpedo," he called out, and then steadied himself in the chair to study the range of new sounds. There were several high-pitched screws and a strange sizzling sound like steaks on a grill. A new frequency band appeared on the display. The sonarman heard the familiar sounds of a nuclear reactor. "Certsub," he declared. "Bearing: one-eight-zero. Range: 11,000 yards. She's diving." Captain Ferlatto ordered the launch of several ASROCs—anti-submarine rockets that deliver lightweight torpedoes. The ASROCS left *Lake Champlain*'s stern missile deck. They glowed as they flew down the bearing of the enemy torpedoes and straight at the panicked Malaysian merchantman. *Lake Champlain* turned to zero-nine-zero—due east—and her turbines came to full power. The frigate *Thach* came hard over to zero-zero-zero and accelerated, too. *Ronald Reagan* and the destroyers *Decatur*,

Gridley, and *Mahan* turned to zero-four-five, with throttles opened. While the big ships ran defense, the littoral combat ship *Fort Worth* swung around and planed like a speedboat toward the contact. *Decatur*'s bowsprit watch spotted the smoky phosphorescent bubble trail of the approaching Squalls and informed the bridge. *Decatur*'s captain radioed the rest of the group before he maneuvered the ship to evade the high-speed torpedoes. With the sizzling sound determined to be rocket-propelled Squalls, *Decatur*'s sonarman localized the other slower torpedoes, matching their acoustic signature to that of a 53-65KE heavy wake-homing torpedo. *More Goddamn Russian fish*, the technician realized. Communicating with the supercarrier, *Decatur*'s captain ordered: "Deploy the Nixie." A giant reel mounted to the American guided-missile destroyer's stern deck paid out a float and line. The float created a second wake behind *Decatur*, and it included speakers that broadcast the simulated engine and reactor noise of an American supercarrier into the water. As *Decatur* went fishing, the Poseidon sub hunter powered in and flew down the threat axis.

The Poseidon scanned the surface with high-resolution thermal cameras and its periscope/wake-spotting radar. A technician inside the aircraft cabin loaded several sonobuoys into launchers, priming the tubes with small pyrotechnic charges. With a whiff of cordite, the sonobuoys shot from the fuselage and rode small parachutes to splashdown. Once in the water, each sonobuoy activated and contacted the Poseidon. Bobbing in the surf, they listened for submerged contacts, and transmitted the compass heading of anything they heard. Then *Lake Champlain*'s ASROCs arrived.

Each ASROC carried a Barracuda light torpedo at its tip. The Barracudas separated from their boosters, dropped to the water, and dove to a preset depth. Once there, they began helical search patterns. As these deadly fish swam about, *Decatur*'s Nixie towed decoy had attracted four heavy torpedoes, though two more of the Chinese wake homers continued straight at for the American supercarrier. Those weapons that homed in on *Decatur* started to snake back and forth within the vee of her wake. *Decatur* increased speed and steered to the south, pulling the weapons away from *Ronald Reagan*. As the guided-missile destroyer turned, the towed float slowed and allowed one of the torpedoes to catch up, exploding it. While this destroyed the Nixie and the weapon next to it, two torpedoes remained, and continued to wind their way toward *Decatur*'s transom. The ship increased to flank, and planed back and forth. One Chinese torpedo shot right up the edge of the wake and detected *Decatur*'s proximate steel hull. The weapon armed its 700-pound warhead. Just a few more feet of travel and the torpedo exploded beneath the American destroyer's twin propellers and rudders. The pressure wave lifted the ship's stern and drove the bow down. The overstressed hull crimped amidships. Cracks propagated through her hull and tore at upper decks.

Decatur stopped and spun in place. Her engine room and aft engineering spaces flooded with seawater. She began to sink by the stern. The second torpedo slammed into the crippled warship's waterline and tore off the rear third of the ship. The separated wreckage pointed to the stars and bobbed momentarily before being sucked under with a belch of trapped air. Even though *Decatur*'s rear decks were awash, her forward watertight compartments kept dry.

Sailors scrambled to rescue those thrown overboard by the blasts, and damage control teams worked frantically within the creaking forward hull as they struggled to keep the broken ship afloat. *Decatur* was clearly out of the fight. The frigate *Thach* peeled off from the main group in order to render assistance.

Ronald Reagan turned attention to the two torpedoes now homing on her mighty wake. At the supercarrier's wide stern, a lattice dispersed, spreading the wash from the ship's four massive propellers, but this lattice could not completely erase the mark left by such a large vessel. The Chinese heavy torpedoes had a 15-knot advantage over the American supercarrier and caught up quickly. They closed to within 3,000 yards. With the threat now inside the inner defensive ring, *Ronald Reagan*'s escorts changed plays. *Lake Champlain* sped up and maneuvered to position herself between the enemy weapons and *Ronald Reagan*.

"Deploy the package," Captain Ferlatto ordered. Rushed to theater and installed on his ship, an experimental wire net shot from a stern canister. Once in the water, it fell back from *Lake Champlain*. One end of the square net bobbed on floats, while the rest unfurled beneath the surface and spread into a curtain array of sensors and transducers. The transducers began to transmit ultra-low frequency waves that formed an outward-focused beam. The sea quivered, and dead fish floated to the surface. The sound, like an amplified bass note, slammed the Chinese torpedoes, crippling their sonars and sensitive critical electronics. One torpedo did a dive toward the bottom, while the other shut down and slowly sank into the black.

"Thank you, DARPA," Ferlatto announced appreciatively. For the moment, *Ronald Reagan* was safe. "Okay, reel it back in. And keep that thing out of my props, understood?" Ferlatto ordered. The watch commander rolled his eyes in dark consideration of the price for fouling the screws: His eternal ass.

American sonar screens were now clear. Much of *Decatur* remained afloat, and her injured and dead had since been transferred by helicopter to *Ronald Reagan*. The Poseidon reported they had to break off the hunt for the offending submarine, and, with no available tankers, flew back to Japan. The Poseidon made a high-speed pass over the Malaysian merchantman, *Bunga Teratai Satu*.

Bunga Teratai Satu's crew, not quite sure what had transpired, counted their blessings nonetheless. They breathed again and chuckled nervously. The midnight shift came on and took the watch. One of the rattled crewmen jogged to his cabin and gulped from a hip flask full of forbidden alcohol.

5: FOG OF WAR

"Secret operations are essential in war; Upon them the army relies to make its every move."—Sun Tzu

With Richard unavailable for lunch, and with no afternoon class this bright sunny day, Jade rode her bicycle past the Widewater and along the Chesapeake & Ohio Canal that paralleled Washington, DC's Potomac River. She followed the path, passing the old locks and pedaling toward Great Falls. Picking up speed, she leaned forward to streamline herself in the headwind.

Jade tried to outrun her conscience and raced against stretched loyalties. She pumped the pedals until her legs burned. Twisting and turning through the strollers, tourists, and joggers, she found herself torn between loving an American and her duty to country and her solemn oath. She turned off the paved path where it crossed the C&O canal, and where it met and skirted the Potomac. The falling river roared, its sound drawing her on. Arriving at one of her favorite thinking spots that overlooked Rocky Islands, she breathed deep and slow. The mist from the whitewater hung in the air, refreshing her sweaty face. She rubbed her aching calf, but then she stopped when a powerful primeval sense tingled: she was being watched. She looked around.

A man leaned against a rock, sipping coffee and staring back through dark sunglasses. He had a neatly trimmed beard with a lick of grey in his brown hair. The man's lips moved and the turn of his head revealed an earpiece. She was under surveillance. She jumped to her bike and took off.

Jade moved at an adrenaline-powered clip, certain somehow that the man was right behind her, keeping up without his legs even moving. She reached where the path squeezed between the C&O and Olmsted Island. She brushed the sharp bark of trees lining the path, and relied on cursing people to get out of the way. She skidded her bike to a stop at Lock 24, the point where the Potomac fell over jagged, steep rocks and flowed through the narrow Mather Gorge. Out of breath again, Jade felt her heart pounding, amid the angst of panic. She picked up her bicycle, and lugged it down a dirt side path that wound between big rocks and crossed small streams. She jumped a low rope barrier, hid her bike, and then tucked herself into a rocky fold. She closed her eyes and imagined the strong, warm safety of Richard's arms.

◊◊◊◊

Richard worked through lunch, though he accomplished little. Instead of attacking the leaning pile of paperwork that occupied his desk, he pondered fatherhood. He shook his head like a stunned dog and tried to focus on the work. He had to propose to Jade...and soon. Ring; wedding; honeymoon; crib; baby clothes; breast pump; college. Richard considered starting to play the lottery. He decided he needed food if he were going to be able to concentrate, so he took out a bag of deep-fried squid chips.

Although everyone else turned their noses up at their sight, Richard loved the chips' briny sweetness and planned to keep buying them from Japantown by the gross. Crunching away, Richard felt the surge of squid power. He looked to the pile of papers and popped a can of soda. On top, he encountered the manila envelope sent over by his liaison at the CIA. He straightened the towering pile to prevent its imminent collapse, flicked squidy salt off his fingers, and grabbed the envelope. On it, he saw his name, the word 'State,' and a question mark scribbled in pen by a low level analyst at Langley. Richard dumped the envelope's contents.

Several photographs fanned out on his desk, apparently taken on the ground in Taipei, with a few shot outside Songshan Airport. One photo showed several Chinese officers as they walked from the terminal to a parked infantry fighting vehicle. Another showed a PLA general atop a light vehicle.

The camera's shutter had caught the general's camo-striped face. Screaming orders at its moment of capture, the greasy face showed lips stretched over yellowed teeth, the face's eyes hidden by sunglasses. The camo and glasses made the Chinese officer tough to identify, so Richard took a magnifying glass from his top drawer and studied the image. The bands of camouflage paint covered a raised cheek scar, and deep lines on the forehead. Richard focused on the open mouth, the missing tooth, and the order of gold caps within. He was sure: This was General Zhen Zhu. He picked up the phone and called the CIA.

"That batch you sent over—photo number three-four-two Charlie," Richard said. "That is General Zhen Zhu, vice chairman of the Central Military Commission, supreme commander of the People's Liberation Army." Richard grinned, proud that he had managed to accomplish what computers and so-called experts across the river had failed to do. "Yep, that's the old bird, himself."

"Could we, you know, take him out?" the voice on the line asked hesitantly. "Legally?"

Richard thought for a moment, and then answered.

"Hey, Zhen's a soldier," Richard snorted. "If he's in-country—on the battlefield—then he's fair game."

Richard sat back and slurped his cold soda, grinning.

◊◊◊◊

The littoral combat ship *Coronado* sat off the beaches of northeastern Taiwan. She had sneaked in, close to the beach, on fast, quiet, water jets. The facets of her trimaran hull deflected enemy radar sweeping the approaches. Her transom gate had been lowered, and two rigid-hull inflatables slid down the launch ramp and into the calm water. A muffled outboard motor propelled each inflatable. Both bristled with the assault rifles of hunched marines. Dressed in jungle warfare fatigues and a brimmed hat, United States Marine Corps Captain Shane Whidby rode the bow of the lead boat as they motored toward a beach cove.

Captain Whidby steadied himself with a hand wrapped in the bowline. His other hand clutched a 1911A1 .45 caliber automatic handgun, and, across his back, he carried a black cylinder. The boat approached the combers that lapped the beach, swerved through the troughs, and then turned into the gentle break to stop. Whidby jumped into the water.

Unconsciously making sure he had not dropped the .45, Whidby squeezed its sharp-checkered grip. The large watertight cylinder strung across his back weighed him down, so he took in some saltwater as he struggled to stand. His throat burned. Spitting water and trying not to cough, Whidby dug in his boots and stood on the slippery rolling rocks. He felt for his canteen and ammo pouch—*Still there*—and watched the inflatables head back to *Coronado*. Sand crunched between his gritted teeth. *If we didn't roll like this, we'd just be army*, Whidby thought with a crooked smile. He emerged from the water and stepped onto embattled Taiwan.

Captain Whidby knelt and waited at the seaweed and garbage-delineated high water mark. An animal sound drew his attention to the shadowy trees at the crest of the beach. Keeping low, his .45 pointed that way, he moved toward the noise. Several soldiers appeared, carrying assault rifles, their helmets disguised with twigs and leaves. Whidby and the soldiers exchanged passwords. The Nighthawks, members of Taiwan's Special Services Company, had clearly been expecting Whidby. Together, they all melted back into the forest.

◊◊◊◊

Secretary Pierce sat in the bunker deep beneath the State Department's Truman Building. She shivered from the air conditioning and adjusted her jacket to keep the breeze off the back of her neck. Richard sat beside her, his face buried in a report. She looked to the video screen that occupied most of one wall. The screen flickered, and live images of the national security advisor, the deputy director of intelligence, and the Pentagon liaison, an army general replaced the screensaver State Department seal.

The deputy director of intelligence opened the meeting with a briefing on growing resistance in Taiwan, momentum regained on the ground, and the infiltration of what he termed 'assets.' The general then cleared his throat and began to speak.

"Afternoon," he offered, with a thin smile. Pierce nodded to the camera on the table. "Okay. Based on State's recommendations, we avoided the Chinese base on Sri Lanka. Instead, a B-1B out of Diego Garcia used its HPM ALCMs to take out the Chinese radar and relay facility on Myanmar's Coco Islands." Seeing a puzzled look on the secretary's face, the general explained that the bomber used air-launched cruise missiles to deliver high-power microwave warheads that disabled electronics and fried antennas at the Chinese base. "Besides the action in the Bay of Bengal," he added, "the attack sub USS *Dallas* fired HPM Tomahawks at, and severely damaged, the Chinese electronics and signals intelligence facility at Changyi." The general leaned forward, his face filling the frame. "The Chinese military is going deaf," he explained, "So, now we're going to poke them in the eyes." The weary general stuck his finger into the camera lens making a cartoonish sound.

◊◊◊◊

A private yacht lay at anchor off Oahu's Iroquois Point. Onboard, a man noted traffic in and out of Hickham Air Force Base. When he heard the thunderous rumble of another aircraft, he raised a pair of binoculars. In the dark of early morning, he saw the flashing navigation lights, and then the form of the jumbo air freighter. Displaying a humped megatop, four gaping turbofans, and ORION CARGO along its side and golden stars on its tail, the airplane seemed like so many others he had seen. He made a note of it, recording it as another civilian cargo aircraft, likely contracted by the US Military

190

Airlift Command to move materiel across the Pacific. What he did not see, however, was the distinctive black nose, or the U.S. AIR FORCE still outlined beneath the jumbo's fresh paintjob. This freighter's strengthened fuselage was not full of bottled water or spare jet engines. Instead, it contained a built-in multi-megawatt chemical laser.

Dubbed 'Gorgon' by the 417th Flight Test Squadron at Edwards Air Force Base, the experimental YAL-1 airborne laser had been rushed out of mothballs, and it now climbed out over Hawaiian waters. In disguise and squawking a commercial code, and flying an Osaka-bound flight plan, the Gorgon steadily gained altitude and turned west over Mamala Bay. It settled in at 41,000 feet, leaving four vapor trails in the sky.

High above the cruising airplane, among flickering constellations, there was a manmade glitter. The Gorgon's nose ball turret swiveled up. A mirrored aperture and infrared sensor were then unsheathed, scanning a patch of the heavens. At an inclination of 63.4 degrees, the technician in the Gorgon's forward battle management cabin found what he sought: China's Hummingbird ocean surveillance satellite. He locked the nose turret on target and initiated auto track. The thermal returns of three satellites showed on his station screen.

Orbiting in a close cluster formation collectively known as Hummingbird, the largest of the Chinese satellites flew on solar-paneled wings, focusing its cameras and antennas on the Philippine Sea It watched and reported in real-time on the *Ronald Reagan* carrier strike group. The other two satellites in formation were small cubes that carried ocean surveillance radar.

The American airman locked the Gorgon airborne laser's tracking and targeting system on the largest of the Chinese satellites, and then passed control to the turret stabilizer and the airplane's autopilot. The fire control operator pressed a red button on her console to initiate the laser's discharge sequence.

At the rear of the Gorgon's fuselage, tank modules the size of minivans mixed chlorine gas and hydrogen peroxide to create oxygen, and a fine mist of iodine stripped photons that bounced between mirrors in an optical resonator chamber. The photons were then squeezed and formed into a beam that entered the optical bench, where mirrors compensated for atmospheric conditions, movement of the airplane and vibration. The beam was then expanded and bounced to the nose turret where final adjustments compressed and focused the beam. The beam, invisible to the pilots in the upper flight deck, instantly bridged the distance between the Gorgon's nose and the Chinese satellite.

"Beam integrity nominal," the airman announced. "Thermals in the green." The beam of light reached into space for 12 long seconds, and heated the gold foil-covered metal skin of the target spacecraft. Asymmetric thrust then pushed the Hummingbird off course, smashing it into one of its mates. Pieces tumbled in all directions; some to begin a fiery fall back to Earth. Others would circle the planet for years.

◊◊◊◊

Legendary Chinese admirals and generals—Cheng Ho; Meng Yi; Shi Lang; Sun Tzu; Zhang Zizhong; and Zheng He—stared from bronze busts and oil paintings that formed a gauntlet in a dark marble corridor within Beijing's Ministry of National Defense. The Chinese president walked the hall, leaning forward as if going uphill and mumbling all the while. At hall's end, the president pushed through tall double doors and burst into a foyer where two soldiers snapped to attention. He waved them away impatiently and pushed into the conference room beyond, where the monitor revealed General Zhen already sitting at his airport terminal desk.

A cloud of tobacco smoke, illuminated by the dim early morning light filtering through an open window in Taiwan, veiled Zhen.

"Mr. President," Zhen exclaimed. "Good to be able to confer with you again."

"General, you assured me we would hold the island by the end of the third day of operations. However, we hold no more than 40 percent of the territory, and the Americans have an aircraft carrier to the south. Who knows how many submarines are lurking out there, and I have just heard that the Hummingbird system is down, likely destroyed by the Americans."

"Please, Mr. President, sit. We must stay unemotional and think clearly. Our destinies are linked. We must cooperate. Yes, the schedule has suffered somewhat. However, our strategic goals are accomplished," Zhen's voice was calming, though the president snorted in disbelief and exhaustion. "President, you are a politician, and I can only imagine the pressures upon you. However, I need you to be strong. China needs you to be strong; as strong as our men on the front lines." Zhen seemed to grow larger as he spoke. The president fell back into an oversize chair. Sensing a power shift, Zhen leaned forward. "Mr. President, you are correct. The Y-9 ocean surveillance system has failed. Before it went offline, however, the satellite provided the current position of the American aircraft carrier. We shall destroy it. Of that, I am certain." The general paused to read the reaction of the president. *He is mine*, Zhen thought and surged. "I regret very much that I must now adamantly request one thing more from you, something only you have the power to grant."

"And, what might that be, general?"

"Release *Liaoning*," Zhen said bluntly. The Chinese president became quietly contemplative. Zhen studied the image of the president's face like one of his battle maps. The president took a deep, nasally breath before nodding acquiescence. Then he stood and glared into the camera.

"And if you fail, general, it will be your head," the president growled, with renewed vigor, as he waved his pudgy finger at Zhen's face. Had they been in the same room, Zhen's instinct may have been to bite it off, but the fox inside told him to bide time instead. *Besides*, Zhen thought, *it is really both our heads on the line.* "Have the missile submarines put to sea, also," the president ordered. "We will need them if this goes wrong."

"Yes, sir," Zhen said and picked up his telephone, as the president clicked off.

Zhen then made a phone connection with the submarine base at Sanya. He ordered two *Jin*-class submarines to set sail from their pens on Hainan Island. Each hauled 12 city-busting Giant Wave thermonuclear ballistic missiles. *The Americans would never risk*

194

escalating this, Zhen wagered. He then pushed a red button on the telephone. "Get me Commodore Shen."

When the naval officer came on the line, Zhen repeated the president's order to get *Liaoning* and the missile boats to sea. Zhen rolled his eyes when the commodore protested with numerous excuses, and then reiterated the order, insisting the 'impossible' be made to happen. Zhen hung up the receiver and settled his face into his palms. Resisting his body's own cries for rest, he knew there was yet one more call to be made. He lifted the receiver and dialed a memorized number.

"*Hundun* (chaos)," the general uttered to another of his Four Fiends.

◊◊◊◊

A People's Liberation Army colonel lowered the telephone, his face betraying an amalgam of amazement, delight, and fear. Determination stepped up, and the colonel left his office to walk through a dark and dimly lit weapons bunker. Long racks of man-sized, brick red and cone-shaped ballistic missile warheads lined the tunnel. The colonel came to a heavy blast door. He removed a lanyard and key from around his neck to unlock it. Inside he observed more warheads and a machine that sniffed the air for biological, chemical, or nuclear elements. Its siren was silent. The colonel touched the casing of one warhead. It was ice cold. *Cold as death*, he reflected, and ran his hand over the orange peel-like texture. He donned thick gloves and primed the 12-kiloton plutonium-powered implosion-type nuclear warhead. He then attached an anti-ship guidance and targeting package to the warhead's base, and used a gantry to hoist and lower it onto an auto dolly. The colonel spray painted over the warhead's distinguishing trifoil symbol and took the dolly's controls in hand, remotely driving the package out of the vault. The blast door closed shut behind him.

The colonel and his nuclear weapon entered another chamber of the tunnel complex. The arched room held a ballistic missile transporter-erector-launcher rail car. Soldiers crawled over the specialized train. A small, yellow crane waited to lift and attach the warhead to its rocket.

Three hundred miles southeast of Hong Kong, the American nuclear attack submarine *Connecticut* met the *Ronald Reagan* carrier strike group, and took her place on point. The frigate *Thach* was surface lead, followed by the destroyers *Gridley* and *Mahan*. Steaming behind this forward screen were the cruiser *Lake Champlain* and the nuclear supercarrier *Ronald Reagan*. The littoral combat ship *Forth Worth* and *Decatur*'s replacement, the guided-missile destroyer *Winston S. Churchill*, pulled up the rear. The carrier strike group steamed due north and made way at 27 knots. Although *Ronald Reagan*'s air wing served as the group's primary air defense, *Lake Champlain*'s task was anti-missile central.

In the cruiser's dark combat information center, Captain Ferlatto and the other sailors watched networked data from US Strategic Command: several ballistic targets had departed China and clearly tracked for the American carrier strike group. Utilizing the remote radar data, *Lake Champlain* launched Standard Missiles; the surface-to-air missiles departing the ship's forward vertical launch system.

The Chinese warheads came within range of *Lake Champlain*'s radar. Hexagonal arrays on the ship's superstructure powered-up, found, and concentrated powerful radio beams on the missiles. With positive track on the inbounds, and the downrange Standard Missiles veering to intercept, the American carrier strike group increased speed and began a coordinated zigzag. In a fountain of fire, *Lake Champlain* put up more Standard Missiles. Smoke ropes climbed through blue sky toward the blackness of space.

Hot from their ascent from Shaoguan, the Chinese East Wind ballistic missiles staged—dropped their booster rockets—and entered midcourse flight in the thin air of Earth's upper atmosphere. Among the flight of conventional East Winds also flew a nuclear ship killer. It fired small rockets around its base; the thrust finely tuning the craft's trajectory. Once on course again, the missile bus expelled gas that spun the warhead to keep it balanced and on course. With its job done, the bus separated from the warhead. As it did so, decoy polyhedral-shaped balloons deployed and inflated. The flight of decoys and warheads began to spark and glow as they arced into denser atmosphere. The Chinese nuclear warhead—its terminal plunge fiery and hypersonic—passed its primary altitude marker. The weapon released the first of several electronic safeties.

Cocooned within the warhead's ablative casing, the warhead's final safety released 500 feet above *Ronald Reagan*'s flight deck, and, at 100 feet, the altimeter triggered 200 pounds of high explosives that surrounded the weapon's nuclear pit. This explosive uniformly crushed the pit to half its normal size, compressing it to critical mass. A fission reaction began and expanded geometrically, burning at twice the temperature of the sun's surface. It filled the sky with brilliant light.

The fireball swelled over the target, and swallowed the American carrier strike group. The surface of the sea boiled. Aboard ship, people vaporized, paint blistered, steel warped, and all jet fuel and ammunition combusted. Infrared light and gamma rays sped in all directions. A blast wave formed and radiated supersonically, creating an overpressure that destroyed everything within a mile. The supercarrier's steel island crumpled and melted. The flight deck collapsed into the lower decks, pancaking and sandwiching everything to the keel. The supercarrier was sinking when the overpressure reached the group's escort vessels.

The burning ships capsized, rolled, and sank; their twisted, unrecognizable metal on an express ride to the bottom. Winds reached six hundred miles-per hour. They shoved the sea into hundred-foot waves that surged from the explosion's hypocenter. Extreme heat and radiation lingered as a massive column of debris, steam, and water rose over the area. The explosion's hot column cooled and expanded as it climbed in the atmosphere, spreading into a giant mushroom-shaped cloud. Ash and smoke were sucked up into the cloud where they mixed with cool, humid air in the upper atmosphere, and began falling back to earth as black rain. Radioactive particles condensed, caught the wind, and began to fall out several miles away.

General Zhen awakened from the fiery nightmare. He felt a moment of doubt, but shook it off and checked his watch. *Soon*, he pondered, *the American carrier will be on the bottom.* Zhen hoped that, by using a relatively small nuclear weapon, the flash, electromagnetic pulse, and residual daughter elements might go unnoticed or be absorbed by the ocean. China would be able to deny the event, and even, perhaps, suggest that an American weapon or ship's reactor was to blame. At the very least, a denial would sow further confusion among his enemies, as well as divide the ever judgmental and sanction-happy international community and its pesky organizations. As General Zhen stared out his office window, the East Winds continued their plunge for the *Ronald Reagan* carrier strike group.

Riding the beam projected by *Lake Champlain*'s radar array, the cruiser's Standard Missiles streaked skyward, their upper stages carrying Lightweight Exo-Atmospheric Projectiles—LEAPs—that had to hit-to-kill to be worth their weight in salt. These American interceptors used onboard homing radar and infrared sensors to orient, and frantically fired thrusters to close with their quarry, the Chinese warheads.

The East Winds crashed through the air; sparking smoking streamers in the atmosphere. Among them, the Chinese nuclear warhead reached another altitude marker and primed the computer-controlled high-explosives. Their radar energized. Small tabs around the warhead's base actuated and maneuvered the weapon into lazy S-turns. As it swerved through Earth's outer layers, a lens at the warhead's base surveyed the chill of seawater. This computer's eye spotted the heat emanated by the American ships. The East Wind's targeting computer locked onto the largest signature it saw.

In the Earth's mesosphere, 40 miles above the *Ronald Reagan* carrier strike group, *Lake Champlain*'s Standard Missiles approached to within 5,000 feet of their targets, entering their kill baskets. The American interceptors and the flight of Chinese decoys and warheads came together at 30 times the speed of sound, generating impacts and explosions.

The nuclear warhead survived and continued to swerve towards it prey. Below, the great blue sea lay and several grey, hot targets steamed upon it. A second volley of American interceptors entered the arena, streaking through the air. There were bright white collisions as more decoys were claimed. A last American interceptor fired motors frantically as its LEAP warhead zeroed on the nuclear East Wind's hot casing. The two war machines collided and vaporized. On radar, two lines became a ball of debris.

Cheers erupted in *Lake Champlain*'s CIC. The watch commander shook Ferlatto's hand, and ordered the last climbing interceptor to be remotely destroyed. The tactical coordinator reported the screen was clear.

In Beijing, General Zhen learned of the outcome of the engagement. He put down the telephone and then stared blankly at the office bookcase.

"Now it is all up to *Liaoning*," he mumbled.

◊◊◊◊

Dense fog had settled over the Chinese Port of Dalian, on the shore of the Bohai Sea. A major city and seaport in the south of Liaoning province, Dalian was the southernmost city of Northeast China and China's northernmost warm water port. Although the sun had risen, its heating rays struggled to penetrate the cool wet blanket that had flopped over the area. At the outer fringes of the murk— where the Bohai yielded to the Yellow Sea— The American guided-missile submarine *Georgia* hovered, lurking within these Chinese territorial waters. This dark, sneaky, huge steel beast had just relieved USS *Ohio*, and her skipper now made a final sweep of the area with the periscope.

Georgia's captain increased the periscope's magnification, and leaned into the eyepiece. Within his circular view, he scrutinized several shadows that emerged from the gloom. He signaled his executive officer who approached and took a peek.

"Looks like a container ship in the lane out of Dalian…or Yantai," the XO said. "Several large tugs following," he added, and peered at his captain.

The captain muttered something, tapped his XO out like a tag-team wrestler, and then leaned back into the eyepiece. The captain's mouth opened and hung in disbelief. Then the captain, his face still glued to the periscope, said: "That's no freighter. That's an aircraft carrier."

People's Liberation Army Navy aircraft carrier *Liaoning* slowly made way in the haze, using the miserable weather to slip from her berth, and break out into open water. *Liaoning*'s upturned prow, emblazoned with a red star wrapped in a yellow wreath, emerged from the swirling mist. Big black anchors hung from the ship's sharp bow, and her long blue-grey hull slid through the water. The carrier's flight deck ran from the thick lip of her ski ramp to her square wide backside. Interrupting her flatness were long horizontal missile cans, and, at the waist, an extensive and tall superstructure that stuck slightly outboard like a saddlebag. What initially appeared to be tugs in attendance were, in fact, small surface combatants. *Georgia*'s captain gawked through the periscope and listened to his executive officer reading a print out.

"*Liaoning*. Refurbished *Admiral Kuznetsov*-class multirole carrier. Launched by the Soviet Union in 1988 as *Varyag*, she had been named for a victorious cruiser in the Battle of Chemulpo during the Russo-Japanese War of 1904. Inherited by Ukraine when the USSR disintegrated, the incomplete vessel was auctioned to a Hong Kong consortium for use as a floating casino. However, *Varyag* was instead transported to Dalian for refit. The Chinese then renamed her for the Chinese province opposite Beijing, and for the river that flows through it. *Liaoning* is 900 feet, 52,000 tons. Presumed armaments include--"

"Destroyers," the captain cursed, and stepped back from the tree trunk-sized periscope. Although *Georgia* had found herself in extreme danger, her captain also smelled an opportunity.

Shedding the thick marine layer of dense fog, the Chinese aircraft carrier picked up speed and warmed her decks in the morning sun. The procession of Chinese ships turned south into the Yellow Sea, and the last of the chaperoning sea birds turned back for shore. Bracing against the stiff breeze, an admiral stood on the carrier's flying bridge, surveying *Liaoning*'s flight deck. The expanse was bare except for a single Helix search and rescue helicopter. The admiral turned to the horizon and strategized: *Beneath the umbrella of land-based air cover, I will take my ship and her escorts off North Korea to collect the air wing. Once I have my aircraft aboard, I will take the battle group into the East China Sea and sail right down the throat of the Americans.* The sound of aircraft then rumbled the sky.

Senior Lieutenant Peng's blue and grey Flying Shark held in the pattern above *Liaoning*. Among aircraft stacked, packed, and racked in the airspace around *Liaoning*, Peng's single-seat air superiority fighter would be the first of 12 to land. The rest of the air wing—specialized two-seat electronic warfare and dedicated anti-ship types—would then come aboard and round-out *Liaoning*'s air wing. Peng banked his big fighter over the battle group.

Arrayed around *Liaoning*, the carrier's surface group consisted of two guided-missile destroyers, *Harbin* and *Qingdao*; the guided-missile frigate *Xiangfan*; and the frigate *Zigong*. Leading the way beneath the waves was Captain Kun's nuclear attack submarine *Changzheng 6*, and, the group's laggard: the diesel-electric attack submarine *#330*. As the battle group passed different Chinese ports, various patrol and torpedo boats came out to join the nautical parade, steaming with the battle group as far as their fuel load permitted. Peng observed the airplanes that now circled above the aircraft carrier. In the haze-diminished daylight, their strobe lights looked like a string of pearls that spiraled skyward. He looked down at his radar screen. It was full of friendly blips.

Liaoning's air traffic center called out to Peng and gave clearance for him to enter the downward leg of the carrier's landing pattern. Peng tuned the radio to the landing officer's frequency, set flaps, dropped the landing gear and tail hook, and then turned toward the ship, settling the heavy fighter onto the glide path. Peng located the search and rescue Helix helicopter that hovered off *Liaoning*'s port forward quarter. He also located the amber lantern—the 'meatball,' as American naval aviators call it—and used the light to stay in the awkwardly offset glide path.

"Aircraft 203, do you have the lantern?" the radio crackled with the landing officer's query.

"Two-zero-three has the lantern," Peng said into his oxygen mask transmitter. He kept the lantern centered horizontally and vertically as he descended toward *Liaoning*. The landing officer on deck began to talk Peng in. Dips, rises and yaws accounted for, the Flying Shark arrived over the carrier's corkscrewing fantail. Fighting gusts, Peng coaxed the airplane down and settled it gingerly on the steel deck.

The tail hook snagged the third of four wire arrestor ropes strewn across *Liaoning*'s after deck. Peng brought the Flying Shark's two afterburning turbofans to full power, to create reverse thrust. The Flying Shark, trapped and decelerating rapidly, Peng slammed forward into his harness. The airplane stopped and, wearing a colored shirt adorned with a Chinese character, one of *Liaoning*'s deckhands confirmed the trap with raised crossed arms. Peng backed the throttles to idle and the engines whined down.

A deckhand came out to the airplane and disengaged the tail hook from the now-slack arrestor rope while another stepped in front of the Flying Shark and directed Peng to a designated parking space. Others swarmed the aircraft, attaching tie-down chains, and a fuel hose. They opened avionics and engine access panels. One technician spotted a hydraulic fluid leak on the main landing gear and began repairs. Senior Lieutenant Peng removed his flight helmet and climbed from the cockpit. He proudly watched the next Flying Shark land, and then Peng headed for *Liaoning*'s interior.

The air conditioning struggled against Washington, DC's late afternoon heat, and dew formed on Secretary Pierce's office window. Richard had already delivered the afternoon brief and provided Pierce with a summary of the day's intelligence traffic. She read it through half-eye glasses while sipping cold homemade sweet tea from a thermos. The brief told her that, via Kyrgyzstan, armaments had been smuggled into China's northwestern province of Xinjiang and were now in the hands of separatists, fanning the flames of dissent and insurgency within the People's Republic. The brief noted that the Chinese army had violently put down peaceful protests in Tibet. In addition, just hours ago in Hong Kong, thousands of demonstrators marched in support of Taiwanese self-determination. Although China's security forces acted with more restraint in the semi-autonomous territory, mass arrests resulted, and hundreds of activists had 'disappeared.' The man who had followed and frightened Jade earlier now stood in the frame of Pierce's open door. He knocked.

Headed for Secretary Pierce's office, Richard walked the hall. He noticed things were unusually quiet and too many heads were down. Pierce had summoned him, and the earnestness of her tone had been ominous. The questions this imparted had quickened Richard's steps. He knocked on Pierce's open office door and entered. Two men awaited inside with her: one seated, and the other standing in the office's corner. With a stern look on her face, Secretary Pierce lifted herself and strolled to the office's door. She closed and locked it. Even more daunting to Richard was when she then lifted the telephone to order that all calls must be held. Richard sat beside one of the strangers, his mind racing. He nervously glanced to the other, who loomed in the room's corner.

"This is FBI Special Agent Hunter Jackson," the secretary said, gesturing to the seated man. Richard extended his hand, which Agent Jackson left hanging. "Special Agent Jackson is in counterintelligence." Richard felt a rush of warm blood that prickled his skin.

"Mr. Ling, you're aware that the penalty for espionage is death?" Jackson asked, his steel-blue eyes piercing. Richard looked to his boss for support, but she looked away. "We searched your apartment," the agent added.

"You... WHAT?" Richard was suddenly more angry than scared. Jackson unfolded a copy of the warrant and handed it to him.

"We found this." Jackson handed Richard a small electronics box with input and output ports. "It's a keystroke logger. Everything you typed on your secure home terminal was copied. It's set to transmit via Bluetooth and it's configured to download to some other device, probably a smart phone." The FBI agent leaned toward Richard, who noticed the empty shoulder holster beneath the agent's grey mid-priced suit. Richard held his penetrating gaze, and told himself he was ready for whatever came his way. "Do you love your country, Richard?" was the question posed. Richard wondered if a white man would have been asked something similar. Anger pushed back against Richard's fear. He looked to Pierce, but she still avoided his gaze. *She's pretending not to be here*, Richard weighed up. He considered cursing them both and then storming out.

"I am not a spy," Richard belted out, and then dropped his face into his hands where he forced his shocked mind to think clearly. Secretary Pierce studied her underling's expressions, and then looked to the federal agent, who nodded.

"Jade," Secretary Pierce stated.

"Zhang Jiao—your Jade—is really Bei Si Tiao, last name first, as in the Chinese manner," Agent Jackson said. He paused to let the information hang in the room like a dark cloud. "Richard, Bei Si Tiao is Chinese Foreign Intelligence Service." Those last four words stabbed deep, and Richard winced as Jackson uttered each one. His heart split into palpitating halves. Then Richard could only mumble incoherently as he shook his head.

"I am *so* sorry," Richard offered the secretary. His tears welled.

"So am I," Pierce offered a sympathetic, though strained smile.

Richard started to stutter an explanation, but the agent cut off Richard's articulations. He said that he knew Richard had not been a willing accomplice, and that he must now, instead, help his country, himself, and even the woman who had betrayed him. Richard lowered his head into his hands again. This time, the tears rolled down his flushed cheeks.

Secretary Pierce stood and went to pat Richard's back.

"Jade could be a dangle," Jackson coldly postulated. Then he sighed and added, "I don't think so. She shows no signs of wanting to turn to our side. So…we want to keep feeding her misinformation."

Jackson stood and practically ordered the crumbled Richard: "I want you to keep on typing your reports at home."

"I'm not trained for counterintelligence operations," Richard complained.

Jackson sighed. "Then I have no choice but to bring Jade in."

Beaten and exhausted, Richard stood, walked to the window, and stared out at the capital. Even though innocent, he realized that he might never be trusted again, and that his career was, perhaps, effectively over. He watched a water droplet as it ran down the windowpane. As he contemplated his fate, almost forgetting that others were in the room, he was handed a business card. He raised it up, ran his fingers over the embossed seal of the FBI, and placed it in his pocket.

Agent Jackson had seen this reaction before; usually presented by the innocent.

"I'll be in touch, Mr. Ling," Jackson promised.

◊◊◊◊

USS *Essex*— a *Wasp*-class amphibious assault ship, the 'Iron Gator'—and the American 31st Marine Expeditionary Unit transited the southern approaches to Taiwan. The size of a World War II aircraft carrier, *Essex* sported a hangar full of jump jets, heavy-lift helicopters, and tilt-rotors, and a well deck full of air cushioned landing craft ready to truck ashore main battle tanks and the eighteen hundred marines that called the ship home.

The dock landing ships *New York* and *Tortuga*, the guided-missile frigate *Hawes*, the littoral combat ship *Coronado*, and the sleek, black stealth guided-missile destroyer *Michael Monsoor* accompanied the *Essex*. Far beneath them all, and making her way at a depth of some 400 feet and some several miles ahead of the surface formation, roamed the nuclear attack submarine *Key West*. Thirty-five thousand feet above flew two aircraft.

One, an olive-drab Marine Corps Lightning II, the Corps' Bravo version of the Joint Strike Fighter, capable of short take-off and vertical landing capabilities, was configured for forward flight. An air force F-22 Raptor air supremacy fighter that had flown out of Guam accompanied the Lightning These two assassins cruised the sky together far above the *Essex*'s group.

Meanwhile, *Essex* carried two unmanned aerial vehicles, sitting on her rectangular deck. These Predators were in air force livery and featured inverted v-tails and pusher props. Remotely piloted from the United States, they began to roll into the stiff head wind. They rose quickly into the air and then droned away.

Lieutenant Pelletier's Lightning II capped at 40,000 feet, doing Mach 1.1. A Growler—an electronic attack aircraft based on the Super Hornet—flew along on her wing. Belonging to *Ronald Reagan*'s 'Cougars,' the Growler carried big jammer pods and HARM high-speed anti-radiation missiles. One of *Essex*'s olive-drab stealth jump jets climbed to join Pelletier and the Growler. Once formed up, the three American aircraft banked in unison.

A Sentry airborne warning and control system aircraft orbited at a distance. Within its long fuselage, controllers studied their screens. Before the senior controller, a tactical display showed all aircraft within range of the powerful revolving radar on the Sentry's back: Eagles out of Guam, Raptors from Okinawa, Pelletier's three-ship maritime strike package, and two very slow Predator UAVs. Although invisible to his scrutiny, the senior controller knew Spirit stealth bombers had entered the area. They had departed Whiteman Air Force Base in Missouri, sweeping west with bellies full of big guided bombs destined for Chinese surface-to-air missile sites deployed on Taiwan's main island. The Sentry controller watched as the Predators approached Penghu in the Taiwan Strait. Pelletier's three-ship lagged behind and, at a higher altitude, the Eagles were ready to keep enemy fighters at a polite distance.

The two Predators flew 1,000 feet over the Taiwan Strait. Ahead lay Penghu. The Chinese surface-to-air missile battery at the island's Magong Airport acquired and targeted the Predators. Meanwhile, Pelletier's three-ship flight had dropped to the deck behind the unmanned aerial vehicles.

The Growler powered up a jamming pod and fired digital streams into the energized Chinese surface-to-air missile radar. Networked to the Growler, US Cyber Command used the digital stream to access and penetrate China's integrated air defense system. Once inside this system, cyber-phantoms seemed to appear on huge flatscreens that covered the wall of a People's Liberation Army Air Force bunker in Beijing.

A massive congregation of aircraft seemed to appear, to the northeast of Taiwan. To the Chinese air defense controllers, the radar returns appeared to be from big, slow bombers, likely American B-52s carrying cruise missiles. They ordered that every available Chinese fighter be sent their way. As the cyber-phantoms drew Chinese attention, real Spirit stealth bombers slipped in from the east and over Taiwan.

Favorit missiles knocked the Predators down. The electronic warfare officer in the Growler's backseat warmed up his high-speed anti-radiation missiles and fed GPS coordinates and enemy transmitter profiles into the HARM's electronic brains. One of the missiles flashed off the Growler's wing rail and streaked away through wispy clouds. A second missile also went, and the American three-ship looped together, coming about for a return to *Essex* and *Ronald Reagan*.

The HARMs crossed the beach at Penghu. They flew over a deserted elementary school's playground, and then over Magong Airport's fence line. The missiles then over-flew a parked Chinese Beagle light bomber, two Flankers, and a Flying Leopard that had taken up residence at the captured field. They then turned for the Chinese surface-to-air missile battery set up at the end of the runway. Even though its radar had shut down after downing the Predators, the missiles remembered the location of the Favorit battery. Two massive explosions announced the HARMs' arrival. The airport's one yellow fire truck dutifully departed its garage.

Warm sun permeated the cockpit of Pelletier's cruising Lightning II. She had just completed a mid-air refueling and taken position at the outer edge of *Ronald Reagan*'s combat air patrol. Pelletier closed her eyes for just a second. Eighteen-hour shifts had taken their toll on everybody. She faded. A spasm travelled her body, and her closed eyes twitched as her brain took her into a dream. Her alarm clock broke through the haze and jarred her awake. The fog lifted from her mind as she realized the alarm was really the cockpit's missile warning.

"Shit," she gasped, and then instinctively dropped decoys before pulling the Lightning II almost straight up. *Enemy fighters? Here?* She wondered with self-admonishment. *Ronald Reagan* came on the radio and stated the obvious: "Bandit, your sector." She rolled the aircraft inverted and pointed its nose back into the threat. With the enemy missile highlighted in her helmet visor, Pelletier dropped the engine into idle, allowing the threat to pass underneath, and then slamming the throttle into afterburner, all while flying upside down. White-hot flames blasted from the Lightning II's gaping maw; her ship quickly regaining air speed. The enemy missile, seduced by the flares, had turned away. Pelletier recognized the weapon as a Chinese Thunderclap short-range infrared-guided missile, and knew its launch platform had to be within nine miles. Her adversary, she realized, had somehow gotten in close. She switched her radar to active scan and flooded the sky with energy. The culprit popped up on the radar screen. Pelletier looked out to the towering cloud her enemy was hiding within and made selections to fire a single AMRAAM. The Lightning II's bay doors opened, and unfolded into the slipstream.

Senior Lieutenant Peng switched from the passive infrared search and track ball in the canopy, and powered up the Flying Shark's radar. He got a faint reflection on his display. Peng sent a Lightningbolt air-to-air missile that way.

Pelletier's own missile was shoved from the bay and ignited. With missile and radar warnings blaring, and the world outside spinning, Pelletier's attention drew to a fault warning on the primary display. One of the weapon bay doors had failed to close. She switched to a backup, but the door mechanism again failed to actuate. Pelletier inverted the airplane to present her stealthy top to the enemy missile. Flying upside down, she hit the chaff and tried the jammed door again. It remained unresponsive. Pelletier climbed the Lightning II in an attempt to slam the stubborn door shut with positive Gs. The flashing red symbol on the dash indicated the tactic had failed. She righted the airplane, and then made inputs to change the view in the helmet-mounted display.

Images from six cameras distributed around the Lightning II fused and projected into her visor. The airplane 'virtually' disappeared, appearing to take Pelletier's lower body with it. She looked down. Her aircraft's specialized camera system allowed her to see below her own aircraft as though it were not even there, so where her lap should be, she only saw clouds streaking by. The effect was that only her eyeballs and brain were flying at Mach 1.2 Certainly, a surreal experience. However, one that would hopefully help her survive. The computer projected a big green down-arrow before her. She lowered the nose and saw the Chinese aircraft, its fuselage outlined by the computer, helping her distinguish its staggered blue and grey paint scheme from the sky. She prepared a Sidewinder on the weapons panel. Small folding doors at the wing's leading edge opened, and a red targeting reticle appeared before her. She turned her head and put the crosshairs between the Flying Shark's canards and wings. The reticle changed to green as the targeting system locked onto the hot exhaust of the enemy airplane's two big engines. Pelletier squeezed the trigger, authorizing the computer to release the weapon.

Spring-loaded arms pushed the Sidewinder clear of the Lightning II. It ignited with a whoosh, and the missile's motor nozzle vanes put the heat seeker into a high-G turn. Pelletier's Sidewinder spotted engine heat and began autonomous pursuit. Hoping to perplex the American missile, the Flying Shark dropped a string of flares.

Senior Lieutenant Peng took his Flying Shark vertical. Speed bled off in the climb. The big airplane rolled over and its nose dropped toward the threatening missile. Momentarily losing lock on the Flying Shark's heat, the Sidewinder switched tracking to the next hottest object: one of Peng's flares. Bringing his airplane outside the heat seeker's cone of detection, he spotted the American airplane in his infrared scope, and recognized its outline as belonging to the new joint strike fighter—the stealthy Lightning II. He could see one of its belly doors was open and the white of its internal weapon bay. The Chinese aviator celebrated the honor and his luck by sending infrared and radar-guided missiles in rapid succession, a nasty one-two punch. In response, the American airplane rolled hard and lit up with afterburner.

With alarms blaring, Pelletier focused on the incoming missiles. She set up the radar for jamming. The Lightning II's active, electronically scanned array directed a high-power beam at the oncoming enemy missiles. Peng's radar-guided missile corkscrewed and did a suicidal dive into the sea, although his infrared one continued after the American's airplane.

Pelletier dropped flares, dove toward the choppy sea, and selected an advanced medium-range air-to-air missile. The computer reopened the one closed weapon bay door, and fired off a brace of AMRAAMs, the missiles kicked out by ejector arms, which then retracted. This time, both bay doors shut and locked. With radar no longer reflected by the door, Lieutenant Pelletier's Lightning II was stealthy again and disappeared from Peng's radar screen.

Peng saw his screen go blank. In hopes of catching a glint of metal or the smoke of an engine, Peng strained to look over his shoulder, scanning the mirrors that surrounded his canopy frame. The radio crackled. A squadron mate from *Liaoning* broadcast that he would be on-scene in less than a minute.

"Where are you, American?" Senior Lieutenant Peng barked, his throat sore from the airplane's arid environmental system. The infrared tracker peered into a dense cloud and found a faint heat signature. Peng fired a Thunderclap and watched it scoot away to pierce a fluffy cloud. The cloud flashed red. *Flares*, Peng realized. The Lightning II popped out, trailed by Peng's missile. Peng yanked his Flying Shark over, grimaced through the radical maneuver, and swooped in to take position on the American's tail. The Thunderclap followed Pelletier through several hard turns. With his opponent on the defensive, Peng selected the Flying Shark's 30-millimeter cannon.

Focusing on the enemy missile, Pelletier dumped more flares and initiated an Immelmann turn, which would end with her jet flying in the opposite direction but at a higher altitude. She gained height and reversed direction on the heatseeker to break its lock, exiting the maneuver upside-down before rolling the airplane horizontal. Tracer fire zipped by like laser beams. She felt a thump followed by vibration. A red light blinked on the Lightning II's console as Pelletier's bird had been hit. Redundant and self-healing systems quickly isolated and aerodynamically compensated for the damage as avionics established new G-force restrictions, preventing the pilot from overstressing damaged areas. With multiple warnings blaring and flashing in her visor, Pelletier initiated another loop. *This guy's good*, she mulled. She pulled the Lighting II over as hard as the computer allowed. Using maximum thrust, she got herself over the enemy.

Peng lost sight of Pelletier and overshot. Unable to shed speed and match her turn, he roared past, screaming curses at the American all the while. Pelletier exited the gutsy move in pure pursuit position. Smack on her adversary's tail, two fiery engine nozzles filled her canopy. Her last Sidewinder begged for release. Pelletier raised the nose to drop back a bit. Then she lowered it again before selecting the impatient weapon. Even throughout violent changes of direction, Pelletier stayed glued to the Flying Shark. About to pull the trigger, Pelletier hesitated, as a chivalrous modern knight. Her foe was down and her blade at his throat, and the crowd in her mind screamed: 'Mercy'—drowning out those who shouted: 'Kill.' Pelletier brought up the radar's function menu and selected the pulse generator. The Sidewinder ended its whine and a yellow star appeared where the red crosshairs had been. The star floated over the Chinese airplane and she pulled the stick's trigger. An invisible beam projected from the nose of the Lightning II, striking the Flying Shark.

Peng's skin tingled, and then itched and burned. Water in his epidermis heated up and began to boil. Crackles of energy started to dance around the Flying Shark's console and cockpit. A zap signaled overloaded electrical systems. The airplane's cockpit display went black, and the stick went dead. The flight computer was cooked, and, without it making hundreds of flight surface corrections every second, the Flying Shark became a flying brick. The big warplane yawed over and entered a flat spin. Peng reached behind him to yank the eject handles. A forceful tug was followed by a rat-tat-tat as explosive bolts fired, releasing the canopy, which was sucked away. Peng got smacked silly by the slipstream. The rocket seat fired, and Peng's spine compressed as he was lifted from the dead airplane.

Lieutenant Pelletier watched the chute deploy and the Chinese warplane tumble away. She called in a search and rescue helicopter from *Ronald Reagan* and turned her Lightning II toward the open parachute and the Chinese pilot who dangled beneath it, buzzing her vanquished enemy with a high-speed victory pass. A beep got her attention. She looked down to see that more enemy airplanes had appeared on the screen. Pelletier shut down the radar, her Lightning II now damaged, low on fuel, and nearly out of missiles. She reluctantly broke for *Ronald Reagan* and disappeared in the glare of the late afternoon sun.

An hour later she was fed, showered, and passed out in her rack. On the small shelf beside her bed rested a silver double frame holding pictures of her cat and her dad.

The White House glimmered in the wash of spotlights. A summer zephyr rustled oak trees. Richard breathed deep and soaked up the cool breeze. Decked out in his best suit, he waited by a fountain outside a Pennsylvania Avenue seafood & grill. Jade appeared at the top of broad, white stone steps. Her silken hair was up revealing her long neck and the pearl-white skin of her chest. *She's*

aglow, Richard thought as doubts of her being pregnant vanished. Richard looked Jade over.

She wore high heels. This was the first time Richard had seen her in a pair. Her toned legs remained warm by black silk stockings. Richard choked to breathe again. She smiled like a debutante before a cotillion review, and descended the steps as gracefully as possible. Without a word, Jade and Richard came together for a long kiss. Richard held the large brass door open, and they entered the restaurant's dining room.

Enticing fragrances of warm bread, grilled meat, and fresh cut flowers wafted to their noses. Led to a table, they passed diners enjoying succulent duck, juicy lobster tails, and steaming risotto. Framed pictures of famous faces lined the paneled walls.

Jade and Richard dropped napkins into their laps and picked up menus. Both agreed coming here was a wonderful idea. He looked over the appetizer list and stole glimpses of the elegant dining room.

A young woman stood at the bar, sipping sparking water. She served as his armed backup. Her presence did not bring comfort, though, as she was just the first of many people that would follow him around for a long time to come. Contemplating such an existence left a stabbing pain in Richard's temples. Jade's voice snapped his attention back to the list of delicacies.

She read the entrées aloud and commented on each with varying levels of interest. Richard decided on a blue cheese-crusted filet mignon. He picked up the wine list. Perusing the establishment's offerings, he looked again to Jade—so beautiful and sexy. He wondered if she carried a concealed weapon, and whether she actually loved him. He wanted to know who Bei Si Tiao really was. Although he had read her unit number, real hometown, and other biographical data, the information did little to explain the creature that sat just three feet away.

"Wow, they have oysters," she said. "You know what they say about those." Jade flashed a wink and broad smile. With her dimpled smirk, the smart sparkle in her eye, and her squeaky little voice, Richard realized he might yet be able to forgive Jade, and that their lives were now forever intertwined. *Maybe*, he supposed, *she had been coerced…Maybe none of this was her fault? Maybe she really does love me.* The heart got the better of the usually logical Richard Ling. Jade realized he was not sharing her excitement for their surroundings and took his hand.

"What's wrong?" she asked.

If he answered honestly, he would say he had just come up with a plan. A waiter arrived with a basket of bread and a plate of cubed butter.

"Nothing, sweetheart. Isn't this great?" Richard smiled and offered her a roll.

6: TIAMAT

"The quality of decision is like the well-timed swoop of a falcon, which enables it to strike and destroy its victim."—Sun Tzu

Jade emerged from the Gallery Place-Chinatown Metro station and walked through Friendship Archway, an ornate gate that spanned DC's H Street. She quickened her pace and weaved her way through the hungry lunchtime crowd, passing under colorful wish lanterns and signs adorned with Chinese characters. Prayer flags flapped in the light breeze. The professor, her handler, had failed to show for the day's lectures. As the dean had stepped in and begun an improvised substitute lecture, Jade sneaked out of the room, and, ignoring protocol, decided to contact the professor. Thinking of Richard and fighting her instinct to turn back, she stood outside the professor's modest apartment. Although she found the front door closed, Jade also found it unlocked. She grasped the butt of the small automatic pistol—a Walther PPK/S—that she had secreted inside her front pant pocket. She pushed the door open.

The door creaked and swung in, revealing the dark. She fell back on training, drawing the weapon and methodically clearing each room of the apartment. In the last room—a makeshift office and study space—she finally discovered the professor, slumped dead in his chair. A bullet had ripped through his shirt and left a small burn mark over his heart, and another bullet a clotted hole in his forehead. His face showed frozen surprise. With heart thundering and an acrid, dry taste in her mouth, Jade felt the urge to scream. However, instead, only a whimper emerged. Jade vomited and ran out of the apartment. As she stumbled down the hall stairs, Special Agent Jackson came up the opposite flight. He found the open door and the crime scene within. He called the Bureau and then his contact at city police.

◊◊◊◊

Commander Wolff had come on with *California*'s midnight watch and stood, nursing his second big cup of black, sweet coffee. For once, somebody had made the brew the way he liked it: steaming hot and strong enough to curl nose hair. Wolff stood between the diving officer and the chief-of-the-watch. He looked to the status board.

California drove on a speed course for a rendezvous with Task Force 24, the new designation for the merged *Essex* and *Ronald Reagan* amphibious and carrier strike groups.

"Slow her down, chief. Let's get the array in the water," Wolff said between sips of coffee.

"Aye sir," the chief responded. "Reduce speed to eight knots. Ready the towed array." The order was repeated several times and the hum of the reactor fell off, while the noise from the churning propeller diminished. After checks, *California*'s microphone-covered cable paid out from a teardrop-shaped chamber on her stern stabilizer. Almost immediately, the passive system detected a noise.

"Conn, sonar. Faint contact," the sonarman announced. The computer began comparing the contact's sound to its vast signature database. While the computer worked, the sonarman began to compile an initial track. Commander Wolff and the executive officer wandered over to the sonar station. "Sounds like a big mother. At least three four-bladed propellers; maybe four," the sonarman reported. A small laser printer churned out a report. The sonarman tore the paper off and read, "One of our *Los Angeles*-class boats recorded something similar in 1990, just outside the Dardanelles in the Aegean. Holy--"

Wolff snatched the paper from the stunned submariner and read it aloud: "*Admiral Kuznetsov*-class multirole aircraft carrier." He whistled like a falling aerial bomb.

The sonarman brought up a three-dimensional graphic of the warship on a video screen, as the computer listed the aircraft carrier's known armaments and capabilities. Wolff perused the data and gave his scalp a contemplative scratch.

"Skipper, I have a 98 percent probability that we're listening to a Russian flattop," the sonarman reported.

"You mean a Chinese flattop bought from Ukraine," Wolff said. The XO reminded his skipper that *Liaoning* had last been spotted in the Yellow Sea, and had been pegged by naval intelligence as a training carrier or temporary helicopter deck. Despite this information, noise from *Liaoning*'s four big propellers and those of her battle group emanated from the bulkhead speaker.

"The mother of all contacts," *California*'s sonarman whispered as he listened to the mechanical music. With a greedy and devious grin, Wolff ordered the sonar station to start a new type on the contact, and then directed the chief-of-the-watch to take *California* up to periscope depth. Both submariners gave their skipper a sharp, "Aye, sir." The chief-of-the-watch began to pass orders down the chain of command.

Wrapped in the comfortable high tech control room, it was easy to forget you were deep beneath the sea. *California*, however, reminded her first-timers that just two metal hulls separated them from death. She creaked, groaned, and popped during the rise, until the boat leveled at 40 feet. The electronic signal mast deployed from the sail and reached up to break the surface for a burst of communication between the submarine and a satellite orbiting overhead. Done, the mast slipped back below the surface, to be replaced by the photonics mast. This mast sent high-resolution thermal imagery to *California*'s control center.

The picture on the screen was undeniable: the Chinese aircraft carrier *Liaoning* and her escort group were sailing some nine miles off the starboard bow. The American submariners watched the huge grey vessel with amazement, and pointed out its bow ramp, spacious deck, and massive superstructure.

"Okay, chief, stow the mast and take us deep," Wolff ordered. The floor began to pitch forward. Those standing grabbed on to something, anything, as the deck became a slide. Leaning against the dive angle, Wolff shuffled to join the executive officer at the tactical table, where he plotted the enemy position on a chart. Bringing up the sonar data on a small horizontal touch screen, the two men concurred that, besides *Liaoning*, they were facing a couple destroyers, frigates, and patrol boats. They reluctantly agreed that enemy subs must be around as well.

"Conn, sonar. Transient, bearing one-nine-two. Designate Sierra One," the sonarman said, and then added, his voice becoming shrill: "High pitch screws. Torpedo in the water."

224

"All ahead full. Countermeasures stand by. Sound collision," the executive officer barked, and the chief-of-the-boat repeated the orders. A horn started and sent men scrambling to collision and damage control stations. Sleeping crew rolled out of bunks, while others on watch shut valves and secured bulkhead hatches.

The captain used 1MC to broadcast an order to all of California's compartments: "Battle stations, torpedo."

The sonarman jumped again, and announced that another submerged contact was bearing two-zero-three.

"What have you got, Jack?" Captain Wolff asked.

"Sir, I heard something; sounded like a trim tank pumping out. Different bearing and range than Sierra One."

"Okay. Good ears, son. Designate the contact as Sierra Two. Peg it as a 'Probsub.'" Wolff could take no chances, and declared the transient sound as a probable submarine.

"Screws and pinging. Another torpedo in the water. This one went active right away."

Commander Wolff ordered flank speed. *California*'s reactor came up to 98 percent, shoving the submarine through the deep. The boat accelerated quickly and topped out at 42 knots. The sonarman warned the center that *California* was cavitating. This meant that, due to blade revolutions, millions of bubbles had formed at the propeller's tips and were collapsing under sea pressure. These implosions coalesced into a rumble that would carry for miles.

"Launch countermeasures," the executive officer ordered. *California*'s hull ejected two small cylinders which began to effervesce. These 'noisemakers' added to the underwater din.

"Rudder hard over." The boat's rudder swung to one side, keeling the boat to an extreme angle and forming a pocket of boiling water.

"Knuckle in the water," the sonarman called out.

With the decoys and swirling knuckle left behind to lure the enemy torpedoes, Wolff had *California* slow down.

Two Chinese heavy torpedoes passed through the curtain of bubbles created by *California*'s noisemakers, but neither weapon detonated. Instead, they both turned for the next sonar return in their path, speeding for the localized disturbance. Below them, in the murk, *California* doubled back.

"Enemy torpedoes passing astern," *California*'s sonarman announced happily. "Sir, Sierra One now identified as Chinese *Shang*-class nuclear attack submarine. Redesignating Sierra One as Shang One."

"Weapons, get me a solution on that sub," Wolff ordered, and then added, "Torpedo room, load tubes one through four with Mark 48s."

The Chinese nuclear attack submarine *Changzheng 6* leaned hard into her turn. Captain Kun had to use the attack center's bulkhead for support. His weapons officer reported that both of their torpedoes had failed to impact and were now in default circular search mode. The man looked to his captain. All submariners knew that, once unleashed, torpedoes presented a danger to both friend and foe alike.

"Sonar, keep an accurate fix on those torpedoes at all times," Kun ordered. "Understood?"

"Yes, sir," was the response. "Captain, submerged contact identified as an American *Virginia*-class nuclear attack submarine."

Kun nodded acknowledgment. He tried hard not to show apprehension; an apprehension imparted by having read all about this type of rather deadly American machine. Fire control announced he had a new solution. Sonar kicked in that 'Virginia One' was running deep and turning toward them. The young Chinese sonarman listened raptly to his headphones and glanced at the digital readout. He then heard something else; something besides the submarine. The sound was a high-pitched whine that emerged from the masking clutter.

"Torpedo," he squealed. "It is running fast."

Kun calmly and quietly thanked the sonar station, before he strolled over to the defensive console to order countermeasures. In the torpedo room, submariners loaded a countermeasures device into the small tube in the compartment's ceiling, locked the hatch, and pulled a lever to eject it into the water.

"Full right rudder. Down 20 degrees. Bring us to one-five-zero meters and fire a torpedo down the angle of attack," Kun said calmly, as though he had just ordered lunch. Kun rested his arms behind his back, determined to be an example of grace under pressure. No one saw his arms shake subtly. Breaking protocol, *Changzheng 6*'s first officer snapped a salute. Then he repeated the orders and turned to the weapons operator.

"Put one right down the path of that torpedo. Do it quickly," he told a subordinate, who scrambled to make it happen.

Most of *California*'s bridge officers congregated at the control center's weapons station. Passive sonar detected a faint noise.

"Sierra Two bearing one-zero-six. No accompanying plant noise. Sir, I think Sierra Two is an SSK," *California*'s sonarman speculated.

Wolff sighed and looked to his executive officer. The XO scrunched his forehead. Both men knew that fighting a nuclear boat is hard enough without adding a near-silent diesel-electric to the mix. This took the melee to a completely new level of danger. The crooked smile on his XO's face told Commander Wolff what he already knew: that the decision rested on his shoulders.

"Power up the active sonar," Wolff said. He had rationalized that the enemy already knew *California* was there. The executive officer could only nod agreement as his own mind swam with adrenalin-fueled aggressiveness plus an equal part survival instinct. The spherical array in *California*'s bow energized. "Hammer."

Steam bubbles formed on *California*'s bow dome. With a low frequency WHOMP, the active sound signal sped through the black water, its waves bounced off *Changzheng 6* and Chinese submarine *#330*, and then returning to *California* like a loyal dog. *California*'s sonar station received accurate enemy ranges, bearings, and fire control solutions for her computer to chew on.

"Conn, sonar. Shang One is at zero-one-nine; bearing one-eight-five. Sierra Two now at one-seven-zero; bearing two-two-two. Both are making turns for about nine knots," *California*'s sonarman reported. A red light flashed on the submariner's console. "High frequency sonar at zero-four-seven. Dipping sonar in the water. Designate as 'Mike One,'" the sonarman added. His voice betrayed the increased stress imparted by the complex tactical situation.

At the dark surface of the East China Sea, high above the sparring submarines steamed the *Liaoning* and her battle group. The Chinese ships turned away from the submerged enemy contact, although they left behind the destroyer *Qingdao* and her Helix anti-submarine helicopter to run interference.

The hovering Helix churned the circle of sea below it as it raised its dipping sonar.

"That would be a Chinese helicopter," Captain Wolff remarked. In his mind's eye, he formed a three-dimensional picture of the battle space: At a depth of 600 feet, *California* was 12,000 yards south of the Chinese submarines that were staggered at depths of 300 and 600 feet, respectively. Wolff had a Mark 48 on the wire. It ran straight and true at 350 feet. Shang One—the Chinese nuclear attack boat—fired a torpedo right back their way. In addition, they had to contend with a helicopter overhead.

"Conn, sonar. Surface contact. Probable destroyer. Designate 'Mike Two.' Identify Mike One as a Helix anti-submarine warfare helicopter. Redesignating Mike One as 'Helix One.'" Refined information appeared on the control center board.

"We've really stepped on a hornet's nest. Recommend we back off, sir," *California*'s executive officer gave unsolicited advice. After all, the XO's job was to be a cautious counter to the commander's aggressiveness. Wolff took a deep breath and explained that, if they could pick their way through the enemy submarines, they would be able to get at the carrier.

"If we sink that bastard—the carrier—we could end this whole damn shooting match," Wolff said, offering a bounty that softened the heavy risk.

"I want to see my wife again," the executive officer said.

"Really?" Wolff prodded his friend. The XO chuckled and relaxed.

"I guess it's a good day to die," the XO surrendered with a shrug. The two old submariners shook each other by the shoulders. Wolff looked around and saw fear in some of the young faces. He knew he had to speak to them; to address their concerns...

"This ship is built to fight. You had better know how," Wolff quoted Admiral Arleigh Burke. These eleven words, spoken by another man so many years ago, were the best Wolff could muster in the speech-making arena.

Big black shadows, the American Mark 48 and Chinese Type 40 heavy torpedoes passed each other in the murk as *California* and *Changzheng 6* moved about the deep. *California*'s torpedo was the first to start pinging, to look for something to hit, as *Changzheng 6* guided her torpedo in. All the while, Chinese submarine *#330* crept along on batteries and sidled for an attack.

"Damn, Sierra Two is quiet," *California*'s sonarman grew frustrated. "Sierra Two is now at two-zero-seven, bearing: zero-three-four." The submariner listened again and heard trickling water in pipes. He knew this sound well, remembering it from recordings presented in training. Although he was more versed in the subtleties of Beasties Boys sampling, he would swear to God that he also knew the sounds of a Chinese submarine's tank transfer system. Therefore, he declared, "Conn, I am calling Sierra Two a Chinese *Yuan*-class diesel-electric submarine. Redesignating Sierra Two as 'Yuan One.' Yuan One is doing revolutions for three knots." While he was in the zone, he also avowed, "designate Mike Two as a *Luhu*-class guided missile destroyer. Calling her Luhu One. Shang One is at one-nine-one and making eight knots and bearing zero-zero-zero. Her plant noise is coming up. Screw noise, too. Enemy torpedo approaching at 37 knots and accelerating. Shang One now bearing zero-zero-two, depth coming down to 500," *California*'s sonarman summarized. Wolff ordered the wires cut on the Mark 48s he had out in the water, leaving the torpedoes to their own devices. The weapon's machine brain took over and sought only to kill without human input. Captain Wolff ordered the chief-of-the-boat to make his depth 250 feet.

"Make it a steep rise, and drop countermeasures," he added.

"Aye, sir. Fairwater planes all rise. Making my depth two-five-zero feet," the chief-of-the-boat confirmed, and then repeated the order. The planesman pulled back on his yoke. *California* pitched up and began her climb through the water column. "Watch your trim; keep her on keel," the chief coached.

Wolff studied the center's tactical display and ordered a speed of 12 knots. A high-pitched ping bounced off *California*'s hull. Wolff's sonarman reported Helix One was in the hover and had dipping sonar in the water at zero-nine-seven some 5,000 yards away. The executive officer made a mark on the table chart, and observed that the helicopter and Chinese destroyer now had enough data to triangulate *California* and fire upon her.

"Got a splash. High-pitch screws. Torpedo in the water," the sonarman confirmed the executive officer's projection. "Torpedo at one-zero-one on a spiral descent."

"Just what we need to spice things up," Wolff said. He made calculations on ranges, speeds, and convergence points in his head. "Okay, chief. Drop countermeasures and take us on a speed course straight at that torpedo," the commander's voice seemed to lack the conviction or confidence it usually portrayed. The chief-of-the-boat noticed the lacking, but acknowledged nonetheless. Then, he turned the prescribed tactics into action. *California*'s reactor and electric motor were pushed to their limits. Two noisemakers were dumped behind as the American nuclear attack submarine made a high-speed dash for the torpedo. Sonar reported the Chinese weapon closing rapidly from 2,000 yards out.

"Sir, if that torpedo goes active before we close the distance--" The executive officer was cut off by the skipper's 'don't tell me what I already know' look.

"Enemy torpedo approaching. One-thousand yards and closing," the sonarman declared. The chief-of-the-boat reported the boat was doing 40 knots on a course of zero-nine-zero.

"Sound collision," Wolff demanded. Inside *California*'s cylindrical pressure hull, crewmen prepared to fight fire, water, or both.

"Torpedo ahead," the chief-of-the-watch called out. Then he looked to his stopwatch and stated, "Twenty seconds to merge." Time was some comfort; a potential to overcome before the inevitable. The sonar station announced that the second enemy torpedo had acquired

232

California's noisemakers and turned for them. "Fifteen seconds. All compartments report ready for collision," the chief-of-the-boat proclaimed. Wolff patted the loyal, patriotic man on the back. He quietly ordered him to take the enemy weapon down the port side of the machine within which they rode, the machine that sustained them; kept them alive. The chief spoke to the pilot and copilot. He coaxed them to gingerly adjust their controllers. Their actions maneuvered the submarine below and to the right of the torpedo's track.

The whining sound of the Chinese torpedo grew louder in *California*'s control center. Some of the American submariners fidgeted, while others sat still. One man closed his eyes, choosing this way to await death. The sound generated by the Chinese torpedo filled the entire compartment. Its din moved down the long length of *California* before it faded away. The executive officer let out a nervous chuckle. As the Americans relaxed for a bit, the Chinese torpedo activated some one hundred yards behind *California*. Commander Wolff had gotten safely behind one torpedo and far away from the other. The remaining pursuing weapon began to run out of fuel. As it dipped in its course and began to sink, both *California*'s chief-of-the-boat and executive officer congratulated Commander Wolff, smacking him on the shoulders, congratulating him for turning a dangerous tactical situation around.

Changzheng 6 released decoys and crash-dived into the icy blackness. Kun took his submarine down to 1,200 feet, close to his hull's official crush-depth. The submarine squeaked, and a low resonance vibrated. Steel in *Changzheng 6*'s sail warped. It banged and popped, reshaping under growing sea pressure. Desperate to enter, water punished the blasphemy of such a manmade void. *Hold together for me just a bit longer*, Kun prayed, while his crewmen twitched nervously with every sound. Despite their overwhelming fear, they nonetheless kept their stations. Kun turned to his sonarman. He watched intently as the young person listened to the American torpedo that searched some 700 feet overhead.

"The enemy torpedo is losing speed; likely at the limits of its range," the boy reported.

"Find our submarine, number *330*. Where is it? And find me that damned American, too." After evasive maneuvers, Captain Kun needed to rebuild his tactical picture, and he demanded the information. Kun ordered that *Changzheng 6* double back while slowly decreasing depth.

California's control center became quiet. Commander Wolff, the executive officer, and the chief-of-the-boat all paced behind technicians seated at terminals lining the curved wall.

"Conn, sonar. Luhu One is at zero-four-three and bearing one-nine-three. Speed: 30 knots," the sonarman informed the officers. Active sonar slammed the ocean and reverberated through *California*'s hull. Like a prison guard throwing a spotlight on a nighttime escapee, the Chinese destroyer *Qingdao* had illuminated *California* with sound, pinpointing the elusive American with the powerful sonar housed in the ship's bow stem.

Qingdao's warfare center lay deep within the destroyer's pyramidal superstructure. Paneled with glowing flatscreens, the center was manned by sailors seated at terminals that showed anti-air, anti-ship, and anti-submarine warfare data. Standing on a small pedestal beside a fold-down table, *Qingdao*'s watch commander ordered the anti-submarine helicopter in for another attack.

The Helix dropped its nose and bolted toward the new coordinates. It arrived quickly, lobbed its second torpedo into the water, and dropped into a hover before dipping its sonar for a good listen. The Helix transmitted the data back to *Qingdao*'s warfare center. Listening to the sonar's microphone, the sonarman encountered a whooshing sound that he did not recognize.

The Helix reeled in the long wire with the sonar transducer at the end. Done fishing at this spot, it readied to move to a new position. The pilot noticed a splash some 300 meters away. He watched as a white canister broached the sea surface and leapt into the air. The canister peeled apart and a puff of smoke and a streak of blue erupted.

As its underwater housing fell back to the water, the small Stinger missile rode its booster into the sky. Once at 2,000 feet, the booster fell away and pulled an oblique parasail from the Stinger's tail assembly. The wing-shaped parachute pointed the Stinger's nose at the water, swinging the missile's infrared seeker back-and-forth in a big figure eight. The Stinger found the Helix's big, hot turbines and locked on. The parachute released, and the main motor fired. The Stinger accelerated through its dive and drove right into the Helix's counter-rotating blades and engine pylon. Seven pounds of high explosives went off and the Chinese helicopter then became a fireball, its wreckage dropping to the sea and sinking like a rock. Next, a big Tomahawk rose from the water's surface. The American anti-ship cruise missile configured for flight and headed for the Chinese guided-missile destroyer *Qingdao*.

Commander Wolff felt he had lingered too long at missile launch depth. Although he had been able to destroy the helicopter and get in a shot in at the surface threat, this lingering had allowed both Shang One and Yuan One to get in behind his boat. *California* dove, picked up speed, and banked into a sharp turn. The sonarman heard the rush of several torpedo shots and called it out. Wolff ordered countermeasures.

Four Chinese heavy torpedoes passed through the noisemakers and activated, *California* directly ahead. Her propeller shredded the water as she dove and turned. All four of the big torpedoes acquired the American submarine and accelerated.

Kun brought his boat behind the fleeing American, while his comrade in *#330* slowed and hung back to become the anvil to *Changzheng 6*'s hammer. High above the scrambling submarines and with a cruise missile headed her way, *Qingdao* maneuvered and prepared to defend herself.

Qingdao ripple-fired her Red Banner short-range air defense missiles. They streaked off and trailed ropes of white smoke, leaving a puffy white cloud that enveloped *Qingdao*'s quarterdeck. One Red Banner collided with *California*'s single Tomahawk anti-ship missile, consuming it in an explosion that scattered debris and wreckage to the water. Driven on by her furious captain perched in the bridge, *Qingdao* rammed through the waves. The Chinese destroyer sped to close the distance on the American submarine's likely position, where the captain planned to bring his rocket-delivered torpedoes to bear.

Despite surprise and initial success, the American nuclear attack submarine was now heavily outnumbered and on the defensive.

California leveled from the turning dive and deployed a towed decoy from the hull dispenser. The decoy broadcasted noise typical of a nuclear power plant, to acoustically tempt the Chinese torpedoes away from the submarine. It worked with the first pursuing torpedo, which zeroed on the decoy, detonated, and committed fratricide on the other Chinese weapons that ran in close proximity. The generated pressure wave caught *California* in the ass and shook her hard. Pipes burst and high-pressure air lines whistled, rocking *California* to her bones. Lights flickered and emergency lighting kicked on in the control center. Panel warning lights began to flash as system after system showed wounds. A worrisome clank broadcast into the water, and damage reports started coming in from the engine and reactor compartments. The pressure wave passed. *California* and her submariners quivered in its wake.

"Come on, Cali' girl, keep it together," Wolff pleaded. In the red shadows, he watched the chief-of-the-boat as he scurried from station to station. Although injured, *California* had survived and the Chinese weapons had been destroyed. The large underwater explosion had also advantageously released billions of bubbles.

"Ensonified area astern," *California*'s sonarman announced. The sonic wall now obscured *California* from *Changzheng 6*'s listening devices, and provided the American submarine the chance to sneak away. In his usual unpredictable fashion, Wolff ordered the sub's propeller stopped and the boat put into a stationary dive, a maneuver last practiced under the Arctic ice sheet. As the propeller slowed and stopped turning, the rhythmic clanking disappeared. This confirmed the origin of the noise: a bent shaft.

"The boat is stationary," the XO reported.

"Take us down, Tom." *California* dropped straight and level into the abyss.

Changzheng 6 passed overhead. The American was not where Kun thought he was. The Chinese submarine let off a single active sonar ping.

"Shoot," Commander Wolff ordered. A Mark 48 departed one of *California*'s bow tubes. The submarine's weapons officer had set the torpedo's engine to run slow and shallow. The Mark 48 tipped back and started to climb through *Changzheng 6*'s baffles.

Changzheng 6's sonar screens were still flooded by residual noise. Her sonarman rebuilt the tactical picture as Kun impatiently hurried him along. The sonarman suddenly looked to the captain. A sound made him grimace as though in pain.

"Torpedo," he screamed. Kun ordered countermeasures and full speed on the motor. *Changzheng 6* accelerated. The American torpedo's electromagnetic coil detected the Chinese submarine's metal hull. Its high-explosive warhead and remaining fuel blew up, forming a bubble jet that expanded into *Changzheng 6*'s propeller. The blades bent, a vertical stabilizer cracked off, and a welded hull seam yielded to the overpressure. Freezing seawater entered the shaft stuffing box and began to flood the aft engineering spaces. The executive officer ordered the pumps activated and the transfer of water to the ballast tanks.

"Blow it overboard," *Changzheng 6*'s executive ordered, pressing his kerchief to the bleeding gash on Kun's forehead.

"The pumps can't keep up," someone announced in the flickering compartment light.

Seawater entered the submarine's machinery compartment. The high temperature gas-cooled nuclear reactor scrammed when its systems shorted. With the reactor shutting down and only batteries left to power backups, *Changzheng 6* slowly began to sink backward.

Despite noisy protests from the propulsor duct, *California* came up to six knots. Her sonarman confirmed the position of the explosion, while listening to the sinking Chinese submarine.

Changzheng 6 tipped onto her side. Captain Kun and his executive landed on a pile of dead and dying men. The shattering hull emanated a crystalline resonance. *It sounds like breaking glass.* This recognition was Kun's very last thought.

A muffled thud emanated from the deep, coming through *California*'s bulkhead speaker. Wolff contemplated the fate of the Chinese submariners. Training told him that, in an implosion, the sea entered so quickly that air within the hull ignited and burned. He shook the horrific thought, and offered a quick, silent prayer for the vanquished men.

"Where is that diesel-electric? And get me an update on that goddamned destroyer." Wolff had been forced to kill, and was angry about it. Angry at the idiots that started this scrap. And angry at those who let the US Navy degrade to the point where the Chinese actually believed they could control the Pacific, thus placing his boat and crew in harm's way.

"Splashes. Multiple torpedoes in the water. They're diving to different depths and starting to search," *California*'s sonarman reported. "Luhu One has turned away and is speeding up; same course as the rest of the Chinese battle group."

Wolff crawled into his enemy's head. The destroyer captain knows one of their submarines was dead, so he's putting a bunch of ordinance between him and me, and heading back to his buddies, Wolff estimated.

"Yuan One?" Wolff asked, worried about that which he could not see. People's Liberation Army Navy submarine *#330* announced her continued presence with a torpedo shot.

Over the clatter of *California*'s damage, the sonarman heard the high-speed counter-rotating propellers of the Chinese weapon, and alerted *California*'s conn.

"Countermeasures. All rise," Wolff had now ordered noisemakers and the fairwater planes set for a steep ascent. Then he ordered a torpedo sent right back at his rival. Although she may not be able to maneuver, *California* could still bite, Wolff resolved.

"Torpedo just went active," sonar declared.

"Can you identify?" Wolff demanded.

"Sounds to me like a Chinese Type 40 heavy, sir."

Wolff turned to the XO and asked, "Hey, Tom, what's the search frequency of that fish?"

Reading his skipper's mind, the XO went to the sonar station, looked over the weapon's specifications, and set the advanced sonar sphere in *California*'s bow dome to match the wavelength of the search sonar on the Chinese weapon.

"Hammer," Wolff ordered, and the XO pushed the button. *California* blasted sound into the water. The noise cancelled seeker transmissions from *#330*'s torpedo and saturated its receiver with hundreds of false targets. Confused, the Chinese heavy torpedo began to veer from *California*.

California's Mark 48 activated just 40 yards off *#330*'s bow. Using staccato pings, the 48 slammed into the Chinese submarine's forward hull, exploding on contact. The shock wave shattered the high-tensile steel and opened *#330*'s pressure hull to the sea. A supersonic liquid juggernaut approached the submarine's control room and rammed its bulkhead hatch. The door warped and burst from its frame, shot across the bridge, and pulverized everything in its way. A jagged hole marked where *#330*'s bow dome used to be. The Chinese submarine flooded and began a final plunge. Her ruin crash-landed on a deep rocky outcropping and, in the aftermost compartment, twelve Chinese submariners lit oxygen-generating candles and exchanged stories of loved ones. One-by-one, however, they succumbed to foul air and freezing temperatures.

"Give these hostile waters a wide berth," Tom, Wolff ordered.

The XO established a course due east.

Commander Wolff knew the war was now over for *California* and her crew. The American nuclear attack submarine limped from the area.

The Chinese aircraft carrier *Liaoning* and her escorts tore through waves, steaming south directly at the American task force. In the dark of night, between the huge, merging naval formations, the last surviving submarine of the Taiwanese navy waited; *Hai Hu*, the Sea Tiger. The diesel-electric attack submarine waited on the surface, where she snorkeled fresh air and recharged her batteries beneath the sparkling stars. *Hai Hu* had just escaped an encounter with two Chinese destroyers, lived through a near hit from a light torpedo, and barely escaped a hail of depth charges. Half of the crew was dead. The other half shivered and gasped at the fresh air that breezed through compartments heavy with stale air. Perched atop the sail, the captain peered up at the Seven Stars of the Northern Dipper. A meteorite's burning trail sparkled for a moment and a warm breeze refreshed his face.

Hai Hu, damaged and alone, could still maneuver, and still had a half charge within her battery bank. Silhouetted against the backbone of night, the captain decided to make a last stand against the Communists. He would take his Dutch-built boat down deep and await the enemy carrier that reportedly headed their way. *Once on the bottom, no one will find me*, his mind slithered like an eel. *Not even Mazu—Goddess of the Sea*. *Hai Hu*'s captain took a final look at the heavens. He breathed deep the wet salty air, held and savored it, and descended into the submarine's sail. The outer hatch shut with a ringing clank.

◊◊◊◊

Jade waited for Richard in their Georgetown apartment. After finding herself under surveillance, and after coming upon the body of her murdered contact/professor, she was surprised to be still alive, and was filled with fear and regret. Sitting in a dining chair, she clutched a pistol; the very one she had considered using on herself. She had gone as far as resting the cold barrel to her forehead. Between sobs, as her finger began squeezing the trigger, she had instead chosen life and decided to face the consequences of her actions. Instead of painting a wall with her brains, Jade had decided to fire the gun on anybody other than Richard Ling who came through the apartment door. Jade perched in a chair and waited. It was then that she began to doze off.

A crunching sound awakened Jade. She remembered where she was, as well as the granulated sugar she had spread about the door's threshold. She observed shadows beneath the door's transom, and brought the gun's barrel up. Keys jingled and then slid into the lock. Jade put slight pressure to the trigger as the door swung open.

"Jade?" Richard asked. He glanced inside, and then retreated from the gun aimed his way. He waved a white kerchief, and Jade laughed with exhaustion. She dropped the gun to the floor with a clunk, swooned and folded off the chair, collapsing to the floor. Richard rushed in. He caught and collected her limp body. Stroking her head, he whispered forgiveness, reassurances, and pledges of love. He scooped Jade up and carried her to their bed.

Richard locked the door. As though it might burn him, he picked up the handgun with the tips of his fingers and placed it in a kitchen drawer. He moistened a towel and brought it to her, draping it across her clammy forehead, and sat beside her. Her eyes flickered open. She smiled, and her eyes closed again. Richard picked up her hand and weighed everything: fatherhood; betrayal; loyalty; career; marriage. He was convinced of what he had to do, and what it would cost him. He strode to his computer desk, brought up an airline website, and booked two tickets to San Francisco. Deciding a train was the best way to get to Dulles International Airport outside the capital, he clicked over to DC Metrorail's website. *I have to keep her safe tonight*, he thought. He was unaware that his surfing was being watched. Richard got two suitcases from a closet and started packing.

◊◊◊◊

Senior Master Sergeant Li and the men of Hill 112 held fast. A few of them had dressed up as civilians, and raided supermarkets and pharmacies for supplies. One man had even located a radio in an abandoned Humvee. Li used it to re-establish contact with Hengshan Command Center and to continue his reports on enemy dispositions at Songshan Airport. Li had also requested relief. Expected any time, a detachment from the 6th Army was to infiltrate up the back of the hill.

Li had designated and deployed a small patrol to intercept and guide them into Hill 112's perimeter, now a warren of camouflaged slip trenches, anti-personnel mines, and foxholes. Soon enough, the platoon arrived with food, water, ammunition, and a replacement radio. Li was astonished to find an American Marine with them—the first Li and his men had ever met—as well as a bunch of Taiwanese special forces. *My little hill has suddenly become important*, Li thought as he ate fresh rations and watched the newly arrived settle in.

The American unpacked and set up a tripod-mounted laser designator-rangefinder. He then unfurled camouflage netting, stringing it between bare tree branches, and mounting a small satellite dish to a splintered tree stump before aligning it with a point in the sky. The American adjusted the laser and tilted it at Songshan Airport. Feeling he watched, the Marine turned to Li. He approached the haggard looking Taiwanese airman and saluted. Li put down his food, stood, and returned the gesture. The Marine offered his hand. Senior Master Sergeant Li weakly accepted it.

"I'm Lieutenant Shane Whidby, 1st Reconnaissance Company, 1st Marine Division, United States Marine Corps. Looks like you guys had quite a party." Feeling better from food, drink, and a vitamin shot, Li forced a smile and adjusted the sling that supported his injured arm.

"Senior Master Sergeant Li Rong Kai. Yes, quite a party, as you say. Why are you here?" Li asked in good English.

"We have a special target that needs attention. Your orders are to cooperate with me. Your countrymen can confirm this. When I am done, you will head out with the Special Services Company for debriefing. You are to be relieved." Like most US Marines, Whidby's voice was hoarse and gravelly from a life-spent shouting.

"Relieved?" Li asked. He remembered his order to 'hold the hill until overrun or relieved.' His duty had been done, Li realized. His chest inflated and he thanked the American. "Lieutenant Whidby, do you have a wife? Kids?"

"Yes," the American said, and smiled for the first time in days. "And I'm sure yours are fine." The American slapped Li on the back, and then walked back to his laser. A soldier came to Li and handed him an envelope. Inside was an official letter informing Li of his promotion to chief master sergeant. Li chuckled. He could not wait to tell his wife. However, the smile faded fast, and the letter went back in its envelope and into Li's jacket pocket.

In the early morning mist, opposite where Chief Master Sergeant Li was finishing his breakfast, two Taiwanese operators led Hill 112's prisoner behind the ruined bunker and off into the jungle.

Unaware of standing orders to summarily execute deserters or spies, Li had brought the airman up on charges of desertion and murder, and placed him in the custody of the military police. Operators from the Nighthawks had other plans and duties for the man, however.

The jungle became the accused's courtroom. The chirping birds: his visitor gallery. A silenced gunshot to the neck was judgment and sentence. Burial: an unceremonious roll down a steep ravine.

◊◊◊◊

Outside Hsinchu City, an old farmer found an unconscious Major Han, hanging in an orchard tree, his parachute tangled in its old limbs. The farmer brought Han home to his wife and visiting niece, who, carefully peeled away the shattered helmet and stitched up Han's slashed scalp.

Han woke to the warm morning sea breeze that wafted through a window. Delicate curtains danced for him. He reached for a glass of water set beside a small radio on the nightstand. His ribs hurt when he sat up. He turned on the radio.

Broadcasting from a mobile transmitter, Taiwanese news was doing its best to cut through Chinese jamming, with more squealing static than words. A knock sounded at the bedroom door.

"Come," Han groaned.

The farmer's buxom niece came in to express her new crush with hot tea and biscuits. With her cleavage in his face, she propped Han up with pillows. She stood and, with hands to hips, declared, "We have to get you strong enough to fight again." Han swallowed some tea. "Anything else I can do?" she said, and cocked her waist. Han smiled and thanked her. He watched her behind as she left, and felt his strength return. A jet roared overhead and his heart raced. *I have to get back to base*, he thought. Han stood dizzily. His best chance was to get to the east coast air base at Hualien City. He would have to cross the mountains to do so. When his host, the old farmer, politely knocked and entered, Han asked to borrow the family car. The old man was happy to help, but insisted on doing the driving.

Major Han, the farmer, and his attentive niece got into the old Swedish wagon. Refusing to let his family be split up, the farmer's wife, daughter, and son also piled into the blue car. Even the farm mutt jumped in.

The wagon struggled to climb narrow winding mountain roads. Stopping for several Taiwanese checkpoints, Han showed identification and talked his way through. The wagon crossed the central peaks, and Han and the family started down the eastern side of the island. The wagon coasted and purred happily most of the way into the valley. Forest opened to coastal plain. As the wagon leaned through a sharp turn, Han pointed at their destination: Hualien City Airport.

The shared civilian-military airport's runway paralleled the coast. Han spotted a Fighting Falcon as it taxied over a wide freeway and toward the base of the mountains, where there was a second runway and tunnels burrowed into the rock face. Han knew the tunnels protected airplanes, crews, fuel, and ordinance from incessant Chinese missile raids. Along with another, smaller facility to the south, enough of Taiwan's air force had been preserved within, able to resist the onslaught. Han observed engineers patching a runway crater with gravel and fiberglass mats, while more men painted a fake crater beside it. The old wagon navigated the switchbacks into the valley and approached the base's main gate.

A heavy machinegun poked from a pillbox. Burly guards emerged to greet them. They checked the family's passports and Han's identification and flight suit. Han saluted the old farmer and shook hands with the rest of his new family. He came to the farmer's round niece and squeezed her tight. Then Han stepped onto base.

A Humvee quickly arrived to transport the valuable pilot inside. Once the base commander had been assured the downed airman was not an infiltrator, Han was sent to the base ward for a once-over, and then on to the mess for a square meal. With one broken rib and three others bruised, Han was wrapped tightly at the torso, and then assigned a bunk. It was not long before a noncommissioned officer arrived. His only question: "Can you fly?" Major Han assured him he was ready to get back in the cockpit.

After pausing at a guard shack for a recheck of credentials and a canine sweep of the pickup truck, Han and his escort were then cleared to proceed into the mountain base. The roadway continued underground, and daylight faded. Short stalactites had formed along the ceiling where moist summer air chilled, condensed, and dripped. The roadway turned at a right angle and then passed an open steel door before it emptied into a vast space cut from the living rock. The man-made cavern was lined with antechambers. Each stored parked fighter-bombers: Ching Kuos, Fighting Falcons, and Mirages. The truck followed roadway markings and passed rows of aircraft in the process of re-arming, refueling, and repair. The driver stopped before a coved bay that held a worn-looking Fighting Falcon.

"It looks as bad as you do," Han's escort joked. As though it were a long-lost love, Han went to the airplane. The Fighting Falcon was light grey with an orange and red sun on its tail. He patted one of its wing tip-mounted Sky Sword air-to-air missiles. Han then ran his hand along the single Paveway 2,000-pound laser-guided bomb tucked beneath the warplane's fuselage. As the pickup truck pulled away, another air force officer walked over to brief Han.

◊◊◊◊

In the deep, dark blue of the East China Sea, *Hai Hu* rested in the bottom mud. The Taiwanese diesel-electric attack submarine had just two hours before she had to resurface and snorkel air.

"Come on, where are you?" the captain wondered aloud. Washed in red emergency lighting, shadows moved about the dripping dark of *Hai Hu*'s control center.

"Sir," the sonarman said. The captain scrambled against the sloping floor and went to the sonar station. "Faint surface contacts." He pointed at his screen. "Approaching from the northwest. One contact is faster than the others. Sounds like a frigate." The Taiwanese submariners remained motionless and silent, listening to propellers, and then the rhythmic thumping of a helicopter. "Aircraft." Then they heard pinging. "Dipping sonar." Then a blast of sound as the Chinese frigate *Xiangfan* fired off her bow sonar. If *Hai Hu*'s muddy disguise worked, the Taiwanese sub would appear on Chinese screens as part of the bottom topography; just a small hill.

The Chinese aircraft carrier *Liaoning* was turned into the wind and making way at 22 knots. In immediate attendance were the guided-missile destroyers *Harbin* and *Qingdao*, as well as the frigate

Zigong. Named for the largest fresh water lake in northern China, the replenishment oiler *Weishanhu* brought up the rear, along with several other auxiliary types, including an intelligence trawler. The forward element of the battle group comprised the frigate *Xiangfan*, diesel-electric attack submarine *#342*, and a variety of small torpedo boats and patrol craft. The guided-missile frigate *Maanshan,* 50 miles away, raced to join *Liaoning*'s battle group. Diesel-electric attack submarine *#286* trailed five miles behind *Maanshan,* snorkeling at the surface and running her diesels in order to catch up. Coming from another direction, Chinese submarine *#111* was unaware she was being stalked from above by an American Poseidon. The Chinese submarine would never make it to *Liaoning*'s side.

In *Hai Hu*'s cold center, the Taiwanese submarine's remaining crew listened to the commotion. The sonarman studied his display, scrutinizing each noise.

"Submarine on creep motors," the sonarman whispered to his crewmates. Another sound grew louder, a propeller that rose and fell as it passed overhead. "That was a diesel-electric submarine, likely *Ming*-class," the sonarman narrated. A sloshing sound came to dominate. The computer reported the sound as the approach of a surface contact. A moment later, the computer identified the contact as a *Jiangwei II*-class guided missile frigate. High-pitched whining flooded the speaker. "Probably small boats—torpedo or small guided-missile types," he whispered. The ships at the forward edge of the Chinese battle group passed over. Their noise reached a crescendo, and then fell off and became part of the background ruckus. A new rumble started low and grew. "The big stuff's coming," *Hai Hu*'s sonarman said, adjusting knobs and dials in an attempt to filter the cacophony into distinguishable parts. He closed his eyes to sharpen hearing. "I hear several large vessels heading our way. Twin propellers. There's also one four-propeller ship," he said, and turned to smile at his captain. "Sir, this has to be *Liaoning*." The men shuffled excitedly. It was true they may not survive, but the prospect of a final stab at the enemy's heart was gratifying.

The captain ordered *Hai Hu*'s last weapons—a brace of heavyweight torpedoes—loaded into the bow tubes. To loosen the bottom's sticky hold on the submarine, trim tanks were flooded in alternating fashion, to rock *Hai Hu* from side-to-side. A storm of silt stirred, and the Taiwanese submarine slowly started to rise. The sail-mounted fairwater planes angled up and pivoted the boat bow high. Pressured air displaced water in the forward ballast tanks. She climbed steeper and faster.

"Aft tanks still flooded. I cannot control rate of rise," *Hai Hu*'s dismayed first officer reported. The men began procedures to regain control of their damaged boat. They angled down the fairwater planes and opened valves to flood the bow tanks. Although a status light showed green, the damaged valves remained stuck closed. *Hai Hu* found herself on an express ride to the surface. In the dark, someone started calling off depth. *Hai Hu*'s pitch exceeded 50 degrees, and somebody tumbled from his chair. *Hai Hu* began to roll. Floors become walls. Anything or anyone not secured started to topple and cartwheel. Although he knew his broken vessel was incapable of complying, the captain ordered all-back-full, and struggled his way up to the navigation station. He whispered an order to the helmsman who now laid back like an astronaut in a space capsule. When the young helmsman grasped what he was being told, his mouth opened in disbelief. Then his face firmed up and took on a determinedly stoic countenance.

"Sonar, go active. Call out range and bearing to largest surface contact," the captain ordered. *Hai Hu*'s bow sonar lashed the water. The sonarman called out the largest return on his scope, and the helmsman moved his control yoke and pedals, swinging the planes and rudder to guide the 220-foot 3,000-ton submarine. "Tubes one and two, open outer doors." The captain looked to the crewman who should have responded. He lay slumped and unconscious. *Hai Hu* rolled again, as she rocketed toward the surface.

Liaoning plowed the water. The Chinese aircraft carrier displaced thousands of tons of seawater that continuously created a sweeping current along her sides. Beneath her, *Hai Hu* ascended from the deep. Ensconced in bubbles, *Hai Hu* penetrated *Liaoning*'s wash and collided with her rounded hull. The submarine's bow dome shattered and her forward casing crumpled. *Hai Hu* was bowled over by the leviathan, although she imparted a second, glancing blow before she violently rolled again and breached. *Hai Hu* bobbed vertically in a pool of blue foam and manmade fluids. Her cracked bow had become a jagged jaw. Water rushed through the forward-most bulkheads and flooded *Hai Hu*, bringing her horizontal again. The Taiwanese submarine rolled over, and her sail smacked the water like a whale fluke. *Hai Hu* bobbed and spun in *Liaoning*'s turbulent wake. What was left of the Taiwanese submarine settled directly in the path of the oiler *Weishanhu*.

Weishanhu put her engines into full reverse. Despite this effort, *Weishanhu* met the submarine's wreckage amidships, sailed up and over her, and shoved her under to trundle along the oiler's bottom. The wreckage ripped into *Weishanhu*'s hull, propellers, and then rudders. *Hai Hu* finally succumbed and cracked at the weld lines, breaking into barrel sections that sank quickly. Unaware of the severity of her injuries, *Weishanhu* continued for a distance, before her bridge crew leaned over the gunwale and found their ship riding low in the water. 'All stop,' was the order. The Chinese oiler started to list to port, and, menacingly, a slick of aviation fuel and bunker oil began to surround her. Sailors scrambled to lifeboat stations and prepared to abandon ship. One group swung a davit outboard, creating a spark. The cloud of fumes ignited with a whoosh. A square mile of ocean flashed in seconds, and burned. Like the herd abandoning a doomed animal, *Liaoning* and the battle group left the burning *Weishanhu* in their wake.

The sunset glowed across the western horizon. On the flying bridge of the Chinese aircraft carrier, the admiral read a typewritten damage report. *Liaoning* had suffered only minor hull damage and one rudder and shaft were out of action. However, he nodded happily. *Liaoning* remained fit for duty.

Meanwhile, General Zhen surveyed the western approaches to Taipei from a hilltop, happy to be far from Beijing and back on the battlefield. He admired the purple and orange sunset that outlined the spiked shadows of the Taiwanese capital's skyscrapers. Zhen took a deep breath of the fragrant breeze and raised his binoculars. *The*

terrain is perfect, he thought. *The hills channel an attacker into the ravine where the #3 Freeway runs and the Linkou mesa isolates the city's west from the sea.* This is where Zhen concentrated his armor and artillery.

Zhen swung his view to the east where he had reinforced the capital's eastern approaches with hordes of infantry. He panned the binoculars to where the Danshui River met the mercurial sea. To deter a waterborne attack on the captured city, the People's Liberation Army Navy had arrayed a force of patrol and torpedo boats, and had at least one attack submarine lurking offshore at all times.

General Zhen turned to the southwestern coast and the container port at Kaohsiung, safely held tight by Chinese marines. And, the same held true further south at Mailiao. Army reinforcements had poured into these ports and expanded their defensive perimeters. The thorn in Zhen's side, however, was the slow arrival of heavy armor from the mainland, leaving his forces dangerously light. Reorganized Taiwanese units were already probing, and enemy operators and bands of armed civilians were now hitting patrols and supply convoys A Vigorous Dragon roared over Zhen on its way to prosecute a target. He contemplated the smoky trail the Chinese fighter-bomber left hanging in the sky. *The People's Liberation Army Air Force no longer enjoys air superiority*, he pondered. The aerial front was now shifted west as Taiwan's supposedly defeated air force staged aerial ambushes from eastern redoubts. This translated into less air cover and less close air support for Chinese ground forces. Zhen shook his head at lost opportunities.

Then he focused on the task at hand. He signaled to his waiting driver that it was time to go.

Taiwan's Major General Tek peered at Taipei from his rooftop command post. He looked back to the map he had been studying by flashlight. Tek imagined arrows and avenues of advance overlaid on the map, following streets and terrain. The entire 6th Army had been placed under the major general's command, and he would soon throw its massive weight against the invaders. As the 8th and 10th Armies prepared to assault the maritime terminals on the west coast, the 6th— with the captured ground across the Toucian River consolidated— would surge northeast to the capital. Both of the 6th's armored brigades had already assembled on the plateau to the west of the capital, in Jhongli and Pingjhen City, and the 21st Artillery Command was moved up to Dasi. To the south-west, the 269th Mechanized Infantry Brigade marshaled in Yangmei while four infantry brigades from the Armed Force Reserve Command united on the coast at Guanyin, with two more brigades held in reserve further south. Tek shone his light on the map. He illuminated Jhubei City's airfield, located beside the Toucian River. Taiwan's 862nd Special Ops Group and the 601st Air Cavalry staged here.

The low thump of the 862nd's and 601st's helicopters drew Tek's eyes to the west, where he focused his binoculars. In the magnified view, he found Super Cobra gunships, armed with TOW missiles and rotary cannons. They led several Black Hawk transports and a Chinook heavy transport, with its double rotor chopping at the air. Tek panned his view toward the freeways and watched his tanks and men assemble at a key intersection along Route 66. He traced the line of fuel bowsers and supply trucks that stretched back in the direction of Jhubei City. Tek lowered the spyglasses and checked his watch. As the second hand ticked down to 0400—X-Hour—the first reports from the artillery echoed among the hills and mountains.

The artillery had now opened up on Taoyuan International Airport. They would soften the way, using airburst anti-personnel, fragmentation, and illumination rounds to keep the Chinese in their foxholes while damaging the enemy combat aircraft parked there. Fire would then shift to the beach north of the airport to pave the way for the marines. The barrage would lift as the air cavalry began its assault on the runways and terminal. While this transpired, Artillery Command would focus its lethal cannons on enemy positions in Taoyuan City and Lujhu and Yingge Townships. All the while, armor, mechanized infantry, and regular infantry would charge east by coastal routes and freeway, thrusting toward their objective: the #2 Freeway that ran north/south along the mesa. Meanwhile, special operators had been tasked with eliminating enemy command and control nodes across the battlefield, as well as to create general confusion in the enemy rear. Tek looked at his map and shifted the circle of light. He shone it on Chiang Kai Shek International Airport, where the navy's 66th Marine Brigade would go ashore and retake the airport from the Chinese invaders. *It is time*, Tek thought. The Taiwanese major general ran to the building's helipad and the machine that awaited him. Saluted as he jumped in, he would be airborne in moments.

◊◊◊◊

As usual, Union Station was a tapestry of people. From this terminal, they arrived at and departed the American capital, to among others, Boston, Chicago, Philadelphia, and New York. Beneath the station's barrel-vaulted, coffered ceiling, travelers scurried to and from trains, and connected with buses, taxis, and DC's subway, the Metro. Jade and Richard hid themselves among the tide of people. She had cut her hair and dyed it a dark shade of red, and dressed in her version of casual: a leather jacket, NY Mets cap, and worn blue jeans. *Even incognito, she's a beauty*, Richard thought. He took and tugged her hand. They had to move faster to their track.

They passed through the doorway and emerged on the platform where a silvery, streamlined locomotive sat at the head of several passenger coaches. On adjacent tracks, local trains from Maryland and Virginia came and went, and Amtrak's Capitol Limited had just arrived from Chicago. A uniformed cart attendant stocked their train's diner car as another man monitored a hose pumping fresh water into a carriage's holding tank. Jade and Richard noticed an armed guard, watching boxes and suitcases being loaded into the train's baggage cart. Richard scanned the platform crowd. His paranoia made him assume that the hot blonde touching up her lipstick was CIA, and the gentleman reading the day's paper was FBI. Although wrong in both cases, what his sixth sense could not suspect was that a Chinese sniper had been situated high in the structure of the station's iron train shed, and had a telescopic sight centered on Richard's chest.

As Jade texted on her phone, the Chinese operator shifted the rifle's crosshairs to her center-of-mass.

"That's not a good idea; using that thing," Richard said, pointing at the phone.

As he eavesdropped on Jade's cellphone microphone, FBI Special Agent Jackson smiled at Richard's statement and silently agreed.

The sniper gently began to squeeze the trigger of the high-powered, suppressed rifle. When other passengers rushing to board the train blocked his shot, he backed off on the pressure. The Chinese intelligence operator muttered curses, and the pigeons that shared his roost blinked blankly. The sniper focused again through the sight. The woman—his target—was now blocked by the porter. Then Richard moved into the sight's view.

"*Fen,*" he silently cursed.

Although the American would be acceptable collateral damage, having Richard's bleeding dead body sprawled across the platform was not this operator's primary goal.

Unaware Richard had now inadvertently saved her life by blocking the shot, Jade handed tickets to the train's conductor, and she and Richard climbed into the silver coach. The capped porter smiled and welcomed them aboard. With all his passengers on the train, the conductor, too, climbed the steps as he checked his pocket watch.

Jade and Richard grew more relaxed with every mile they put between themselves and downtown DC. They arrived at Dulles International Airport station, hopped a bus to the terminal, were felt up by security, and boarded a cramped jet. Despite the wafer-thin seat cushions, they both fell fast asleep. Later, a bump of turbulence woke them.

The seatbelt sign was on. Richard raised the blind of the oval window and squinted through sleepy eyes, pressing his face against the cold pane. The jet's extended flaps and low altitude told them they were on final approach. The marine layer of fog cleared and San Jose were evident below. Green and red salt-ponds, and the lush marshes that outlined the southern half of San Francisco Bay, glistened in rays of sunlight that stabbed through the murk. The long viaduct of the San Mateo Bridge passed beneath them as the landing gear came down with a bump and sucking sound. The surface of the bay drew closer. Seeming about to land on water, the airplane finally settled onto the runway that jutted out into the muddy shallows. Spoilers on the wing deployed, and with the roar of reverse thrust, the jet slowed and turned off toward its waiting gate.

With 'California Dreamin' playing on the PA, the cabin attendant cited the local time and weather before welcoming the travelers to San Francisco. Richard peered out at the collection of foreign airlines assembled on the tarmac and at the terminals. He suddenly realized: *This is my first time in San Francisco*. Then, sadly, he concluded, there could be no Fisherman's Wharf, Golden Gate Bridge, or Palace of Fine Arts on this visit. He was, after all, just passing through. *A run-of-the-mill traitor and his foreign spy girlfriend*, he realized. Despite increased anxiety and disbelief at the course they had embarked upon, Richard forced a smile for Jade. He looked back through the taxiing aircraft's window. *Just passing through*, he pondered again. *Never to return*. The airplane slowed next to another before it stopped at the gate. The cabin chime sounded and a jetway extended and bumped the fuselage at the forward cabin door. Everyone else raced to get up, to stake a claim in the aisle. Richard watched as they elbowed each other. Overhead compartments yawned open and regurgitated carry-ons that did not quite fit the space within which they had been crammed. Swimming in doubt for the first time in his life, Richard was unable to picture the future. He looked to Jade for strength. He thought of the baby that grew within her womb. He gently touched Jade's belly, and leaned in for a long, reassuring kiss.

They deplaned and walked down the jetway, their footsteps reverberating on the carpeted aluminum, emerging into the terminal where every face that turned their way seemed to threaten: The Asian couples were Communist agents, Jade thought. The young guy with the crew cut was an American assassin, he concluded. Of course, the cop by the coffee stand had to be clutching their mug shot. Richard pretended to admire a gauntlet of art pieces arrayed along the terminal's moving walkway and breathed deeply to calm himself. He looked at Jade. She was a rock. They followed the tide to baggage claim.

Richard swiped his credit card to rent a Smarte Carte bag trolley. He then realized he should have used cash instead of a card that registered his exact location and the time of the transaction. He looked at the plastic rectangle with the Visa symbol on it. *I am a slave, you are my shackle*, he pondered, before tucking it back in his wallet. As he did so, he realized that he might be in way over his head. They silently collected their bags from the carousel, and then boarded an elevated train driven by computers. *God help us*, Richard thought. *Machines are in control*. Watching the white headlights that streamed along CA-101, the train headed for the airport's international departures terminal. The robot engineer pulled them into the airport station. They stepped across the platform threshold and realized things were about to get more serious.

Security at the international terminal was far heavier than they had considered. A Transportation Security Agency worker towered over and scanned the mob. Although Richard arrogantly thought that the person would be cleaning his apartment if they were not checking identification and boarding passes, he avoided the man's gaze nonetheless, and occupied himself by pawing at the contents of his carry-on. Richard's American diplomatic passport was reddish-brown, and Jade's—one of many provided her by Chinese intelligence—had been 'issued' by the Republic of the Philippines. They both took out the small books and wielded them like shields in battle.

Richard's diplomatic credentials triggered politeness from the woman who clacked away on her keyboard, and happily, no US agents swarmed them in an enveloping maneuver. Despite beating hearts and rapid, shallow breaths, Jade and Richard received their half cardboard/half paper boarding passes, and saw their baggage labeled and chucked onto the conveyor.

They shared a look of relief. As they strolled away from the counter, they began to feel home free. Then Richard reminded himself his home was here—the US—and that, leaving it, he would never be free again. Suppressing this voice of reason, he remembered duty to Jade and the unborn child tucked in the sack of her belly. No longer encumbered by luggage, they quickly navigated the crowded terminal, and then ducked into their airline's first class lounge.

Inside the privileged oasis, Richard led Jade to a large vase behind which the couple landed on a corner sofa. Killing anxious minutes with small talk, they heard their flight number and destination finally announced. Soon the speaker said first class was ready to board and they stood, anxious and ready. They both collected carry-on bags and headed for the lounge's door. There were several uniformed police officers when they exited. One of them noticed Richard's strange reaction, but went back to scanning for their own fugitive. Jade nudged Richard along to their gate.

Gate 12 served as a simple portal; a door to the airplane that would carry them away. Jade hooked her arm through Richard's. They handed over boarding passes to the woman in uniform who held a hand out at the jet-way entrance. Then, they strolled through the gate's door.

7: THE LAST DAY

"The opportunity to secure ourselves against defeat lies in our own hands, but the opportunity of defeating the enemy is provided by the enemy himself."—Sun Tzu

A People's Liberation soldier, one of many now on Taiwan, lay in his foxhole. Although he was loyal and had believed all he had been told and absorbed all the films and lectures, he now entertained other thoughts. Now, on a foreign island fighting other Chinese, with explosions that lifted earth all around him, he cocked his rifle again and centered on a man's shadow in the sight before he pulled the trigger and terminated a life. However, before he did so one more time, he asked himself: Why?

He looked to the next man in the hole, a man caked in mud and blood who screamed as he emptied his assault rifle. The scream that emanated from his mouth made his lips a square shape beneath the slits of squinted eyes. Fire licked from the barrel of his weapon and illuminated everything in a yellow strobe.

Such hatred, the soldier thought. *Such blind hatred.* Then he looked through the iron sight of his own rifle. A parachute flare caught a shape in its cone of light. A shadowed face showed. *He could be a colleague; a friend; or, even, a brother*, the Chinese soldier thought, although he aimed his rifle anyway, ready to fire. Then, fighting indoctrination and training, he stayed his trigger figure and let his heart decide.

"You *are* my brother," he whispered to the Taiwanese soldier who charged his position. "I love you." He dropped his weapon and looked for a means of escape from the hellish fire, flying mud, and whistling shrapnel, and, most of all, from the murder. That is when he saw General Zhen.

Zhen had pushed his way to the front. For several minutes, he ran from foxhole to foxhole, shouting inspiration to those he led. But then, when the enemy's determined faces had appeared too near, and explosions blossomed around him, Zhen dashed for his command vehicle. Tripping on the way, he tripped atop a mangled comrade, and received a gash on his forehead from the pavement. The unfortunate's bloody exposed entrails soaked his uniform. When Zhen reached his vehicle, he scurried inside its steel cocoon, opened the compartment meant to hold maps or other paraphernalia, and found his small flask of whiskey.

He drew a deep gulp from it; a gulp that was meant to be one of relief, but with every swallow, every rise and fall of his Adam's Apple, it told him 'You are weak. You are defeated.' As if to reinforce the sentiment, a Taiwanese rocket destroyed another vehicle, and the shockwave shook his old bones. Soldiers of Taiwan's 6th Army poured over the line. They shot and bayoneted anything that still moved. When a nearby Dragon Turtle light tank received a missile and popped like an overcooked sausage, Zhen's vehicle sped off in retreat.

Four hours after Taiwan's armies launched their counterattack, a dented and scorched infantry fighting vehicle pulled up outside Songshan airport's terminal. The rear hatch squeaked open and

General Zhen stumbled forth. A soldier ran to assist, while signaling for a medic. Crackles of gunfire could still be heard in the near distance, and the thud of artillery drew closer.

"The enemy is coming," observed the medic who attended to General Zhen.

Zhen hissed and his eyes filled with poison. If he had not dropped his sidearm, he may have shot the man for stating the unfortunate, obvious truth.

Once his wounds had been stitched and bandaged, Zhen's hearing began to return. Zhen ripped the drip needle from his arm and dizzily stood from the cot. A doctor protested, but Zhen brushed him aside. General Zhen emerged from the hangar that housed the makeshift hospital, blinking away the bright sun of the early morning. A guard snapped to attention. Zhen walked away, back to his terminal office, where he nursed his headache with coffee. Surrounded by maps and timetables, Zhen mustered energy and reluctantly turned on a teleconferencing terminal. A green light indicated that a secure connection had been established, and that the camera and microphone functioned.

"General Zhen Zhu, reporting, sirs," he stated firmly to the camera. The president and vice president of China appeared on the video screen, staring with hostile anticipation.

"I deeply regret to inform you that the enemy hit us with unanticipated numbers. My force has been...negated," Zhen said, lowering his head in shame.

"Negated?" the vice president gawked. The president turned away for a moment, but turned back and pounded a fist, shaking his camera and the image on Zhen's screen.

"General Zhen, you are hereby recalled. Return to Beijing immediately," the president ordered, before storming off screen. The stunned vice president stared back at the general.

"There is still hope," Zhen muttered.

"Hope? My dear general, there are over 200,000 people standing in Tiananmen Square with candles and flowers. Tell me: How is there hope?" the vice president asked.

"Sir, you must clear the square immediately. I beg this of you. And get the president to reconsider. Get him to send me another armored division. I also want follow-up strategic strikes against Guam and Hawaii."

"By strategic strike, General Zhen, I assume you mean nuclear weapons?"

"I do. A chemical strike against Guam would suffice, however." Zhen straightened up. A digital silence hung between the two men.

"General, listen carefully. You are recalled."

"Yes, vice president," Zhen conceded.

"At once. Or must we have you collected?"

"No, sir. I am recalled. I understand. I will obey," Zhen said. He turned off the camera and video screen with a trembling hand. He touched his tender head and gabbled to himself.

Chief Master Sergeant Li awakened in his tent as the sun rose, struggling to peek through thick forest. Among the smoky, sweet smell of a campfire was that of brewing coffee. Captain Whidby waited by his tripod-mounted laser designator. Having been up most of the night, he rubbed tired eyes. He picked at a tin of peaches, and, between bites, Whidby continued to stare through binoculars, concentrating on the airport. Li walked over to the coffee and poured them both a cup. Whidby accepted the steaming mug, thanked Li, and pressed his face to the binoculars again. Whidby spotted something of interest and removed a photograph from his thigh pocket.

"That's him," Whidby said, and began removing a protective cover from the business end of the laser designator. He checked battery power and turned on the contraption. Li approached and drew a sharp glance from the American that said: 'Do not interfere.' Whidby leaned into the laser's sighting eyepiece. Li stole a glimpse of the photograph that balanced on the edge of the trench, recognizing the man in the photo. It was General Zhen, Politburo Military Commissioner and Supreme General of the People's Liberation Army. Li nodded approval. Whidby looked up and took one last comparative look at the photograph, and then asked Li to confirm the target's identity. Li took the binoculars, and, amazed with their magnification, settled on the Chinese officer on Songshan's tarmac.

"It's him."

"Okay, let's start the show." Whidby mumbled to the breeze. Then he spoke into a radio, giving his identification and a code word.

Captain Whidby's transmission had gone to nearby Hualien Air Base. Major Han and his Fighting Falcon took off just three minutes later and climbed over the mountains toward Taipei.

Whidby disengaged the laser's safety and leaned back into its eyepiece. He kept Zhen in his sights, pressed a trigger, and fired an invisible pulsing beam. Li got his own pair of binoculars and fixed his magnified gaze on Songshan.

General Zhen had driven up to one of the airport's hangars, with 'Taiwan, Touch Your Heart' painted across it in big, colorful letters. Two Chinese soldiers snapped to attention as the general stumbled from the vehicle, wobbled, and pressed the bloody gauze wrapped around his head.

"Nobody, not even Chairman Mao himself, enters this hangar after me," Zhen ordered. "Understood?" The guards saluted. Zhen entered, shut the door, and locked it behind him. The guards crossed their bayonet-tipped assault rifles in a menacing 'X.'

Zhen's fully fueled private jet awaited inside, ready to take him from defeat, and into the hands of consequences. However, the general did not climb the narrow steps to board the jet. He instead headed for a corner of the hangar where several wooden crates were stacked against the wall. Padlocked chains wrapped one large crate. Zhen spun the lock's combination, opened the shank, and released the chain. It ran; fell heavily, to the floor. He raised the crate's lid and pulled a cord that tore a foil seal. Beneath padded fire blankets lay a black steel cylinder the size of a refrigerator. The cylinder, marked '596,' displayed a radiation trifoil painted on its side, and a parachute container at its base.

"You are my hope," Zhen said to the 100-kiloton hydrogen free-fall bomb.

Whidby now had his laser designator was trained on the hangar with General Zhen inside. The American centered the reticle on the structure's big tourism slogan. Han's Fighting Falcon arrived 20,000 feet overhead.

Han armed the big Paveway laser-guided bomb slung beneath his warplane.

General Zhen attached a cable to the bomb and plugged it into a small keypad. From his chest pocket, he removed a command authority card as well as a second card that only an authorized pilot on a nuclear bomber mission should be in possession of. Zhen entered his command code to disengage the bomb's primary tamper safety. A hum emanated from the weapon as batteries started up its internal electronics. Zhen input the pilot's code, and the bomb's second tamper safety unlocked. He quickly set its controls for a ground burst. As soon as the bomb's altimeter detected sea level—plus or minus 100 meters—a thermonuclear detonation would be triggered. *There will be a great light*, Zhen imagined, *and the banking, commercial, industrial, and government heart of Taiwan will be incinerated.* Some two million enemy citizens will die as a single glorious blast ends the Chinese Civil War once and for all. There will be victory for the Communist Party, and General Zhen's place in history and among the pantheon of great Chinese leaders will be assured. As the radioactive fallout blows harmlessly to sea, Mother China will then care for the hundreds of thousands of injured and dying Taiwanese. The island province will then be rebuilt, and China will finally be one. *And I will be a hero*. General Zhen cracked a devious smile.

In the sky over Songshan, Han put his Fighting Falcon into a gentle climb and then released the Paveway. It separated from the airplane and wobbled weightlessly. Tail fins sprang into position and the Paveway nosed down. Han rolled over, dumped chaff and flares, and then dove away. The Paveway's laser detector spotted the laser beam that splashed the hangar wall, and the small onboard guidance computer matched and verified the laser's coded pulse. The Paveway zeroed in on the invisible light and adjusted its silent fall. The Paveway broke through wispy clouds that hung over the airport.

Zhen slowly turned the bomb's commit key. A green light illuminated on the control panel. Zhen cackled as he started typing the hydrogen bomb's final arming code. A gust of wind came from above, shaking the hangar. Zhen looked up.

The Paveway pierced the hangar roof and entered, uninvited. Its ton of high explosives detonated and sparked the fueled airplane within. The hangar burst, and wall and roof panels blew away and fell as leaves caught in the wind. Crackles echoed as Chinese anti-aircraft batteries fired angrily and blindly into the clear afternoon sky.

Li and the American watched the fireball rising from the airport. Neither man realized how close they had come to a mushroom cloud rising over Taipei. Tired of violence, Li rubbed his eyes. He pictured his daughter and wife, and hoped the surgical strike would help end the war and get him home. Hoping the same, Captain Whidby methodically powered down the laser designator-rangefinder and began its disassembly.

"Thanks for your hospitality," Whidby said.

"Do you think it will all be over now?" Li asked the American Marine.

"Chief Master Sergeant, it ain't over until the fat lady sings –an American idiom," Whidby answered with a wink.

◊◊◊◊

Despite one gimpy shaft, *Liaoning*'s turbines drove the giant to near 30 knots. On picket guard were the destroyers *Harbin* and *Qingdao*, the frigates *Maanshan*, *Xiangfan*, and *Zigong*, as well as several fast patrol boats. They formed a ring of protection around the Chinese aircraft carrier, training their anti-ship missiles on the horizon. Submarines #286 and #342 struggled to keep up with the battle group, but were still available to the Chinese admiral sitting high in *Liaoning*'s armored superstructure. One of the group's JZY-01 radar planes reported in. It had detected surface contacts. The Chinese ships turned toward the enemy and reported the Americans' position to the mainland

The People's Liberation Army fired East Winds. The medium-range ballistic missiles were tasked to saturate the area ahead of the American warships in order to corral and channel them toward a freshly sown minefield. It was the admiral's plan that, as the Americans absorbed mine and missile hits, shore- and carrier-based aircraft would finish them off.

◊◊◊◊

The horizon was colored twilight pink, even though the sky still showed shades of dark blue and gleamed with hanging stars. US Navy Task Force 24 had slowed for replenishment some 300 miles from the Chinese carrier battle group, and the oiler *Yukon* steamed alongside *Ronald Reagan* with wires and hoses strung between the two big ships. With the transfer of aviation fuel and supplies complete, this link was severed. *Yukon* peeled off and opened the distance. Rear Admiral Kaylo watched from *Ronald Reagan*'s flag bridge.

A sailor delivered a message: The US submarine *California* had encountered and engaged the Chinese carrier battle group 300 miles from *Ronald Reagan*'s current position. Kaylo knew his combat air patrol had just knocked down a Chinese maritime patrol aircraft as well. With the news from *California*, he was certain they would be having full-blown combat by lunchtime. He turned back to his planning table, which displayed small blue models that represented the ships of the Task Force. *Ronald Reagan* held the table's center point. The old mariner leaned over them. Kaylo's guided-missile ships—the frigate *Thach*; the destroyers *Gridley*, *Mahan*, and *Winston S. Churchill*; the cruiser *Lake Champlain*; and the littoral combat ship *Fort Worth*—were all arrayed around the supercarrier in a diamond formation. There were several green models on the table as well, at the table's east side; they represented *Essex* and the other amphibious assault ships of the group. In addition, at the table's northern edge lurked a small, blue submarine, *Connecticut*. The sub steamed at the forward edge of Kaylo's armada. Then the American rear admiral found one last small blue model and picked it up. This one was shaped like a modern day *Monitor*: low to the waterline and with a faceted castle. It represented Kaylo's newest warship, the stealth guided-missile destroyer *Michael Monsoor*. Kaylo placed *Michael Monsoor* next to *Connecticut* on the table as these two warships sailed

272

on a special mission. He went to the window and peered at the big cruiser that steamed nearby.

Although his stateroom was nearby, just a few passageways away, *Lake Champlain*'s tactical action officer had fallen asleep in the combat information center, slumped at the table next to the radio monitor. Captain Ferlatto sat in CIC as well, sipping a cup of bug juice, the Navy's neon version of fruit punch. He was about to wake the sleeping officer when a clattering printer did it for him. The tactical action officer jumped up, ripped the paper, and then wobbled. The sailors guffawed. The TAO smiled, blinked away sleep, and read.

"What's up?" Ferlatto asked.

"Sir, Commander, Pacific Fleet has informed us of a Chinese missile launch. Initial plots have them splashing down in our neighborhood. We should be picking them up any second now."

Rear Admiral Kaylo ordered *Ronald Reagan* to come about and double back on her course, and also notified the rest of the task force about the inbound enemy rockets. The ships of the task force spread out to give the supercarrier room and prepare for a coordinated wheeling maneuver. *Ronald Reagan* slowed down for the turn while *Lake Champlain*'s radar began to scrutinize the Chinese attack.

In the guided missile cruiser's CIC, Aegis presented a frightening picture: lines extended from the belly of China and reached for the American task force. Each represented a ballistic missile track. Mesmerized by the scene, Captain Ferlatto stood.

"My goodness," was all Ferlatto could muster.

"Sir, SM-3s assigned to the outer kill basket," the tactical action officer told the captain. "*Gridley* and *Mahan*'s weapons have been slaved to Aegis." The fire control station sported a block of green lights. Its technician called out: "Weapons ready."

"Fire at will," Ferlatto said. He was handed a telephone. The American rear admiral planned to reassemble the ships on the leeward side of the turn and land a few airplanes. Although Rear Admiral Kaylo and the task force currently played defense, he also held a dagger behind his back: the stealth destroyer *Michael Monsoor*.

Michael Monsoor steamed at high speed. Instead of riding the waves, her pointed tumblehome hull pierced and broke them over the weather deck. The foamy wash splashed her retracted deck guns. Half as big as the supercarrier, *Michael Monsoor*'s faceted hull absorbed and refracted radar. It sucked in seawater that then piped around the ship to cool engine exhaust and electromechanical systems, making *Michael Monsoor* nearly invisible in most of the spectrum. Riding shotgun 300 feet below *Monsoor* was another stealthy beast: the nuclear attack submarine *Connecticut*. Both American warships were tasked to outflank the Chinese group's forward element and attempt to sneak up on *Liaoning*. A column of seawater erupted from atop *Michael Monsoor*'s black monolithic superstructure. Replacing bulky antennas, the water column pulled in transmissions from *Lake Champlain*. The report concerned *Thach*. *Michael Monsoor*'s captain read that rising mines had hit and damaged *Thach*, and Chinese ballistic missiles continued their advance on the task force. In *Michael Monsoor*'s bridge/combat information center, a sailor announced that *Liaoning*'s electronic emissions had been localized, and firing point procedures for the ship's electromagnetic rail guns were set in motion.

Horizontal sea doors on *Michael Monsoor*'s forward gun vaults opened. Barrels rose from the stealthy containers.

"Two bells," the fire control technician announced. "We're charging now." Electricity coursed into capacitors—some 40 megajoules—and two horns sounded. "Charge has stopped." A video screen showed the stealth destroyer's forward deck.

Michael Monsoor's sea-search radar activated and fed targeting information to the fire control computer. The rail guns swung over. Stabilized by gyroscopes against the pitch and roll of the hull, the guns maintained a fixed point-of-aim. The gunner closed the firing circuit, and electricity shunted to magnets that lined the gun barrels. With no telltale flash, recoil, or report, both *Michael Monsoor*'s deck guns discharged in unison. The projectiles were already hypersonic when they departed the gun bores. They immediately found GPS's precise positioning service and adjusted their flight paths accordingly. The guns discharged again. Two more projectiles were sent at the Chinese.

The frigate *Xiangfan* steamed at the outer edge of *Liaoning*'s defenses. Suddenly, something slammed into her forecastle and shook the ship to her keel. It pierced the forecastle's steel and penetrated to an ammunition elevator. A deep rumble emanated from within *Xiangfan*. A massive explosive bulged and then ripped open her decks. Flame and smoke jetted to the sky. An accompanying torpedo boat skimmed over on hydrofoils. As it neared, it slowed and settled back into the water. Deckhands prepared to pluck several of the burning ship's sailors from the sea. Chinese diesel-electric submarine *#342* had surfaced, and watched through her periscope. Disgusted and filled with hatred and the desire for revenge, the submarine dove again and leveled out at 200 feet. *342*'s introduction to *Connecticut* was not a pleasant one:

"Submarine. American. *Seawolf*-class. Torpedo in the water." These were the last frantic words spoken aboard the Chinese submarine...

Meanwhile, moving at over 1,000 miles-per-hour, Lieutenant Pelletier pulled her Lightning II through 50,000 feet. She flew at the outer boundary of *Ronald Reagan*'s air defense zone with two Super Hornets flying lower and 20 miles behind her. Pelletier kept her radar off and instead pulled in data from the less stealthy Super Hornets. A beeping drew her attention downward, where several bogeys had shown up on the radar screen. They failed to return identification. Therefore, the computer immediately reclassified the bogeys as bandits, and listed their approach altitude, bearing, and speed.

Six of *Liaoning*'s Flying Sharks rushed the Super Hornets. The Chinese heavy fighters fired off Lightningbolts at extreme range. The Super Hornets then fired back with their AMRAAM air-to-air missiles. Pelletier added four of her own AMRAAMs to the Hornet's counterstrike. The missiles streaked off. Their smoke and vapor trails lined the sky and crisscrossed as they headed toward their opposing targets. Pelletier hit the afterburner and maneuvered her Lightning II to get in behind the Flying Sharks. The Super Hornets continued their merge with the raiders and prepared for the imminent arrival of enemy missiles. Chaff bloomed behind both aircraft formations.

The Flying Sharks broke into two groups of three planes each. One group went high, the other, low. One of Pelletier's missiles speared a Flying Shark and the ones fired by the Super Hornets took out two more. A Lightningbolt struck a Super Hornet and zapped it from the sky. Another of Pelletier's missiles detonated in the face of a Flying Shark, killing the pilot and ripping the Chinese warplane's nose off. Confused by the multi-axis attack, the last two Flying Sharks dove to gain speed. They squirted chaff and flares as they rolled over. The Super Hornets fired two Sidewinder heat-seekers as Pelletier brought her Lightning II around. Should the Sidewinders fail to bring down the Chinese heavy fighters, Pelletier decided she would come in from the side and fire her own close-in missiles. The Sidewinders chased down the two Flying Sharks and practically flew up their tailpipes before their warheads exploded. Both Flying Sharks became burning balls that somersaulted and ripped apart in the sky. Pelletier looked around for parachutes, but spotted none. *One airplane for six,* she counted. Having lost one friend for six strangers, the cost was still too steep, she determined, although the admiral would certainly be happy. The Super Hornet peeled off for the boat. Pelletier turned to meet another one that had already pulled tanker duty.

Fifteen Flying Leopard fighter-bombers flew in from Hainan Island, belonging to the South Sea Fleet, 9th People's Liberation Army Navy Air Force. The Flying Leopards began a low-level attack run on the American ships. They yanked up and fired Eagle Strike supersonic anti-ship missiles that winged off in a deadly flock. Climbing, the Chinese fighter-bombers continued to charge the American formation. *Lake Champlain*'s Aegis combat system scrutinized the horizon and detected the threat.

Sea Sparrows and Standards burst from their launch cans and vertical cells on *Lake Champlain*, *Mahan*, *Ronald Reagan*, and

Winston S. Churchill. They whooshed into the sky, their blastoff enveloping the task force in a bank of propellant smoke. The Standard Missiles were still climbing out when the Sparrows intercepted several Eagle Strikes that skimmed in over the water. More of the Sea Sparrows then reached the Flying Leopards that were coming in high. Able to penetrate the American defenses with sheer numbers, the Chinese anti-ship cruise missiles threatened *Ronald Reagan* herself.

Power from the supercarrier's twin reactors was diverted to laser turrets arrayed beneath the ship's flight deck. They fired and held their beams on the lead Eagle Strike. The Chinese missile heated and exploded. *Ronald Reagan*'s laser turret swung over to the next target.

Lake Champlain kicked in a Rolling Airframe Missile that burst from a stern-mounted turret and skipped off. The task force's Gatling guns came alive. Their ripping sound added to the chorus of sea battle. Eagle Strikes were cooked by laser, shredded by Phalanxes, or knocked down by RAMs. Some of them exploded so close that they sprayed the American ships with debris. Part of an Eagle Strike's ramjet crashed onto the deck of *Mahan.* Otherwise, Task Force 24 was undamaged.

Lieutenant Pelletier broke her Lightning II from the tanker's drogue hose. *Ronald Reagan*'s air controllers immediately put her on a vector to intercept the incoming bandits. They advised her that eight Super Hornets had just launched, as well, and that an EA-6 electronic attack aircraft was already on the prowl. Pelletier's Lightning II turned hard and rushed at the bandits.

Seven People's Liberation Army Air Force Flankers joined the fray, dashing for the American supercarrier with loads of Krypton supersonic anti-ship missiles. The Chinese pilots locked their missiles on the largest surface target and fired. Ramjets sprinted the Kryptons to over Mach 4 as the launch aircraft turned back to the mainland.

Lake Champlain's Aegis combat system selected *Mahan*'s surface-to-air missiles for a defensive broadside. The Evolved Sea Sparrow Missiles ascended from *Mahan*'s missile deck. Already damaged by a mine, *Thach* maneuvered to shelter on *Ronald Reagan*'s starboard side. *Lake Champlain* reported that Standard Missiles had brought down several Chinese ballistic missiles that threatened the group. Rear Admiral Kaylo enjoyed a fleeting moment of relief. Then a new missile report came in. More ballistic and cruise missiles had departed the Chinese mainland. Kaylo looked to the sparkling sea and worried his defenses were being overwhelmed, and contemplated retreat for a fleeting moment. Then he pushed this dark and disheartening thought from his mind, got back to work, and had *Essex* put up two fighter-bombers to round out the task force's combat air patrol.

Kicking up spray from Essex's wet deck, an olive-drab Lightning II stealth jump jet rolled several feet and then leapt into the sky. Its engine nozzle, lift fan, and roll jet balanced the machine until adequate forward speed had been achieved. Once there was enough forward speed for the wings to generate adequate lift to keep the heavily loaded machine in the air, the engine nozzle rotated to horizontal and the lift fan door closed. A second stealth jump jet followed. It rose vertically on a cushion of black fumes, retracted its landing gear, nosed down, jetted off, and the two Marine Corps Lightning IIs met up and went supersonic. *Ronald Reagan* launched two Super Hornets. The American combat aircraft united and climbed to their patrol sector.

Task Force 24's fast boats—the littoral combat ship *Fort Worth* and the guided-missile frigate *Gridley*—put themselves in front of the inbound Kryptons. The warships put up clouds of chaff and a wall of metal from their Gatling guns. *Gridley* kicked in an ESSM as well, firing it at near point blank range. An explosion low to the water confirmed a hit. *Fort Worth*'s close-in weapon system sprayed more big bullets and sent fratricidal rounds into *Gridley*'s rear deck, impacting and ricocheting around her helicopter hangar, shredding the walls, stowed equipment, and personnel working on a Seahawk engine. A Krypton homed in on *Fort Worth,* and she took the supersonic ship killer amidships. *Fort Worth* rocked with the energy of the hit. The Krypton penetrated her superstructure and went off inside, blowing her top off. With her bridge gone and the rudder locked over, the burning American littoral combat ship began to circle.

Sneaking past the task group's outer defensive line, one Krypton screamed in at 2,000 miles-per-hour. *Lake Champlain* fired a Rolling Airframe Missile, and *Mahan*, her Phalanx. *Ronald Reagan* powered up her close-in lasers. Before the RAM and Gatling gun bullets hit, before the lasers had time to cook it, the last Chinese anti-ship cruise missile slammed into *Ronald Reagan*'s side just above the waterline, and took a deep supersonic stab at the American titan. It sliced through the supercarrier's outer hull and penetrated her secondary skin. The Krypton's mid-body warhead triggered a half ton

280

of high explosive. Pipes burst, wires were ripped, fires kindled, and sailors died.

Several Flying Leopards continued their drive on the American ships. Frictional heat from the Chinese fighter-bombers forward quarters displayed on Pelletier's cockpit screen and those of the two Marine Corps Lightning IIs on her wing. Three minutes later, burning wreckage tumbled from the sky. One Flying Leopard's hot engine slammed into the water near *Michael Monsoor*.

Michael Monsoor kicked up sea-spray and punched through choppy seas. She slipped to within 90 miles of *Liaoning* as the nuclear attack submarine *Connecticut* crept in even closer. Vertical launch cells along the American stealth destroyer's periphery yawned open. Tomahawk anti-ship cruise missiles rose and flashed off into the black night. Then *Michael Monsoor*'s deck guns emerged, elevated, and fired 12 shots in rapid succession before tucking back into their vaults. *Michael Monsoor*'s engines surged and she sped from her firing position.

"Intermittent surface radar contact," *Liaoning*'s surface warfare officer announced. He had spotted *Michael Monsoor* for a moment, although the blip on his screen had disappeared again.

"Air-search radar has several projectiles coming in. Profile looks like cruise missiles," the air warfare officer cried out.

Michael Monsoor powered up her sea-search radar, got a quick fix on the Chinese vessels, fired off six more railgun shots, and shut it down again. She rapidly changed course and then sped off. As *Michael Monsoor* misbehaved topside, *Connecticut* glided quick and quiet through the dark waters.

"Shoot," was the order from *Connecticut*'s captain. Eight Harpoon anti-ship cruise missiles slid from the submarine's torpedo tubes. *Connecticut* crash-dived and accelerated away as the Harpoons broached and climbed out on boost motors. With Harpoons and Tomahawks on their way, the Chinese carrier battle group readied to take them down and slammed the water with sonar, trying to sniff out the enemy submarine that had to be close by. With her two big destroyers blocking the axis of attack, *Liaoning* prepared to lash out.

Liaoning's deckhands opened the missile canisters forward of the carrier's island. Inside the waterproof cylinders were the pointed intakes of fighter plane-sized missiles. Machinery started and gears turned, and two Granit surface-to-surface missiles were coaxed from inside their enclosures. They displayed shiny silver bodies with menacing skull and crossbones painted upon them. These long bodies tapered at the tail and ended with folding stub winglets and a stunted fin. Sailors in fire suits and gas masks attached hoses to the missiles and began filling their tanks with liquid propellant. When fueling was complete, the Granits' turbofans started up.

Black smoke covered *Liaoning*'s flight deck as the missiles burned off a film of factory oil. A technician checked readouts and began programming the missile guidance packages with the American supercarrier's approximate position. Onboard flight computers completed preflight checklists and brought engines to full power. The Granits' launch rails were cranked-up and angled skyward, and personnel cleared the area.

With a howl, rocket assist packs lifted the Granits into the sky, where they dropped free and skipped into the sea. The huge Chinese cruise missiles leveled off, dipped to wave top, and flew toward the horizon. When done with this latest launch, *Liaoning* added her surface-to-air missiles to those already put up by *Maanshan*, *Qingdao*, and *Zigong*, and Chestnut-shaped turrets around *Liaoning*'s deck fired their Gatling guns and small Grisom surface-to-air missiles.

Several intruding American anti-ship cruise missiles were taken. Finally, getting dangerously close, the last Harpoons were knocked down, and a Tomahawk also succumbed to the hail. Two Tomahawks fought through, however. The stealthy American cruise missiles popped-up, climbed for a moment, and then nosed over to dive into *Liaoning*'s flight deck.

From *Liaoning*'s towering island, the Chinese admiral saw the American cruise missiles arcing in and instinctively crouched against the blast. There followed the sickly tearing of metal followed by a rumble from deep within his ship. He touched one of the bulkheads and felt *Liaoning* shimmy. The admiral stood and bellowed to his stunned officers: "Start damage control sirens and automated firefighting systems."

Ronald Reagan was still turned into the wind. A brisk sea-spray drenched her flight deck and her hulk rose, fell, and rolled in the chop. Most of her air wing was in the air. Her decks were bare, save for yellow aircraft towing and weapon hauling equipment. A bright reflection emanated from close to the sea. One of *Ronald Reagan*'s deckhands pointed it out.

The big, shiny Chinese Granits approached low, skimming just over the white-capped waves. *Lake Champlain*'s radar spotted the Chinese cruise missiles, but the sea's state interfered with targeting.

Aegis sent several missiles anyway. When they missed, *Mahan*'s forward Phalanx opened up and shredded one supersonic missile in a hail of tungsten bullets. A sickly greenish-brown cloud formed where the Chinese missile had been. It expanded and drifted like an unholy fog. *Lake Champlain* fired two Rolling Airframe Missiles and *Winston S. Churchill*'s Gatling gun spit fire. The Granit approached and crossed the American supercarrier's stern.

The Chinese missile dispersed an aerosol. The Granit overflew the flight deck and left a mist in its wake. Once over water again, the missile was slammed from three sides by bullets and missiles, and exploded in a huge fireball off *Ronald Reagan*'s port side. Rear Admiral Kaylo watched from the supercarrier's flag bridge, believing his ship had survived a near miss. Then, when several sailors on deck began to convulse and grab at their throats, Kaylo went to the plate glass and pressed against it. Men flopped on the ground, gasping for air like fish out of water. Something was terribly wrong. Kaylo called the bridge to order countermeasures.

Ronald Reagan's wash-down system pumped seawater through thousands of deck sprayers. Vents in the supercarrier's air handlers were isolated from the outside and the public announcement system ordered everyone to get below decks. Those caught outside began to super-convulse as a nerve agent caused violent muscle contractions. Their contortions snapped bones and ripped tissue. When the VX was done tearing bodies apart, flaccid paralysis set in and shut down respiration. With his face pressed to the flag bridge's thick green glass, the American rear admiral watched his kids die a painful death. He pounded the window with his fist and swore. *Lake Champlain* sailed through the periphery of the toxic cloud the Granits had created over *Ronald Reagan*.

Ferlatto ordered *Lake Champlain*'s wash-down system activated, and her sailors to event positions, sealed stations that protected against biological, chemical, and radiological attack. Ferlatto turned the cruiser radically to avoid contamination and blew the horn to warn of his unannounced maneuver. Although *Ronald Reagan* remained undamaged, the Chinese nerve agent had delivered a mission kill.

High above the scrambling American ships, a Hawkeye airborne early warning aircraft spotted and announced a new raid.

Fresh Super Hornets climbed from lower-level combat air patrol position to replace Pelletier, and then new orders came in. Although her bird was getting low on fuel, *Ronald Reagan*'s controllers sent Pelletier at the inbound bandits, and informed her that the raiders profile indicated Flankers. "Busy night," Pelletier mumbled through an exhale. She touched the cockpit display. The weapon load-out came up and showed that just two Sidewinders remained. *The cupboards are bare*, she thought.

Pelletier dropped her thrust back to minimize the Lightning II's heat signature and fuel burn, and began a slow climb to gain altitude. A solid tone indicated that the bandits were now within the engagement envelope of the Sidewinders and that they radiated enough heat to offer her heat seekers a target. In Pelletier's helmet, the two enemy aircraft were highlighted and '30,000 feet' and 'Mach 1.8' were listed beside the red diamonds that framed them. Pelletier stepped her Lighting II up in altitude again, climbing to 45,000 feet.

Despite the whine from the Sidewinders, she hesitated to take unreliable frontal shots with the last of her weapons. Instead, she planned to use stealth to sneak around on her enemy's six. *Then I'll fire my snakes right up their ass*, she thought.

A cockpit alarm interrupted Pelletier's sly stalk. She instinctively fired off decoys, and then pointed the aircraft's nose down and over. Pelletier called out to the Hawkeye and *Ronald Reagan*, and pleaded for information on any other known bandits. Air controllers confirmed just the two known plots and reassured her that back up was three minutes out. That is when streaks of tracer fire zinged past the Lightning II's canopy. Pelletier jerked the airplane away hard and punished herself with extreme G-force. More flashes of tracer fire. She screamed with frightful surprise, powered up the radar, and looked back over her shoulder. Shrouded and illuminated by shimmering plasma, Lieutenant Pelletier's 'black knight' slid into view.

"That's no Flanker," she declared aloud, noting the enemy's canard delta layout, canted vertical stabilizers, stealthy body shaping, and frameless canopy. Looking at her rear-facing radar, Pelletier saw only sporadic reflections from her new challenger. As the big jet pulled up high, she caught a glimpse of the big red star on its dark grey airframe. Pelletier recognized the supposedly experimental Chinese stealth air superiority fighter and muttered reiteration of an intelligence brief: "J-20 Black Eagle: Not yet in service." She gave an ironic laugh. The missile warning sounded again.

Pelletier pushed the boundaries of consciousness as she dove and turned. The grey grew bright again, and she had the presence of mind to recognize the alarm and release decoys. Then she grunted into the radio: "Stingtown One, totally defensive." Pelletier zagged instead of zigged, and heard and felt thumps as rounds ripped into her machine. "Fuck," she exclaimed. The airplane jerked. With a sharp crack, her wing's aluminum beam failed, and the Lightning II lurched. Composite wing skin tore and peeled away. Finally, the wing folded, bending at a right angle.

Pelletier's helmet slammed against the canopy.

A vision flashed: Her father looked sad. Hobbes the cat meowed and gave a nictitating blink.

The wing ripped from the fuselage and knocked off part of the airplane's tail. The Lightning II went into a violent flat spin. Pelletier's head was pinned to the canopy. The world outside swirled. Pelletier struggled to stay conscious. A wave of nausea swamped her, and her vision tunneled. As Pelletier was about to pass out, there was a burst of white light.

Cynthia saw herself at a big dining room table wearing a birthday cap. An aroma from a cake baking in the oven, and wax candles slowly melting away teased her nostrils. Her boyfriend from high school was there, and in this vision, made a handsome husband. They had a beautiful daughter as well. The little girl drew a deep breath, and with puffed cheeks and a wish, blew out candles on a frosted cake. Pelletier's father bounced in his chair and clapped loudly.

He froze suddenly, looked at Cindy, and screamed, "Wake up, Cindy." Pelletier came to and pawed for the Lightning II's ejection handle. G-forces had pinned her arms in her lap. Chimes; red flashing lights; and, a whooping warning assaulted her senses. The mortally wounded Lightning II bucked. Pelletier's head was thrown backwards. With a sickening pop, her helmet split. She tasted blood.

Just one more jarring yaw and a deep rumble…

And then, a bright light, warmth, and peace.

An explosion bloomed over the Pacific. From it, fingers of smoke and debris reached down to the water's surface.

"Stingtown One?" *Ronald Reagan*'s controllers called out and repeated. No response.

◊◊◊◊

A black tailless flying wing pierced Pacific skies. Named *Spirit of Louisiana*, it was the 21st and final Spirit strategic stealth bomber built by the United States. After a long flight from Missouri and heavy with two Massive Ordinance Penetrators; 30,000-pound bunker-busters, it was open for business. Quick bursts from the Spirit's look-down radar built a three-dimensional picture of the Chinese naval formation. The American airmen selected the biggest ship and locked its coordinates into the targeting system. The stealth bomber's bay doors folded open and, one after the other, two giant MOPs dropped free.

Latticed tail fins extended, stabilizing and guiding the huge bombs as they nosed down. The bombs pierced a wisp of cloud. Below them and coming up fast was *Liaoning*'s flightdeck. One Chinese sailor heard a rush of air and looked up to see the two bunker busters. The first bomb hit. It ripped through the flightdeck and disappeared into the ship's bowels. Hah, the sailor chuckled. *It's a dud. Liaoning* shook and the hole in the flightdeck erupted like a volcano. The sailor and hundreds of his comrades did not live long enough to see the second MOP impact and rip into the Chinese aircraft carrier.

Ordinance and fragments of ship hit the sea around *Lake Champlain*. Black and white smoke trails crisscrossed the blue sky. Ferlatto adjusted his helmet and flinched as the Gatling guns once again spewed flame. He saw a huge flash in the distance, and after a few seconds, a pressure wave arrived, slamming into his ship. Low, prolonged thunder rolled in, and a massive cloud of black smoke rose at the horizon…

Meanwhile, *Connecticut*'s passive sonar array registered two very large consecutive explosions. Her captain brought the submarine shallow to peek above the surface. "We're at 60 feet, sir. Neutral bubble," *Connecticut*'s XO reported.

"Very well. Steady as she goes and periscope up," the captain ordered. The periscope climbed from its well, piercing the waves. He leaned in for a look.

A column of smoke rose from *Liaoning*. Now she listed to port and blazes vented from gaping, jagged holes in her flight deck. Several patrol boats slowed to pull sailors, blown overboard, from the water. *Liaoning* heeled further to port as she felt the effects of unbalanced flooding. *Connecticut*'s captain considered putting a spread of torpedoes into the hapless warship when the sonarman interrupted. A destroyer had turned *Connecticut*'s way.

"Take her deep, chief," he reluctantly ordered.

The guided-missile destroyer *Qingdao* hammered the water with her bow sonar, but lost *Connecticut* as she slipped beneath a substantial thermocline. Then, *Harbin* and *Qingdao* turned for *Lake Champlain* at full speed. They fired anti-ship missiles and opened up with their deck guns. Two torpedo boats—*Huchuan*-class semi-hydrofoils—joined the charge, spitting two torpedoes each along the axis of attack.

"Okay, I would say they are pretty mad," Ferlatto half-joked. "Present minimal aspect. Ready the Mark 45. I want those fast boats dead. Put two Harpoons on each of those destroyers." *Lake Champlain* turned at the charging ships, her deck gun turned and elevated. The 5-inch gun recoiled and spit smoking brass casings onto the foredeck. Geysers of water erupted around the Chinese torpedo boats until rounds found them, ripping into their decks, and sinking them.

A sailor on *Lake Champlain*'s bridge lowered his binoculars, turned to the captain, and reported, "Torpedo tracks. Closing fast."

"Sir, cruise missiles inbound," another man announced, just as *Lake Champlain*'s vertical launch system loosed four Harpoons. "Likely CSS-N-8 Saccades. Subsonic profile. ACS is engaging."

Several Evolved Sea Sparrow Missiles departed *Lake Champlain* to intercept the approaching Chinese Eagle Strike anti-ship missiles.

"Where are those torps?" Ferlatto asked.

"Zero-one-five. Three thousand feet off. Bearing one-zero-three degrees. They're doing about fifty knots."

"Okay, hard over to starboard, increase speed to flank. Let's see if they turn with us or are straight shooters."

Lake Champlain turned and sped up. The Chinese torpedoes followed.

"Goddamn it."

"Sir, ESSMs have missed. Sea-whizz."

Lake Champlain's Phalanx close-in weapons systems found and locked on the enemy sea-skimmers. A zipping sound vibrated the bridge as the robotic Gatling guns opened up. A large explosion shook the ship. Bullets from one Phalanx met a missile and detonated its fuel and warhead.

"Mother fu--" Another explosion, but this one shook *Lake Champlain* violently and knocked sailors to the cold, hard bridge deck. Thick black smoke began to infiltrate the bridge via the air circulation system. Alarms sounded and warning lights flashed. *Lake Champlain* had been hit. Speed dropped off rapidly, and the hull rose and fell as the wake wave caught up.

"Torpedo terminal."

"Brace. Brace. Brace for impact," Ferlatto shouted. Then an immediate, violent jarring and a bright flash rocked Ferlatto's ship.

At the moment *Lake Champlain* was lifted, broken in two, and crumpled back on herself, People's Liberation Army Navy multirole aircraft carrier *Liaoning* succumbed to her wounds and slipped beneath the rippled sea. She pulled down with her over 2,000 souls.

Qingdao ate a Harpoon that crippled her, but *Harbin* blasted Lake Champlain with her 100-millimeter gun. One life raft left *Lake Champlain*'s side just before a salvo of three Eagle Strikes slammed into her. She went down fast after that. Three hundred, twenty-five sailors went with her, Captain Anthony Ferlatto among them.

With their mission finally accomplished and *Liaoning* now a future reef and fish sanctuary, the contaminated supercarrier *Ronald Reagan* led Task Force 24 from the area. When the Chinese departed the area, too, an Osprey tiltrotor from *Essex* found *Lake Champlain*'s lone life raft and hoisted the last of her crew to safety.

◊◊◊◊

Richard woke from a disturbing dream and frantically scanned the dark, windowless room. Soaked with sweat, he touched his aching temples and blinked his eyes. Lying on a cot, he focused on the peeling green paint. What happened? He tried to remember. He had been with Jade, waiting for their flight. Then they were walking down the jet-way, and had reached the last corner, where folded strollers and oversized carry-ons are left. After that, nothing. Blackness. He felt a bump on his neck. An injection site? A tranquilizer dart? Richard began to panic.

"Jade," Richard murmured, his throat dry and hoarse. He tried to sit up and wondered if he was still in San Francisco. He scanned for details. Not even an electric outlet to tell him which country he was in. Unrestrained, Richard stood and wobbled on feet of clay. Someone outside the heavy door yelled in Chinese. It unlatched and swung open, and a People's Liberation Army officer burst in, and shouted at someone out in the hall. He stood over Richard. His smile was a wicked curl. The Chinese officer asked for something, and got agitated when Richard did not comply. He smacked Richard, who trembled.

"I don't know Chinese...Mandarin," Richard stuttered. The officer went nuts and grabbed for his pistol. Richard held his hands up in surrender and begged for his life. The officer's snarling face smiled again. Then the Chinese officer began to laugh and slid the weapon back into its holster.

"Sorry, Richard," he said in perfect American English. On cue, Richard's favorite FBI counterintelligence officer, Special Agent Jackson, waltzed in, wearing a smug smile of satisfaction.

"Thanks, Sam," Jackson acknowledged his counterpart in the Chinese uniform. "Richard Ling, meet Special Agent Sam Wu." Richard deflated with exhaustion. "Sorry, I couldn't resist. You have been bad, Richard. *Very, very* bad." Wu left Jackson alone with Richard. "Where exactly were you going, Richard?" Jackson asked.

"I don't really know anymore," Richard stuttered, and sat back down on the cot. "Where is Jade?"

"Richard, Bei Si Tiao made a deal with us. In exchange for clearing you of charges, she gave us some valuable information. Then she left the country, never to return." Jackson handed Richard a small bottle of water. He choked it down. "Look," the special agent continued, "I'm a father, too. There is something hardwired in our brains that makes us do anything to protect our children. It's like with birds: One day you're free and winging it, the next, you're puking up worms. Know what I mean?"

"Throwing up sounds good," was all Richard could say. The blank look on Richard's haggard face spurred simplification from Jackson.

"What I'm trying to say is: I'm not sure I blame your poor decision-making these last few days. I would add that I believe Jade lied to you about being pregnant and used that lie to manipulate you

further. I hope that helps a little." While alleviating some of
Jackson's nagging, empathic guilt, Richard took little comfort in the
words. "By the way, Richard, you're back home in DC. Come on,"
Jackson said. "Let's get out of here."

◊◊◊◊

China National Television broadcast news of a glorious sea
battle with the Americans and the great victory of Chinese naval forces
over the imperialist power. According to the state-controlled
propaganda machine, two American aircraft carriers were afire at sea,
soon to be finished off by Chinese submarines. Despite this version of
the news, however, most Chinese had gotten information from western
websites and Taiwanese transmitters that broadcast into the mainland.
By the time Beijing released the official story, reports of disaster had
spread like wildfire, and close to 1,000,000 people had gathered in
Tiananmen Square and its surrounds.

The People's Liberation Army deployed to encircle Beijing's
city center.

8: AFTERMATH

"The art of war is of vital importance to the State. It is a matter of life and death, a road either to safety or to ruin..."—Sun Tzu

The moon hung high in the young night as the *Harry S. Truman* carrier strike group steamed into the East China Sea. Rushed from the Persian Gulf, the American nuclear supercarrier was accompanied by the guided-missile cruisers *Antietam* and *Bunker Hill*, the guided-missile destroyer *John Paul Jones*, and, running near the surface and leading the way, the nuclear attack submarine *New Mexico*. The American ships set headings for *Ronald Reagan* and Task Force 24.

Ronald Reagan was now sufficiently decontaminated to resume flight operations. Severely damaged, the destroyer *Gridley* had tugs alongside, shoving her along to the Philippines. With the arrival of the *Harry S. Truman* carrier strike group, over a half-million tons of warships were under the command of Rear Admiral Kaylo.

Dressed in formal whites, and standing over the planning table on *Ronald Reagan*'s flag bridge, Kaylo positioned the three cruisers in a wedge around his two supercarriers, then put destroyers in the leading and laggard positions, the two attack subs on the flanks, and repositioned the dock landing ships and amphibious assault ship as trailers. The stealthy littoral combat ship and guided-missile destroyer brought up the rear, with the last attack submarine anchoring the entire formation. Satisfied with the positioning of his ships, Kaylo straightened his uniform.

"Form the task force up like this," he ordered a commander, pointing to the table. The rear admiral adjusted his cap and mentally prepared for somber duty. He made for *Ronald Reagan*'s hangar.

Ronald Reagan's number-one elevator, now suspended over the water and serving as the site of a memorial detail, was ready for duty. All available hands gathered in the hangar deck's opening. Rear Admiral Kaylo led the service. Senior Lieutenant Peng stood among the attending aviators, marines, and sailors. One of *Ronald Reagan*'s search and rescue helicopters had plucked him from the sea, and his wounds had been treated. Kaylo had granted Peng's unorthodox request to attend the memorial. He felt Peng's presence appropriate, especially once he learned of Pelletier's gallantry. Nevertheless, he ordered armed marines to watch Peng's every move while outside the brig.

Rear Admiral Kaylo read the name and rank of 162 American aviators, marines, and sailors, each followed by the toll of the watch bell. When Kaylo said: "Lieutenant Cynthia Pelletier," Peng snapped to attention and raised cuffed hands in salute. Peng would always know this name. In the years to come, even when his own children had to refresh his fading memory, Peng would recognize the American woman who had brought him to the edge of death, and then chosen to spare his life. The honor roll complete, *Ronald Reagan*'s salute gun discharged. For those claimed by the sea, a wreath was thrown into the supercarrier's wake, and the chaplain prayed for resurrection from the cold deep. The collection of American ships—now accompanied by several surviving Republic of China Navy vessels—steamed into the Taiwan Strait.

296

Two weeks later…

Jade enjoyed a scorching shower that fogged her hotel room window, obscured the sparkling towers of Singapore. She wrapped herself in a luxuriant robe and plopped into the soft clean bed, flicked her wet hair aside and turned the television to an international news report. She sighed with exhaustion and began to towel-dry her hair. For the first time in days, Jade felt like she could relax. She closed her eyes and reviewed her escape, a flight from San Francisco to Jakarta, then one to Hanoi. After a few days in the bustling city, she had then left for Singapore, arriving in the port city-state early in the evening.

Jade's sister had arranged for a wire transfer she expected in the morning. Delivered to the hotel's front desk, it would provide her with a fistful of Singapore dollars. *So, for now, everything is going according to plan*, Jade supposed. *I'm hungry.* She finally heeded her growling stomach and reached for the leather-bound room service menu on the nightstand.

Jade called in an order of several hors-d'oeuvre and an aperitif of gin and tonic to calm her nerves. She hung up the phone and considered the fluffy pajamas she had neatly tucked in the room's drawers. Deciding the PJs could wait, she fell backward onto the cool quilt. The sound from the television filtered into her drowsy head. The voices became gibberish as she dozed off.

A loud knock startled Jade from her sleep. She wiped drool away and jumped from the bed, slipped into some complementary hotel-provided slippers, and paused at the hall mirror for an adjustment of her spiked but still-damp hair. Then she opened the door for the female attendant with the cart full of goodies.

"Room service," the woman said in English, with a smile.

Jade gestured her into the room.

The attendant lifted a small table leaf and cast out fresh linen before carefully positioning polished silverware. She removed a small, green bottle of alcohol, and placed it next to some bubbling tonic, wedges of fruit, and a bucket of ice. Jade said she would eat at the bed, and the cart was wheeled to its edge. The attendant continued her duties and set a place, putting everything just right. Jade turned to the television's picture as she waited.

On the screen, she saw the East Room of the White House. Seated at a long table were the President of the People's Republic of China Xu Wai Li, President of the Republic of China Bing Rong, and President of the United States William Keeley. Jade recognized the Chinese Ambassador to the United States Fan Wei and People's Liberation Air Force General Piao Bai. Also in attendance was Taiwan's recently promoted Lieutenant General Tek Foo Chek, the hero who rallied his army and pushed them into Taipei. Vice President Elias Campos squeezed in behind the American president, as did Secretary of State Georgiana Pierce, and National Security Advisor Nathaniel Westermark. The three presidents signed documents, exchanged pens, and shook hands. The television shot widened, and, at the periphery of the smiling, clapping congregation, Secretary Pierce pulled Richard Ling in to share in the happy moment he had 'unofficially' helped broker.

Surprised, Jade smiled with delight. The British newscaster narrated and summarized that remaining Communist forces on Taiwan were now departing peacefully. Reports also mentioned widespread, peaceful demonstrations in China. Unsupported rumors abounded that the army, ordered to fire upon the demonstrators, had refused. Some soldiers reportedly stacked their weapons, stripped uniform shirts, and joined the black-haired masses in their vigil. Soon thereafter, the government announced general elections would be held within one year, and a commission would sit to draft a constitution. Furthermore, Taiwan was to be recognized as an independent nation and granted a seat in the United Nations General Assembly. Statements also provided that parts of China—Tibet in particular—were now free to examine their own political status. Chinese forces appeared to be thinning on the Indian frontier as well.

The room service attendant cleared her throat, interrupting Jade's mesmerized stare. The attendant gestured to the table and raised a silver dome. Dim sum—literally 'touch the heart,' savory, steaming dumplings—were revealed. Jade remembered her appetite, but also realized her hunger had departed her. She eyed the bottle of gin, sat on the bed, unfurled a napkin, and retuned her concentration to the television. The camera caught Richard's smiling face again. The attendant lifted the other domed silver food cover.

On the white plate lay a Chinese pistol fitted with a suppressor. With a fluid motion in Jade's peripheral vision the attendant picked up the gun and placed its cold metal on her temple. On the television, Richard smiled and shook hands with delegates. A tear ran down Jade's cheek. She clutched her swollen belly. A puff of hotness, and then blackness.

Followed by a double tap to the heart for indemnity, the single shot to the brain of Bei Si Tiao, AKA Zhang 'Jade' Jiao, had ended her life instantly. Her unborn child took longer to die, however. The assassin disassembled the pistol, stashed its components about her clothes, and left the smoky room. She hung a 'Do Not Disturb' sign on the door handle. The scene would go unnoticed until tomorrow's checkout time.

◊◊◊◊

Rear Admiral Kaylo finished watching the White House ceremony and moved to the flag bridge's window. He marveled at the sparkling lights of Hong Kong and the fireworks that burst over its skyline. Kaylo stepped outside and breathed deep the fresh sea air. *Ronald Reagan* rose and fell gently in the swells. A sailor came outside and handed Kaylo a transmission from national command: CEASE ALL HOSTILITIES. MAINTAIN ALERT STATUS. END. The cessation of hostilities having been an unofficial fact for more than a week now, the command was still a welcome sight.

Rear Admiral Kaylo smiled, crumpled the paper, and tossed it to the wind. It danced there for a moment before tumbling to the sea's foamy surface. Kaylo retreated to the warmth of the bridge.

◊◊◊◊

Major Han Ken walked up the dirt road toward the farm outside Hsinchu City. He passed the crop fields and spotted the old tree in which he had landed. He noticed a shred of his parachute still fluttering from the twisted branch that had torn it. Han turned a bend in the road. There, ahead, he saw the old farmhouse. One of the kids had waited at the entryway and now dashed inside.

The old farmer and his family emerged. The last to come outside was the niece, wearing a big smile and waving enthusiastically. Han greeted everyone. He shook the old man's hand, kissed the farmer's wife, ruffled the children's hair, and then embraced his future bride.

◊◊◊◊

Chief Master Sergeant Li Rong Kai, his wife, daughter, and mother sat at the Italian eatery in Neihu. Even though his mother had offered to watch the little girl so Li could steal away with his wife, he wanted them to all be together. The restaurant sat in the shadow of Hill 112. Li watched a construction vehicle turn up the winding road toward the hilltop.

Around Taipei and the rest of the island nation, a monumental effort had begun to repair the ravages of war, although a semblance of normal life had already returned. Li's wife showed their little girl how to twirl the spaghetti on a fork—the first time the little girl had used such a strange utensil—and then to suck the noodles into her mouth. Li smiled at his daughter's sauce-covered grin, leaned over the table, and kissed her forehead.

◊◊◊◊

It was raining hard in DC, but Richard happily entered his townhouse on Olive Street. He flopped his soaked trench coat over a kitchen chair. Jade's favorite perfume still wafted through the place and traces of her abounded everywhere: a textbook; a magazine; and a pile of clothes left behind during their hasty departure. Richard went to his desk.

Raindrops wiggled their way down the windowpane. The yellow streetlight decorated Richard's face with their streams, as he thought of Jade. He hoped she was okay and happy. As much as he missed her, he missed most of all the idea that he thought he would be a father. He had forgiven Jade her deception, and was thankful he had come to realize a desire for family that now permeated his entire being.

"Goodbye, Jade," Richard whispered. "Be well." A tear rolled down his cheek, lost among the rainy rivulets that the streetlight painted on his face.

◊◊◊◊

Although the runway and pockmarked terminal at Taipei's Songshan had already been opened to limited commercial and military traffic, and much of the litter of war was cleared, the airport remained under repair. A cluster of hangars at the far end of the field was particularly devastated and needed to be razed and rebuilt. A bulldozer began to clear one of the wrecked hangars.

The bright yellow machine's blade pushed into the burnt piles of aluminum sheet, concrete, and fallen trusses and shoved the debris into piles. The bulldozer backed and rushed forward again. Something large and heavy, however, stopped its progress hard. Beneath a pile of wood planking and other flotsam, the operator saw a large, dented black cylinder. Upon it was a tangled cable that linked the cylinder to a small blood-caked and charred control box.

The bulldozer's operator swore and backed off. The machine's toothed blade caught and, as it retreated, the blade dislodged the control box, which tumbled down. Within it occurred a spark and a puff of smoke, and an electronic hum began to emanate from the black cylinder...

Printed in Great Britain
by Amazon